CONFIDENCES

CONFIDENCES

PENNY HAYDEN

DOUBLEDAY

NEW YORK   LONDON   TORONTO   SYDNEY   AUCKLAND

LOVESWEPT®
PUBLISHED BY DOUBLEDAY
a division of Bantam Doubleday Dell Publishing Group, Inc.
666 Fifth Avenue, New York, New York 10103

DOUBLEDAY and the portrayal of an anchor with a dolphin,
and the word LOVESWEPT and the portrayal of the wave device
are trademarks of Doubleday, a division of
Bantam Doubleday Dell Publishing Group, Inc.
All of the characters in this book are fictitious,
and any resemblance to actual persons, living or
dead, is purely coincidental.

Library of Congress Cataloging-in-Publication Data:

Hayden, Penny, 1950–
    Confidences / Penny Hayden.—1st ed.
        p.   cm.
    "Loveswept."
    I. Title.
    PS3558.A82885C6   1992
    813'.54—dc20   92-14058
                                                            CIP

ISBN 0-385-42596-1
Copyright © 1992 by Penny Hayden
All Rights Reserved
Printed in the United States of America
December 1992

1   3   5   7   9   10   8   6   4   2

First Edition

In memory of Con Sellers,
mentor and generous friend.

Special thanks to Stephanie Bartlett, Sheila Straus, and the rest of my writing group for their constructive criticism and unflagging support; Jack Davis, Pamela Burkholder, Michael S. Morey, Diane Williams, M.D., and Jura Sherwood for their assistance with technical details; the members of my playgroup and women's group for keeping me sane during the three times I lived through the "terrible twos"; my agent, Andrea Cirillo, for her insight and faith; and to Curtis, Alex, Catherine, and Juliet for not interrupting me too often while I wrote.

PROLOGUE

July

SAN FRANCISCO

It wasn't anyone's fault. At least that was what Mom and Dad and his doctor kept telling him. It wasn't his fault; it wasn't his parents' fault; there wasn't a damn thing to blame except some stupid cells gone crazy.

Turning his face toward the hospital room window, Doug Sommers blinked hard to keep back the tears stinging his eyes. He wished everyone would leave so he could cry instead of having to act so goddamn brave all over the place. He was only seventeen, for Christ's sake. He didn't want to die.

While Dr. Levison droned on to Mom and Dad about white blood cells and platelets and chemotherapy and bone marrow, Doug aimed the remote control at the television and zapped it on, then flicked through the channels until he found MTV. By the time he got out of the hospital, summer would be over, school would have started, and there'd be a whole new bunch of songs on the top-ten list.

Some senior year. Instead of playing football, he'd be taking a mess of drugs that would make him feel even worse than he did now; instead of going out with Jennifer, he'd be getting stuck with needles and his blond hair would be falling out in handfuls. He'd read *Brian's Song* in seventh grade—he knew what to expect: first they tortured you; then you died. He poked a button on the control, and the television clicked off.

"So, how does that sound, Doug?" Dr. Levison's voice was low and pleasant, but direct, not at all syrupy like those doctors who went around saying, "And how are we feeling today?" He had to hand it to her; at least she was honest. She smiled at him as if she expected him to be pleased by whatever it was she'd been telling his parents.

It was easy for her. She wasn't going to die before she'd ever really lived. He shrugged, his grip tightening on the remote control as he fought the urge to heave it at the window. All he wanted to do right now was scream and cry and break things. But every time he looked at Mom and Dad, at the love and grief engraved on their faces, he tensed against the horrible rage twisting his guts, invading his blood like the malignant myeloid cells the tests had discovered. It wasn't their fault, he reminded himself again, for the hundredth time. He had to keep it together for them.

"I'm sorry," he said. "I sort of spaced out."

"I was just explaining to your parents what doctors call a *protocol*, what I think is the best treatment plan for you. The first goal is to get you into remission." Dr. Levison nodded at his parents. "That's accomplished through induction therapy—or chemotherapy, in your case. At this point we may not need to resort to radiotherapy."

"Then I won't lose my hair?" His face flushed as soon as the words were out. What the hell did it matter if he was bald when he died?

"Some drugs may make it a little thinner, but, no, you probably won't lose it all." Her tone was serious, matter-of-fact, as if he'd asked a perfectly reasonable question. "There are a number of other possible side effects of the drugs we use to induce remission. But if we're successful, there's the possibility of a bone marrow transplant, where we replace your diseased marrow with a donor's healthy marrow. It's still experimental, but the overall results have been good, and some transplant patients are still in remission after more than eight years. I was just going to explain it to your parents. Should I come back later or are you ready to hear about it now?"

His cheeks grew even hotter. She seemed to understand how angry he was, and she didn't seem to mind at all. "I guess so," he mumbled, laying the control on the bedside table. He spread his hands out over the white covers and stared at them. Maybe it wasn't so hopeless after all. Suddenly, eight years looked like a lifetime. He could do a lot in eight years—finish high school, graduate from college, maybe even get married. At the very least, he wouldn't die a virgin; he'd make damn sure of that.

"You have a lot of points in your favor," she said. "You're young; your general physical condition is excellent; your internal organs appear to be in good shape; you've never been treated for blood cell diseases before." She turned to his parents. "The biggest consideration in bone marrow transplants, however, is finding a prospective donor, someone with a matching HL-A type. We find that out by testing the lymphocytes in the blood to see if they share the same antigens and by culturing the donor's blood with the patient's to see if the cells attack each other." She smiled at Doug. "You have two younger brothers, right?"

"Yeah." He pushed himself up straighter and cocked his head, the warmth of hope loosening the constricted, cold feeling in his chest. "But what have they got to do with it?"

"Well, an identical twin would be ideal because he would have the same chromosomal inheritance as you. But since you don't have a twin, we'll look at your brothers. Genetically speaking, there's a 25 percent chance for each one to be a good match. Parents are a possibility, too, though the chances are much slimmer."

Doug's mother drew her breath in sharply and glanced at his father. "Genetically?" she whispered, then cleared her throat.

3

Dr. Levison raised a dark eyebrow and looked back and forth from his mother to his father. "Is that a problem?"

For the first time during the two days since the blood tests for his football physical had shown there was something wrong, Mom's eyes filled with tears. She opened her mouth to speak, but no words came out. Finally, she buried her face in her hands.

Dad put an arm around her shoulder and pulled her close. He shook his head slowly, then touched Dr. Levison's shoulder. "May we have a few minutes alone with Doug?"

"Certainly," she said. "I'll be at the nurses' station."

Even though the room was silent after she left, Doug's ears buzzed. Mom and Dad had been so calm about everything. Until now. He took a deep breath of the disinfectant-laden air, then broke the silence. "What's up?" he said, pushing his lips into something he hoped resembled a smile. "First good news I've heard, and you guys—"

Mom's hands dropped to her side, and she lifted her head. Tears streamed down her cheeks, and she clenched her teeth. "We meant to tell you a long time ago, but somehow—" Her voice broke. "We love you so much. It never made any difference, not even after your brothers were born."

Bitter-tasting saliva flooded Doug's mouth. "*What* never made any difference?"

Dad sucked in a deep breath. "We adopted you when you were a week old. We have no idea who your biological parents are."

CHAPTER 1

August

ASHLAND, OREGON

The best thing about having playgroup in Lithia Park was that no one had to clean house or fix lunch—or pick up after four busy toddlers when they'd finished demolishing the place. Sheri Riley leaned back, resting her elbows on the big red blanket she and her friends had spread over the lush grass bordering the playground. Of the four women in her mothers' group, she was probably the most relieved when they met like this. Liz had a housekeeper and usually hired a caterer; Naomi loved to cook and give parties; and if Meredith ever got flustered by anything, she sure as hell never showed it.

Liz the real estate broker, Naomi the scholar, Meredith the lawyer —and Sheri the cocktail waitress. As usual Sheri was amazed that she was actually close to three women so classy you'd never hear the word *classy* escape their lips. Their age was what had drawn them together—

they'd all been over thirty the day the four of them met in a childbirth education class at Ashland Community Hospital. They'd stayed in touch afterward, forming a little playgroup when the babies were barely old enough to sit up, let alone play with each other.

And what was even more amazing than her being a part of their group was how nice they all were—real people, not pretentious or snobby despite their wealth and their accomplishments. And they were truly her friends, not backstabbing little bitches like the girls she'd gone to high school in Ashland with, girls who'd envied her for her dark-haired beauty and sneered at her for her poverty. Meredith and Naomi and Liz accepted her as one of them.

A furious squeal interrupted Sheri's thoughts. Across the blanket, sitting yogi-style with her Birkenstocks placed neatly next to her, Meredith Marshall wiped the tears from her daughter Justine's cheeks and pulled her into her lap. They made a beautiful pair, Sheri thought, the way Meredith's long, thick auburn hair mingled with Justie's soft golden-red curls. They shared the same dark brown, almost black eyes and pale olive coloring—a striking contrast to the rich red glints in their hair.

Meredith whispered a few words in Justie's ear, then set the child on her feet and nudged her toward the other children. Justie hesitated a moment, her thumb in her mouth, watching the kids run around in circles on the grass, then fall down and laugh uproariously. Finally, with a last glance at her mother, she trotted over to join them. "Whew," Meredith said. "We'd better talk fast while we have the opportunity."

Naomi Chandler popped a green grape into her mouth so she wouldn't be quite so tempted by the plateful of her famous oatmeal cookies occupying the position of honor in the middle of the blanket. She watched almost resentfully as Liz crunched away on a cookie—her third at least, and Liz probably never weighed an ounce over 115 even though she was a good three inches taller than Naomi. Liz always made her think of a tall, willowy, pixie-haired Tinker Bell, flitting through life, sunshine on the outside but with a backbone of steel. On the other hand, Naomi thought of herself as Dumbo the Elephant—before he realized he really could fly.

Naomi swallowed her low-cal grape, glancing toward the kids to make sure that her teenage stepdaughter Kristin and Sheri's eight-year-old daughter Felicia had everything under control. She jerked her head toward Kristin and said in a low voice to the other women, "I found a package of rubbers in the washing machine yesterday." Sighing, she shook her head. "She's only fourteen. I'm not quite sure how to handle it."

Meredith pushed her long hair over her shoulders and straightened her back. "You could always tell Richard and let him take care of it. She's his daughter, after all." She fixed Naomi with her no-nonsense, Merciless Meredith stare, but her voice was soft with concern. "You don't have to do everything for everyone, Naomi."

"Yeah," Liz chimed in with a laugh, hoping to diffuse Meredith's intensity. Meredith always took everything so seriously. Just like Fletcher. Whenever people met the four of them together—Meredith with her husband Ted and Liz with her husband Fletcher—they always got the couples mixed up.

It was easy to understand why, too. Fletcher and Meredith were both lawyers, both a little on the radical side where their causes were concerned—Meredith and her women's rights and Fletcher and his environmentalism—and they both dressed with an eccentric flair while she and Ted were much more conventional in all areas. Fletcher, with his beard and wire-rimmed glasses, was a familiar sight riding around Ashland on his bicycle when he wasn't driving his ancient VW bus; Meredith looked colorful and exotic with her long auburn hair, Birkenstock sandals, and expensive ethnic clothing. Perhaps that was why Meredith and Fletcher's legal partnership had been so successful—they were attuned on so many levels. And maybe that was why Liz and Fletcher's marriage wasn't so great—they had nothing in common except Brookie.

Well, that wasn't something she wanted to worry about right now.

Liz shoved the unpleasant thought away. "You know, I wasn't a lot older than Kristin the first time I ever did it."

"You mean, as in the first time you ever *fucked?*" Meredith asked. "I can't believe I haven't heard that story yet. Tell us."

Naomi's grin was just a little wicked. "If it takes as long as the act, you should be finished in about ten seconds."

Liz hooted with laughter, Sheri blushed, and Meredith just shook her head. Kristin stared at them for a minute, the corner of her lip hiked in teenage disgust at the idiocy of adults, especially female adults. She was never going to be that stupid when she grew up.

Liz started to reach for another cookie, then pulled her hand back. "These things are addicting, Naomi," she said. "You ought to go into business selling them or something, like that Mrs. Fields did a few years back. I read somewhere that she's a millionaire now."

A rueful smile touched Naomi's lips. "A *fat* millionaire, undoubtedly. At least I would be. Even fatter than I am now, that is." Richard had made another of his snide comments that morning when she'd gone through three pairs of shorts before finding ones that still fit. Damn him! She was trying her best to take off the extra pounds she'd gained when she was pregnant with Leah, but it didn't help much when he made her feel like a lard-belly. And a lazy lard-belly at that—he'd coupled the jibe about her weight with the observation that she was using the time she'd set aside to finish her doctoral thesis on the women in Shakespeare to cavort at the park with Leah and her women friends.

Sheri frowned at her. "You're not fat, Naomi. I wish you'd stop saying that."

"Enough, already," Naomi said. "Pleasantly plump, then." She smiled at Sheri, easily one of the most beautiful women in Ashland, with her wavy brown hair tumbling over her shoulders, long green eyes framed with dark lashes that weren't fake but looked it, and a body to die for. Sheri was truly gorgeous but so sweet you couldn't hate her for it. Not too much anyway.

Naomi turned her attention back to Liz. "I want to hear about the first time you got laid. Go for it before the kids get bored."

8

"I'll talk fast," Liz said, craning her neck to check out how Brooke was doing. Her daughter's thick white-blond hair gleamed in the sunlight as she toddled around after Kristin.

Liz stretched her legs out and crossed her ankles. "It was the summer after I graduated from high school. I had this really wonderful boyfriend. Kevin Sawyer. God, he was cute. And smart. And nice, too. We'd been going together all during our senior year at South Eugene High, king and queen of the prom, all that stuff. We were *totally* in love. The only thing was that he was going to Stanford, and I was going to stay in Eugene and go to the U of O."

Liz sighed and shook her head. "We actually talked about doing it, about me taking birth control pills, but we decided to wait until we got married. Then the day before he left for Stanford, we got carried away. It wasn't as earth-moving as I thought it would be, but I loved him so much it didn't matter."

Meredith drew her heavy dark eyebrows together and stared at Liz. "What happened to him?" she asked. "I don't remember you dating anyone named Kevin while we were in college."

Liz smiled, but she could feel the tiny tremor in her lips. After all these years it still hurt, but she hated letting anyone else know. She took a deep breath. "He'd gotten a new car for graduation, and he insisted on driving it down to California. He never made it. A drunk driver hit him head-on right outside Redding." Even now, she worried unreasonably every time Fletcher drove somewhere, sure that after she kissed him good-bye, she'd never see him again.

"Oh, Liz," Naomi said, tears welling up in her round brown eyes. "That's so sad."

Liz forced herself to smile even more broadly. It was dumb of her to have brought the subject up, but she hadn't been thinking about the end of her story when it occurred to her. Fletcher was right; she ought to spend a second or two contemplating what she was going to say before she opened her mouth. "It was a long time ago," she said. "I've gotten over it completely."

"I was even younger than you," Naomi said. She grimaced. "Actually, I hate to admit it, but I wasn't much older than Kristin. I was fifteen." Glancing at Kristin, she lowered her voice even though the girl couldn't possibly hear their conversation above the kids' happy shrieks. "Of course, nowadays, that'd probably make me almost over the hill. Then, though, I thought I was pretty damn daring."

"Who was the boy?" Meredith asked.

Naomi squirmed a little. "Leave it to the lawyer to cross-examine the witness," she said. "Actually, I'm not particularly proud of that part. I'd come out to Oregon to spend the summer with my cousin Rose in Portland. We were the same age and had always been great friends." She winced, twirling a strand of her frizzy black hair around her finger. "I slept with her boyfriend. She was pretty hurt and upset, but she found someone else and forgave me by the next summer when I came back out again." Her chuckle was humorless. "Maybe Richard is my karmic justice. I never thought of it that way before."

"Give yourself a break," Liz said. "You were only fifteen; Richard's almost fifty. I hope karma, whoever or whatever that is, is more fair than that."

Naomi shrugged. "So, anyway, I went back to New York at the end of the summer. We wrote to each other for a while, until he found another girlfriend."

"Did you ever see him again?" Sheri asked.

"No," Naomi said. "After I got over being hurt, I realized what a schmuck he was, dropping Rosie like that just because she wasn't putting out. That's what he called it—putting out. In order for him to put it in, some dumb girl had to put out. I was hot, I was convenient, and I was stupid. I thought he loved me, but the only thing he loved was his dick. And his car, which was where we did it. It was an old Rambler— the seats folded down flat, like a big lumpy bed."

Naomi sighed, remembering how disappointing it had been when it was all over. "All in all, the best thing about losing my virginity was that I only had to do it once. Not that the other times that summer were much better."

"That's the truth," Meredith said, then fell silent as Kristin and Felicia approached them with the little herd of toddlers.

"They want to swing," Felicia said. "Is it all right?"

"Sure." Sheri smiled at her daughter. Felicia was always such a big help with the little kids.

The children trooped off together to the baby swings at the far end of the playground. "Where were we?" Naomi said. Sometimes she thought the hardest part of being a mother was remembering what you were talking or thinking about through the dozens of interruptions. She'd read somewhere that being pregnant and having babies killed brain cells. Well, she was living proof—either that or she was developing a premature case of Alzheimer's.

Meredith leaned forward and plucked a couple of grapes from the bowl next to the cookie platter. "I *decided* to get rid of my virginity when I was twenty," she said. "I had no illusions about being in love. It just seemed like it was about time. During the summer before my junior year at the University of Oregon I went backpacking in the French Pete wilderness area with a guy I'd met in a lit class. You know, the poetic type—sweet, romantic, crazy about me. We zipped our sleeping bags together, and that was that. The best thing about it was the clear sky and all the stars. I just watched them winking at me and waited for him to get through."

She shook her head, then tossed the grape into her mouth. "Unfortunately, he *wasn't* a virgin, and he prided himself on how long he could keep at it. I was so sore the next day I could hardly walk. And it was a five-mile hike back to the damn car."

"That was right before I met you, wasn't it?" Liz said. "You were two years ahead of me, and I started at U of O in the fall of 1973. Did I ever meet him?"

"I'm not sure," Meredith said. The memory wasn't particularly pleasant; she really didn't feel like talking about it anymore. She gestured toward Sheri. "You're the only one who hasn't fessed up."

Sheri felt her cheeks redden. The other women were always so casual about things like this, but it was still real hard for her to reveal anything personal after all those years of hearing her mom say, "What goes on in this family is no one else's business."

She curved her lips into what she knew was a sheepish smile. "You wouldn't believe I'm still a virgin, would you?" she asked.

Everyone howled with laughter. "I didn't think so," Sheri said. "Okay. Well, it's true I wasn't even a virgin when I married Mike. He had a hard time with that. Of course, his own experiences didn't count because he's a man and everyone knows that's different."

Meredith uttered a little snort. "It never fails to amaze me how that works." She'd seen it over and over again in her family law practice—a man who cheated on his wife expected to be forgiven, or if not, at the very least to leave the marriage with all his possessions and self-esteem intact while a wife foolish enough to confess or be caught usually ended up with nothing.

"Yeah." Sheri nodded. "Sometimes Mike still gets jealous over guys I dated fifteen years ago. Anyway, my first time was right before my senior year in high school. I'd had a crush on the boy practically since fifth grade—he was a few years older and really a big shot, so I never actually expected anything to come of it. In fact, I hardly ever saw him after he graduated from high school and went off to college, and I think I'd pretty much outgrown my infatuation. But I went to this big party up on Mount Ashland with some of my friends, and there he was. We both got drunk and ended up sneaking off into the bushes." She laughed, shaking her head. "I must have passed out or something because I don't even remember what it was like."

"You probably didn't miss much," Meredith said. "I wish I'd thought to stow away a pint of vodka in my backpack." She uncrossed her legs from her lotus position and wiggled her toes just as the kids descended on the blanket. "Well, I guess our meeting is adjourned for this month," she said, scooping Justie into her arms.

San Francisco

The television screen filled with an avalanche of brightly colored geometric shapes, and Doug let the Nintendo control pad drop from his hand. He'd been able to beat the very highest level of Tetris no sweat before they'd started pumping him full of drugs. Now he got so dizzy he couldn't even complete level one.

He leaned his head against the back of his beanbag chair and squeezed his eyes shut to keep from crying. Nothing had been the same since the day he found out he was adopted. Sure, he had a horrible illness, but there'd been hope and his family had been behind him 100 percent. And he'd known who he was, who his parents were.

He didn't know anything anymore. Sometimes he wondered if Mom and Dad were sorry they adopted him now that he was causing them all this grief. Or maybe it was easier for them because he wasn't their *real* son. Maybe they thanked God every night for sparing Andy and Nick.

He shook his body like a wet dog to drive the doubts from his mind. Of course, Mom and Dad loved him. They told him so over and over. He was a fool to think otherwise. It was his biological parents who didn't give a damn about him.

His bedroom door swooshed open, and his father stepped into the room. "How's it going?" he asked, sounding genuine instead of phony cheerful the way he did after they'd first found out about the leukemia.

Doug lifted a shoulder. "Okay, I guess. At least I've been able to eat today."

"That's good news." Dad sat down on the foot of Doug's bed. "I've got some myself. Dr. Levison says it looks as if you're heading into a remission—and a bone marrow transplant is still a possibility. All we have to do is find your birth parents and keep our fingers crossed for a good match, either with one of them or with a sibling, if you have one."

Doug sat up straight. If only he could get over that first hurdle—remission—everything else would be easy. He just knew it. "Now that's truly excellent news!" He calmed down a little when Dad didn't join in. "Is it going to be hard? Finding them, I mean."

"I don't think so. Since you were born in Oregon, I've been on the phone all morning with a lawyer in Portland. He says all we have to do is to present a petition to the same court where the adoption decree was filed. You'll have to write an affidavit explaining why you need to know who your birth parents are—they even have contingencies for emergencies like this in the law. Then when the judge grants the petition, they'll unseal the file, and the lawyer will have access to the information in it. Your birth mother's name. Your birth father's name." Finally, Dad gave in and grinned at him.

"Wow!" Doug slapped his hand against his father's. "They couldn't possibly turn me down, then?"

"I sure as hell hope not."

Doug nodded. Look out hurdle number two. He was on his way.

CHAPTER 2

A thin spiral of smoke curled above the Waterford crystal ashtray on Liz Berenson's desk, and she stared at it with disgust. Only three weeks without a cigarette this time, and she'd caved in already. She picked it up and took a deep drag of the crisp, mentholated smoke, then stubbed it out. It was a good thing she didn't have too many vices—or a weight problem—because willpower had never been her strong suit.

Still, she hadn't smoked the whole thing, so maybe it didn't count too much. She was at her office—not at home where Fletcher would sniff out the evidence and look at her with that damned eyebrow of his raised above the wire-rimmed glasses he'd worn since college. He'd given up his pipe over two years ago without a single relapse. Anyway, that's what he claimed. Just the thought of his condescending attitude rankled so much she pulled another Salem from the pack in her desk drawer.

Someone tapped at her door. She hurriedly stuffed the cigarette into the drawer and tossed the ashtray into the wicker wastepaper basket at the side of her desk. She'd retrieve it later. Waving her arms about in what she knew was probably a futile effort to dispel the incriminating odor, she called, "Come in."

Her receptionist Ursula poked her head in the door. "Naomi Chandler is here to see you. With a friend."

Liz smiled. "Send them in." She always liked seeing Naomi; the monthly playgroup meetings just weren't frequent enough, as far as she was concerned. In the beginning they had gotten together so that the kids could play. But after the first few gatherings, they discovered that it benefited the mothers more than the children. And, as Meredith—always the logical one—had pointed out, a mother's sanity was pretty important to a child's welfare, so it was still a good thing for the little ones no matter why they met.

Naomi stepped into the office, Leah riding her hip and a tall, good-looking man following her. As usual, Naomi looked as if she hadn't had time to finish anything she'd started: her chin-length black hair was frizzy, her pants wrinkled, and her lipstick smudged. Motherhood was even more complicated for Naomi than for the other women in playgroup—except for Sheri, the rest of them only had to worry about one small child while poor Naomi mothered not only Leah and her stepdaughter Kristin but also Richard and a whole host of other people who by all rights should have been able to take care of themselves.

"Hope I'm not bothering you," Naomi said. She glanced behind her. "This is Alec Whittier. He's going to be filling the Shakespeare chair at SOSC this year." She motioned Alec forward. "I just picked him up at the airport. He mentioned he didn't have a place to live yet, so I told him I had a friend who owned a real estate and property management company and brought him straight here."

Liz rose and walked to the front of her desk, her hand outstretched. Well, Naomi had found herself another orphan, it appeared.

Not that Liz blamed her. She wouldn't mind taking in this orphan herself. She liked the way his hazel eyes sparkled as he shook her hand,

16

and his Michael Caine Cockney bad-boy accent was certainly not going to hurt his popularity with women. It would serve that bastard Richard right if this great-looking guy charmed his way right into Naomi's bed.

Knowing Naomi, though, that was unlikely to happen. Despite realizing exactly what Richard was up to, she chose to ignore most of it, make jokes about the rest, and keep up the facade of a happy family. Naomi was too good for her own good.

Liz waved Naomi and Alec toward the chairs in front of her desk. "Glad to help," she said. "Just tell me what you need."

Naomi sank into one of the cane-backed chairs and settled Leah on her lap. The child frowned at Liz and popped her thumb into her mouth. Naomi stared at Alec, an anxious little smile fluttering across her lips.

"Thanks." Alec sat down, rubbing his chin with his forefinger. "A one-bedroom place near campus should do quite nicely."

"That's easy enough." Liz scribbled a note on her calendar. "Why don't we get together tomorrow afternoon and look at some of the things I've got available?"

The office door opened. Jeff Haviland stood in the doorway, backlit like a model in *Esquire*, perfect hair framing an equally perfect face. "Sorry," he said. "Didn't realize you were busy." Smiling sheepishly, he backed out. "I'll talk to you later."

Liz's cheeks flushed. She hastily bent her head over her appointment calendar. She'd hired Jeff three weeks ago, and so far every time she saw him she found herself reacting like a gawky teenager. She blushed, stammered, forgot what she was going to say no matter how much she rehearsed it beforehand. His obvious attraction to her was flattering, and God knew she enjoyed it, especially since lately Fletcher managed to make her feel about as desirable as a little sister with a runny nose.

Still, Jeff had never so much as hinted that their relationship should extend beyond business. All he did was treat her like a beautiful woman; she was the one getting carried away by her daydreams, lustful little vignettes of the two of them engaged in the kind of behavior that

Fletcher had apparently lost all interest in. Her cheeks cooling a little, she said to Alec, "Two o'clock okay?" and scribbled his name next to the slot after he nodded.

Alec stood and offered his hand again. "I'll see you tomorrow, then."

After Alec, Naomi, and Leah left, habit propelled Liz's hand to the desk drawer where she kept her cigarettes, but she stopped it midway there. No. She would not give in.

Jeff stuck his head in the door. "Okay now?"

Everything about him shined—his sleek light brown hair, his green eyes, his regular white teeth. Not even his crisp pale blue shirt could disguise his broad shoulders and beautifully muscular arms. She couldn't keep herself from imagining what it would feel like to rest her head on one of those shoulders, to feel those strong arms wrapped around her, to touch her lips to his—

"Y-yes," Liz said, her cheeks burning again. She set her teeth. Despite their problems, Fletcher was a good husband. It was her own fault she wasn't happy. She forced herself to take a deep, calming breath. No. She would not give in to her daydreams, either.

CHAPTER 3

SEPTEMBER

Meredith paused at the living room entrance with the vacuum cleaner trailing behind her like some kind of prehistoric pet. Sunlight streamed through the windows, illuminating every single speck of dust on the furniture and old hardwood floor. Damn! She was going to have to choose—after Justine's messy accident in the sandbox and her second bath for the day, there just wasn't enough time left to dust the living room *and* vacuum the family room. Everyone was going to arrive in ten minutes.

Hurriedly, she dropped the vacuum cleaner, then let down the blinds, angling them so there was still some light but not enough to show the dust. Actually, she didn't know why she bothered cleaning the house *before* playgroup. Two minutes after the kids arrived, it would look worse than it did before she started. Still, she liked creating the illusion of calm for her friends—hard as they all worked, they certainly deserved a few minutes of luxuriating in a tidy room, one they hadn't had to pick up themselves. She supposed that was the reason why she made the effort.

Clutching the vacuum, she headed toward the family room as the phone rang. Damn again. She raced to catch it before the second ring, hoping against all experience that it wouldn't awaken Justine. All she needed was a few more minutes.

"Hello," she said, cradling the phone against her shoulder.

Her mother's voice rasped at her ear. "Meredith. How are you?"

Meredith looked up at the ceiling. Her mother had an unerring sense of timing. It never failed—in college, when she was drunk or stoned or in bed with someone and the phone had rung, it was always Eva. Ted hated the interruptions so much he'd come home one day with an answering machine. "For your mother," he'd said. "I'm tired of coitus interruptus." Meredith had laughed and told him that they'd have to start using another form of birth control then.

"Fine, Mother," she said. "But I'm really busy right now. Could I call you back later?"

"Won't take a minute," Eva said. "Just wanted to let you know I'll be coming down to see you and Justine next weekend."

It was always "you and Justine." She never mentioned Ted. When Meredith had confronted her about it once, Eva had denied that she disliked Ted. "He's so shallow," she'd said. "What's there to dislike about him?"

There was a tug at Meredith's blouse, and she looked down. Justie wrapped her arm around one of Meredith's legs and sucked noisily at her thumb. "Fine, Mother," Meredith said. The doorbell rang. "Look. My company's at the door. We'll see you when you get here." She hung up before Eva could say anything else and headed for the door, dragging the vacuum cleaner and Justie behind her.

Shaking her head, she opened the door. Five years ago she'd never have believed this scene possible. She'd always thought of herself as a professional, a lawyer, not a mother. In fact, she'd never really allowed herself to yearn for motherhood—her doctors had always told her the chances were slim because her mother had taken DES while pregnant with her.

But then along had come the miracle of Justine. At first Meredith had thought she'd stopped having periods because of yet another side effect of the DES. She'd been so afraid of a tumor, of cancer, that she'd insisted on having an ultrasound, and the tumor had turned out to be a lively little fetus.

Now Meredith smiled down at the former lively little fetus, jumping up and down as she spotted her friends clinging to their mothers' hands. "Come in," Meredith said.

Liz let go of Brooke's hand, and the little girl scampered inside. Liz hugged Meredith, surrounding her with the potent aroma of freshly applied Obsession. "What's that?" she said, pointing at the Electrolux stretched out behind Meredith.

"It's called a vacuum cleaner. Those of us without housekeepers still find a use for them."

"Don't let her fool you," Liz said, turning to Sheri. "It's a prop. Meredith is just trying to impress us."

Sheri nudged her older daughter and little Timmy inside, then followed them and shut the door behind her. "Well, I, for one, am already impressed. Especially if she can talk Ted into vacuuming for her." Her chuckle sounded a little brittle to Meredith. "I wish I could convince Mike . . ."

Meredith lifted an eyebrow and exchanged a glance with Liz. Sheri never said much about her husband Mike, but Meredith had been suspicious ever since the first time Sheri arrived at playgroup wearing a pair of sunglasses she'd declined to remove. A fair number of women sporting dark glasses indoors had sat across a desk from Meredith since she'd begun her practice in family law a dozen years ago, and most of them hadn't been the victims of allergies, sties, or an ophthalmologist's eye drops. If Mike's only flaw was his failure to vacuum the carpet, that would be surprising.

She motioned Sheri and Liz toward the family room. "Liz is absolutely right. I didn't really use this thing." She shoved the vacuum cleaner into the hall closet. "As I'm sure you'll notice." The doorbell rang again. "Naomi," she said. "She's not even ten minutes late."

Naomi stepped into the entry, Leah perched on her hip, as always. Meredith sometimes wondered if that child ever walked anywhere.

Naomi put Leah down in front of her. "Sorry—"

Meredith held up her hand. "Don't apologize," she said. "You're so close to being on time today it doesn't even count."

Liz enveloped Naomi with a hug, then tucked her arm through Naomi's and pulled her toward the family room. "I finally found a place for your friend Alec." She winked at Naomi before turning to the other women. "Wait until you see this guy Naomi dragged into my office right after the last playgroup meeting. Tall, lean, lots of thick dark hair, great crooked smile, and a wonderful, wicked gleam in his eyes that sent shivers down to my toes." She wiggled her eyebrows like Groucho Marx ogling a beautiful dame.

Meredith grabbed Naomi's other arm. "Have you been holding out on us?"

"Yes," Liz said. "This is an inquisition. You have to tell us everything you know about Mr. Alec Whittier."

The smile froze on Sheri's face. They were talking about her English professor.

Naomi grinned over her shoulder at Sheri as they followed the children into the family room. "I'll bet Sheri could do a better job. You've made quite an impression on Alec," she said. "He told me all about his Shakespeare on Stage class, about how he's going to cast *The Taming of the Shrew* and put on an actual production at the Shakespeare Festival's indoor theater at the end of the term. What a great way to study Shakespeare! Then he described this gorgeous woman in his class, and I just knew it had to be you. So I asked him her name." She waggled her finger at Sheri. "Why didn't you tell us?"

Sheri seated herself in Meredith's old-fashioned oak rocker, her cheeks burning. She should have known she couldn't keep a secret in Ashland. Everyone didn't *really* know everyone else, but sometimes it seemed that way. She didn't mind her friends finding out—it was Mike she was worried about.

Maybe going back to college had been a stupid idea after all, as stupid as Mike always said it was. "Just look at me," he'd said whenever she brought up the subject. "Four years of college and I end up building houses because it's a hell of a lot better paying job than just about anything I could do with a degree in social science."

She took a deep breath to calm the rapid beating of her heart. If Mike found out she'd enrolled in a class at SOSC, he was going to be pissed at her. Not telling him was pretty much the same as lying, but it was the way her mom had always handled her dad. It was sure as hell safer.

Unless she got caught. Sheri shrugged and tried to laugh, but it sounded strained even to her own ears. "I guess I was a little embarrassed," she said, glancing at Felicia. The little girl was too busy organizing the four toddlers into a game of hide-and-seek to pay any attention to the mothers, thank God. "Thirty-four and going back to school. I felt foolish." She'd had to quit after her sophomore year at SOSC when her dad had died in a logging accident and Mom needed her help with the kids still at home. That had been fourteen years ago, and even though she'd dreamed of going back, for one reason or another—mostly men, money, and babies—she just hadn't made it.

Meredith narrowed her eyes at Sheri, but her voice was gentle. "Did Mike give you a hard time about it?"

"He doesn't know. I haven't told him." She cleared her throat. She might as well get it over with. She lifted her chin and met the eyes of each one of her friends, relieved to find their faces filled with compassion and worry rather than with disgust. "And I'm not going to."

SAN FRANCISCO

Doug grabbed the glass from the bedside table and gulped a mouthful, then swirled the cold water around his mouth, bathing the sores for a few seconds of relief before he swallowed. He had no idea which of the drugs gave him the sores—or the nausea or the diarrhea or the hair loss, for that matter. Each one had a list of possible side effects a mile long, and he hadn't bothered to remember which drugs caused what horrible thing to happen to him. It was hard to believe that this was the cure when it made him feel so goddamn awful. It kept getting worse instead of better, and a week ago Dr. Levison had insisted he go back to the hospital.

Attitude check time. He gritted his teeth. Positive thoughts. He rubbed the sore spot on the back of his hip from the latest bone marrow test. Any minute now he'd find out the results, and he had to keep his mind positive. It was a kind of game he'd devised after the second week of chemotherapy. His blood was the football field; the drugs were the home team; and the Blasts were the opponents. Every negative thought was a first down for the Blasts; every positive thought was one for his team, the Lymphocytes. Christ, he hoped the test showed he'd made a touchdown.

Or that he'd won the game. That was the way he thought of remission. He closed his eyes and visualized the flashing scoreboard and the screaming crowd. He'd won. Goddamn it, he had to win.

"Doug?" Dr. Levison's quiet voice sent the football game off into the ozone.

Doug jerked his eyes open and pushed himself up straight in bed. He stared at her, trying to read the test results by the expression on her face. Impossible. They must give classes at medical school on how to look noncommittal. "What?"

She took a deep breath, and he knew. Bad news. She got a C in her facial expression class, and he flunked the big one.

"The blood tests looked good, but the bone marrow sample still shows blasts."

"Do my parents know?"

"I called them. They're on their way here."

"So what's next? You gonna nuke the sons-of-bitches?" Bad attitude. A fifty-yard run for the Blasts, but he didn't give a damn.

"Radiotherapy?" She shook her head. "Not yet. There's still one more drug I'd like to try before we resort to that."

Dr. Levison paused as Doug's mother, her eyes shiny with tears, rushed into the room. Shoulders slumped, his father trailed after her. Dr. Levison turned toward them. "I was just telling Doug about another drug I think we should try," she said.

Mom stepped up to the bed and rested her hand on Doug's arm. He knew she wanted to smooth his hair the way she used to do when he was little and running a fever, but she was afraid to now because it was so different, so patchy and thin. He laid his hand on top of hers and squeezed.

Dr. Levison handed Dad a small brochure. "It's called L-Asparaginase. It's an enzyme that works by breaking up one of the ingredients that blasts need to make protein, and it's been fairly effective. But—"

Doug rolled his eyes at his mother. Here it came, the list of tortures, the side effects.

"—some people are very allergic to it. The only way to find out, unfortunately, is to give it to you and wait and see. Are you game?"

Doug forced himself to smile at his parents. No point in making them suffer, too, anymore than they already did. "Sure, I'm game," he said. "What the hell have I got to lose except more hair?"

CHAPTER 4

OCTOBER

Something thudded in the family room next to the kitchen, and Naomi tensed, waiting for the loud wail that always followed one of Leah's frequent, but fortunately minor, accidents. She quickly stuck her hands under a stream of water to rinse off the sticky bread dough. Sometimes a half minute or more elapsed before Leah let loose with her famous yowl, but usually her scream would be bouncing around the house before now. Wiping her hands dry on the seat of her pants, Naomi trotted into the family room.

Leah sat at the bottom of the short stairway leading to the kitchen, a small cut oozing blood on her forehead and a dazed look in her eyes.

Naomi let out her breath. At least it wasn't anything major. She scooped Leah into her arms and headed toward the bathroom. "You're all right," she said, cradling the little girl against her chest like a baby.

"Mommy'll clean up the blood and put on a sparkly purple bandage, and then you can look at yourself in the mirror."

Suddenly, Leah arched her back and flailed her arms and legs. Her whole body stiffened, and Naomi clutched her even more tightly. Leah's eyes rolled upward and she gagged, her tongue thrusting out of her mouth. Then she went limp.

"Oh, my God!" Her heart pounding wildly, Naomi ran back to the kitchen with Leah in her arms. She grabbed the phone with trembling fingers and pushed the buttons for 9-1-1. When the dispatcher answered, Naomi gasped out, "My baby's dying! Send an ambulance to 408 Iowa. Hurry!" Her voice sounded tinny and far away, as unreal as what was happening.

She hung up, then knelt, laying Leah on the floor in front of her. CPR. That was it. What the hell was she supposed to do first? Why hadn't she listened better? Richard would know what to do. Richard always knew what to do. Richard. Her hands shaking even harder, she dialed his office number and let it ring six times. No answer. She slammed the phone down. He was never there when she needed him. When Leah needed him. How was she ever going to tell him their child was dead? And that it was her fault. Something she'd done wrong, maybe picking Leah up after her fall. Or something she hadn't done right, like the CPR.

The instructions came back in brief snatches. She tipped Leah's head back, opened her mouth, and made sure there wasn't anything inside she might have choked on. Then she sniffed, but all she could smell was Leah's sweet baby scent, no odd or poisonous odor, and tears blurred her eyes. Her baby couldn't die. All she'd ever asked of God after Leah's birth was to let her live to see her child grown and let her die before Leah did. That was all.

Willing herself not to cry, she put her lips over Leah's nose and mouth and breathed into it, then pressed lightly on her chest. Again. Then again.

Minutes passed, and still Leah lay limp and motionless, her eyes closed. Finally, the faint sound of one siren, then another reached

Naomi; and as she continued breathing, pressing, breathing, the sirens grew louder until they stopped in front of the house.

She picked up Leah, ran to the entry, and flung open the front door. Two ambulances were parked at the curb, one yellow and white one from the fire department and the white Ashland Life Support ambulance behind it. Two men jogged up the walk, followed by two more with a stretcher. The red-haired medic in front stretched out his arms, and Naomi placed Leah carefully in them. "Is she dead?" she whispered, her throat aching from unshed tears and unuttered screams. "I gave her CPR, but nothing happened."

The medic's fingers closed around Leah's wrist. He shook his head and looked at Naomi, just the ghost of a smile touching his lips. "She's got a pulse," he said. "She's breathing, but it's so shallow you might have missed it. She probably didn't need the CPR, but at least it gave you something to do before we got here."

Naomi closed her eyes for a second. Thank God Leah wasn't dead. "Is she going to be all right?"

The redhead knelt and laid Leah gingerly on the stretcher, and the young medic behind him handed him a pair of scissors. Carefully, the redhead cut Leah's pink sweatsuit off.

"Is she going to be all right?" Naomi repeated.

The medic kept his eyes on Leah's still body. "We're doing everything we can."

Naomi's throat tightened even more. Leah still might die—that's what he meant even though he didn't say it. She held her breath as the four men gingerly lifted the stretcher and carried it to the idling Life Support ambulance. They moved so slowly she wanted to scream at them, but she choked back the words. They had to know what they were doing.

Carefully, the medics slid the stretcher into the back of the ambulance, and the redhead helped Naomi climb in behind. "Don't break your neck," he said to the driver. "Just get us to the hospital with as few bumps as possible."

By the time they wheeled Leah into the emergency room, Naomi's heart was constricted with pain and her whole face ached with the effort of holding back her tears. The phone rang as she signed the admission forms, jarring Richard back into her mind. "May I use it?" she asked the clerk. "I need to call my husband."

The clerk directed her to the phone at the end of the counter. Her fingers stiff and cold, she jabbed at the buttons and listened to the rings. Where the hell was he? His classes met in the morning, and he usually spent his afternoons in his office.

Leah's shrill cry ended Naomi's speculations. Her vision blurred, and she smiled through tears at the clerk. "I never thought I'd be so happy to hear that wail," she said, the phone still dangling from her hand. "Thank God." Quickly, she called the English department office, left a message for Richard with the secretary, and hurried into the emergency room.

Leah lay on an examining table with a doctor bending over her. Her eyes were open, but she appeared dazed and listless.

"Is she—" Naomi's throat constricted.

"I'm Dr. Jackson. Your daughter seems to have had some sort of seizure, but it's over now. She doesn't have a fever, so that rules out a febrile seizure. Can you tell me what happened, exactly?"

Naomi described Leah's attack, stopping occasionally as Dr. Jackson jotted notes on the chart. When she finished, she waited silently while he added a few more sentences. Finally, he said, "I'd like to admit her overnight for observation."

"All right." Almost afraid to ask, Naomi cleared her throat. "What do you think it was?"

Dr. Jackson peered at her over the top of his half-glasses. "We'll need to run some tests to be more sure," he said. "But my guess is that she had an epileptic seizure."

There was something reassuring about the smell of a hospital to Naomi, something brisk and efficient in the mingled odors of alcohol and disinfectant. Someone else was in charge; there was absolutely nothing she could do for Leah except sit by her side while she slept through what Dr. Jackson called the "postictal" state that followed a seizure.

Naomi settled back in the chair next to Leah's bed and recrossed her legs. Now that the most horrible part of her terror was past she had time to conjure up visions of what had become of Richard. Three hours since she'd talked to his secretary, and still he hadn't shown up.

And when he finally did, she knew exactly what his excuse would be. He'd spent more time in the goddamn library in the last month than he had at home—or so he claimed, just as he always did whenever he was having an affair. Research, hah! She'd had to bite her tongue to keep from asking him if he'd gone into partnership with Masters and Johnson. Except that instead of being one of the researchers, he was a researchee.

Leah stirred, and Naomi leaned forward. It seemed strange to see Leah lying so quietly. She was always so active; she snorted and jabbered and scooted all over her crib, exuberant even while she slept. Watching her now made Naomi sad. Still, that was better than hysterical, which was what she'd come too damn close to a few hours ago.

She stood and paced to the window, looking out at the maple trees in the courtyard, at the scattered yellow and orange leaves on the green lawn. She'd always expected that she'd love her child, but she hadn't been prepared for the overwhelming, all-consuming passion she'd felt for Leah from the day she'd been born. If anything happened to her baby, Naomi knew her own life would be over. By comparison, Richard's affairs seemed almost unimportant. She loved him, but he was just a husband. He could be replaced. That was something he should be able to understand—she was his third wife, after all.

But Leah. That was different. Sure, she could have other children. A dozen if she wanted. None would be Leah, though; and if Leah died, the hole in her heart would never heal. She'd known that from the moment the midwife had placed the slimy, yowling little baby on her belly. Bonding, the psychologists called it. Too mild a word as far as Naomi was concerned. Fusion was more like it.

Once she'd imagined she felt the same for Richard, but her love for him had turned out to be so fragile, so conditional. He'd left too many holes in her heart, too many crater-sized scabs she could never resist picking at, each one with a name. Julia Reynolds. Mary Lawrence. Karen Henderson. She stared through the fading daylight at another dying leaf drifting to the ground.

A light tap sounded at the door, and she turned. Richard stood in the doorway, worry etching deep grooves in his handsome face.

"Jesus Christ, darling," he said. "I'm sorry it took me so long to get here." He glanced down at the floor. "I just got your message a little while ago. I was in the library."

CHAPTER 5

"You want me to sue your *father?*" Repeating her client's words, Meredith stared at the young woman sitting on the edge of the light green club chair across the desk from her. Yvonne Giroux was probably no more than twenty or twenty-one years old, but something in her pale blue eyes made her seem much older. She looked as if she'd seen plenty so far, most of it bad. But the set of her jaw and the slight jutting of her chin contrasted strongly with her limp dishwater blond hair and the way her white hands fluttered when she talked. She was not as weak as she appeared at first glance.

Sticking her chin out even further, Yvonne nodded. "I know it sounds strange, but I have a good reason." She took a deep breath and peered into Meredith's eyes for a long moment, as if she were searching for something there, some sign that it was all right to go ahead, that Meredith wouldn't condemn her afterward. Finally, without taking her eyes from Meredith's, she said, "My father forced me to have sex with him. I was twelve when he started, and it went on for four years."

Meredith sucked in her breath, trying to keep the full extent of her horror from registering on her face. Yvonne was working hard to keep things matter-of-fact; she owed it to her not to make it any more difficult than it had to be to reveal something like that to a stranger.

"Your *biological* father?" As soon as she said them, Meredith wished she could recall her words. What difference did it make whether the girl's abuser was related or not? Logically speaking, raping a child was abhorrent no matter who did it. Emotionally, though—now that was a different matter.

But Yvonne didn't seem to think her question at all odd. "My real father," she said. "Not a stepfather, or anything like that. It was my dad, and I loved him. At least I did before. Afterward, I didn't know what to think for a long time. Then I started hating him."

"What about your mother?" Meredith pressed the tip of her pencil so hard into the yellow legal pad on her desk that the lead broke off. Usually, it was a little easier for her to keep her emotional distance from her clients. She empathized with their anger and their suffering, but she didn't identify with them. The battle was theirs, not hers; she was a mercenary, not a patriot.

Yvonne shrugged. "She still doesn't believe me. When I told her a few months ago, she called me a vicious liar. Now she refuses to talk to me at all."

"You didn't tell her at the time it was happening?"

"I was too scared. Dad threatened to take away my horse if I said anything, and he told me no one would believe me anyway." Narrowing her icy blue eyes, Yvonne snorted. "Turns out he was right—about her anyway."

Meredith planted her elbows on her desk and leaned forward. A lock of her thick auburn hair fell over her shoulder and she impatiently tossed her head. "What made you decide to tell now?"

"I want to ruin his life the way he ruined mine." The girl's voice was hard and angry, but she didn't raise it. "He took something important

33

away from me. Now I want to take something important away from him. A fair trade—my childhood for his reputation." She lifted a pale eyebrow, sizing Meredith up as if she were interviewing a prospective hit man. "Can you help me?"

Meredith settled back into her old oak office chair and tapped her pencil on the pad. "I think so," she said. "You have some choices to make, though, both legal and moral."

"Give me the legal ones first. I'll think about moral later."

"First, exactly how old are you?"

"Does it make a difference?" Yvonne squinted at Meredith. "Twenty-two."

"Good. Then we won't have to worry about the Statute of Limitations. Normally, it's two years, but there's a special provision that extends it for five years after the plaintiff's eighteenth birthday for child abuse accruing before eighteen years of age. Since you're under twenty-three, we don't have to deal with finding a way to toll the statute. That makes everything more straightforward."

Meredith stood, dropped the pencil, and perched on a corner of the antique partners' desk she'd found at a flea market right after she moved to Ashland. She tugged at her long, hand-woven Guatemalan skirt to straighten it under her, then crossed her legs. "In fact, we may even be able to settle out of court."

"No. That's not what I want. I want it made as public as I can get it. I don't give a flying fuck about the money. He's got so much it wouldn't matter to him anyway."

"In other words, you want vengeance?"

Yvonne shook her head vigorously, and her dark blond hair swung across her face. "Justice," she said. "Only justice."

Meredith nodded. It made her a little uneasy, but she couldn't help feeling that what the girl said made a lot of sense.

Richard eased into the classroom and sat in an empty seat at the back as a red-faced boy stumbled through the last lines of an incredibly mutilated version of Mark Antony's funeral oration. He caught Alec's eye and smiled, sharing both his amusement and his sympathy for the poor kid. It took guts to audition in front of a roomful of your friends, especially when you were pretty sure you were going to make an ass out of yourself even before you started. The fact that it was an assignment and everyone else would have a chance to do the same didn't make it any easier.

While Alec offered a few encouraging comments to the young man, Richard glanced around the room until he spotted Heather Austin's blond head bent over her open Shakespeare text. Either she hadn't seen him sneak in or she was pretending she hadn't for everyone else's benefit. SOSC was a small college, and Ashland was a small town. He had to be a lot more careful here than he had at NYU—and even there, it had been hard to keep things quiet.

Although sometimes he didn't know why he bothered with the pretenses. Naomi had made it clear enough at the hospital that she knew something was going on, but she hadn't said a word about it since, just treated him the same as always, as if he were last on her list of priorities. In fact he doubted he was even on her list now that all of her attention went to Leah. He'd tried to talk to her about it after three days of her obsession with Leah's every breath, but then Leah'd had another seizure and there'd been all those EEG's and CAT scans to live through, and he'd finally just given up. Every time he said something she accused him of not caring enough about his daughter.

God knew nothing could be farther from the truth. He loved Leah every bit as much as she did, but he had his own life to live, too. Since Naomi was so involved in Leah's life—and at least a dozen other people's as well—thank God he had Heather.

Alec called Heather's name. She rose slowly and walked to the front of the room, her wonderful thick hair a cascade of strawberry blond curls to the middle of her back. It had been that wild mane of hers that had caught his attention the first time he saw her. She'd been waiting in line during registration. Then she'd turned around, caught his eye, and smiled at him with an open acknowledgment of his interest in her. Two seconds later he'd been standing by her side asking her to have a cup of coffee at the Union with him when she finished. She'd reeled him in as if he were some kind of prize marlin; he hoped she never found out he was actually about as exciting as a trained dolphin.

When she faced the class, her eyes skimmed the room until they found his. Unlike the student who'd auditioned before her, she seemed to relish being on stage. She leaned against the blackboard without any signs of self-consciousness while Alec addressed the class.

"You probably couldn't help noticing when you looked at the list of characters in *The Taming of the Shrew* that there are only three parts for women. That's not uncommon in Shakespeare's plays. Does anyone know why?" Alec waited for a few seconds, then called on the only person with a hand raised, a slender dark-haired woman in the front row.

She turned sideways in her chair before she answered, and Richard recognized Sheri Riley's perfect profile, the small straight nose, high cheekbones, finely arched black eyebrows. Now there was a beautiful woman. Long, cat-green eyes and hair with a sheen like silk. He vaguely remembered Naomi mentioning that Sheri was going back to school, but Naomi talked so much he didn't listen to most of what she said. Other people's troubles simply didn't interest him the way they did her. He had plenty of his own to worry about.

"Women weren't allowed on stage then," Sheri said. "All the actors were male, and young boys played the women's roles."

Alec smiled at her, and his whole face lit up with pleasure, and not the kind that derived from getting a correct answer. Intrigued despite himself, Richard leaned forward and stared at Alec. It looked as if the poor fellow were falling for a married woman. That, at least, was one transgression Richard had never committed.

Alec kept his eyes on Sheri. "That's why there are so many girls disguising themselves as boys in the comedies," he said, then turned back to Heather. "Anyway, we've got a lot of competition in here for the two main female parts. Are you ready, Heather?"

Heather nodded, her solemn manner signaling how seriously she took the audition. She'd begged Richard to attend—even when he'd worried about how it might look—because she thought she could do her best only if he were there. She hesitated for a moment, then plunged into Juliet's balcony scene speech begging Romeo to forgive her for being so forward. Her eyes were riveted on Richard throughout the entire performance, and several curious students turned in their seats to see what she was looking at so intensely. A slow warmth moved up Richard's neck into his cheeks. He pretended to scribble notes on the tablet he'd brought with him. Damn her for calling attention to him like this.

Heather sat down amid a smattering of applause. She turned to the back of the room and flashed a triumphant smile at Richard first, then Alec. Richard had to admit that she hadn't been too bad, although her Juliet seemed more bitchy than innocent. Maybe she'd make a good little shrew, after all. He sighed. He certainly had a knack for picking difficult women.

Leaving now would call even more attention to himself, so Richard remained seated while Sheri got up to face the class. "I'm doing Portia's speech from *Julius Caesar*," she said, her hands clenched stiffly at her sides. "She's Brutus's wife, and she's complaining that he doesn't treat her as his equal partner."

Sheri closed her eyes for several seconds before she spoke the opening lines. Her tentativeness completely disappeared; and by the third or fourth line, a confident, angry woman squared off with her invisible husband. Sheri's rich, throaty voice resonated with conviction and love, and by the time she reached the final line, there wasn't another sound in the classroom.

When she finished, she bowed her head. For a long moment, the room was utterly silent; then everyone clapped loudly, Richard among them. He glanced over at Alec and nodded. He knew what the poor bastard was suffering.

Meredith struggled awake through a haze of horror, just as she had the previous five nights, ever since her first meeting with Yvonne Giroux. It was the same dream she'd had sporadically for years, more frequently since Justine's birth, but amplified lately to nightmare proportions. Somehow it was all connected to Yvonne.

She opened her eyes to darkness, relieved to be awake even though it was still the middle of the night. She'd rather get up exhausted than risk going through the torture of the dream again. She'd read somewhere that lying in bed quietly was almost as good as sleep. It would just have to do.

Next to her, Ted snored softly. To keep her mind occupied, she turned on her side and stared at his perfect profile. Television cameras loved his face; women were always telling her how lucky she was to have such a hunk for a husband; but his good looks had never meant that much to her. He hid it pretty well from most people, but he was smart, a lot smarter than he needed to be in order to succeed at his job as a television reporter at KDRV in Medford. They kept trying to promote him to anchor, but he kept turning them down. It was more fun out in the field, he claimed.

And having fun was what made Ted tick. The lack of it had tocked him right out of law school, where they'd first met fifteen years ago. She didn't see him again until three years after that, when she and Fletcher had started their practice in Ashland. One day she turned on the news, and there he was. She called him up just to find out how he was doing, and he asked her on a date. A year later they'd gotten married.

Eight years later, she'd gotten pregnant, and that was when all their troubles had started. Meredith rolled over onto her back and stared at the ceiling. She'd never really thought much about having a child until she found herself pregnant at thirty-five, and Ted would have been content for things to go along the way they had been, the two of them having fun together, completely free from the constraints of parenthood, able to do almost anything they wanted whenever they wanted.

But Meredith surprised both of them. She really wanted the baby. For one thing, her pregnancy was practically a miracle. Because Eva had

38

taken DES while she was carrying Meredith, Meredith's doctor had told her she quite likely would never get pregnant, and if she did, there was a large possibility she wouldn't be able to carry the baby to term. Despite Ted's objections, she decided to try.

That was when he accused her of refusing to compromise. "Compromise?" she'd screamed at him. "How can you *compromise* about having a child? It's not something you can do halfway. What you're talking about is capitulation. You get your way, and I capitulate. Some compromise."

He'd backed off after that, but nothing had been the same afterward. Her pregnancy had been horribly unpleasant, but she managed to get through it. Then Justine had been born, and although Ted fell in love with her every bit as much as Meredith did, something inside Meredith went awry. The bad dream of her childhood started again, and it awoke her in the middle of the night as often as the baby did. She knew it was neurotic, but she couldn't bear to leave Justine alone with Ted. Making love turned into sex; sex turned into duty; and the duty became disgusting to her. She had to work hard to keep from shuddering every time Ted touched her.

The dream. Sex. A child. Yvonne. They were all interwoven somehow, but how—and why—continued to elude Meredith. She crossed her arms under her head and called up some of the disjointed images of her nightmare. She was on a merry-go-round and the music kept getting louder and faster and then something hard pushed up from under the saddle, jabbing at her through her panties. Then the scene changed and she was in her bed and something was in there with her and it was touching her all over. And then she was up high in the air, sometimes over water, other times over tall trees, her crotch pinned to a clothesline, the kind that moved when you tugged on one end of it. Mommy was pinned next to her and they were both screaming as Daddy cranked on the handle, pulling them closer and closer.

That was when she always woke up, her heart pounding and her nightgown soaked with sweat. It was the last image in the dream—her father's face getting closer and closer, his horrible grunting sounds as he pumped the handle up and down—

All at once the dream vision turned into a memory so real Meredith stuffed her fist in her mouth to keep from crying out. Suddenly it all became terrifyingly clear. This time she knew she would never be able to forget it again.

CHAPTER 6

The only thing Mike Riley hated more than fixing a clogged-up kitchen drain was stepping in dog shit. Especially when it wasn't his fault—except to wash his hands, he never used the goddamn thing anyway. He gave a final twist on the wrench, and the pipe came apart, dirty water and Drano flooding over his hand and splashing into the bucket. He jerked back and banged his head against the top of the door. "Fuckin' a—" he bellowed.

"What happened?" Sheri appeared in the doorway, a worried look on her face like some stupid ass dog about ready to roll over on its back and piss all over itself.

"What the fuck have you been putting down this drain?"

She cowered some more. "Just the dishwater."

"Just the dishwater," he mimicked. "Well, dishwater doesn't plug the damn thing up. Grease does. And food."

"I'm sorry." She backed out of the kitchen.

"Make yourself useful," he called after her. "Bring me the snake from the garage. It's your goddamn friends who're coming in an hour, not mine. Mine are already halfway to Klamath Falls by now." Which is where he would've been, too, if it weren't for the sink and goddamn playgroup. The day before deer season opened, a hunting trip he'd planned months ago, and here he was farting around with a fucking drain.

Sheri came back with the snake dangling from her hand. "Is this it?"

"Yeah, that's it." Mike snatched it out of her hand, and she cringed away from him like he was going to smack her with it or something. Shit, he'd never hit her when he wasn't drunk—she should know that by now. Not that he didn't feel like it sometimes, but he could control it better when he was sober. Unlike Pop. He rubbed at the scar on his chin where Pop had taken a belt to him once, buckle end first. Sheri was lucky he wasn't as mean as his old man.

"Can I help?" Her voice trembled a little, but she stood her ground.

Something inside him snapped. He'd been looking forward to this day for so long, to riding to Klamath Falls with Bob and Carl, setting up camp, drinking a few beers, then getting up before dawn so they'd be ready when the mule deer season opened a half hour before sun up. They'd gone ahead without him, saying they'd meet up with him at Ye Olde Towne Club in Klamath Falls that afternoon. But if the two of them got started drinking too long before he got there, he'd be lucky to find them anywhere, let alone the Towne Club. He worked too goddamn hard. He deserved this trip.

"Sure," he said, the bile in his stomach turning into sarcasm in his voice. "Why don't you just take care of the goddamn thing yourself?" He slammed the snake to the floor and stalked to the refrigerator, his fists clenched. "I'm outta here." He grabbed a can of Blitz, popped the top, and let a stream of the cold beer pour down his throat. "You and your fancy fucking friends can go piss up a rope." He stomped out of the house, slamming the front door behind him.

A minute later, Sheri heard the pickup roar out of the driveway. She knew how important his hunting trip was to him, but she still didn't like it when he got mean like that. Nine years they'd been married, and she always ended up crying whenever he yelled at her. If only she could stand up to him and tell him what she thought, but even the idea started her stomach churning.

Tears stung her eyes as she stared at the mess Mike had left her with. Meredith and Liz and Naomi and the kids would be knocking at the door any minute now, and she'd wanted so bad for everything to be perfect that she'd even hired the teenage girl next door to watch the kids while she cleaned up. A spotless house wasn't much to offer, but even that was better than this.

She brushed the tears from her cheeks. She never felt she really belonged in Timmy's playgroup. She was just a cocktail waitress, the only one without a college degree; and Mike was a contractor, not a professional like Fletcher and Richard or a local television celebrity like Ted. She was always embarrassed when it was her turn to hostess—her tract house in Quiet Village looked so different from the modern castle on the hill that Liz lived in or Naomi's meticulously restored Victorian or even Meredith's cute but comfortable farmhouse on the edge of town. The others served lunch on their Dansk or Lenox or unmatched but antique china; all she had was dingy, knife-scarred Melmac and cheap stainless from Bi-Mart.

She drew in a shuddering breath and made up her mind. If Mike could afford a hunting trip, she could afford lunch at Dairy Queen for her friends and a plumber to fix the drain. If she didn't tell him, he'd never know.

Liz fastened her seat belt and snuggled back against the soft leather seat in Jeff's new Mercedes. Ever since she'd hired him, she'd found herself looking forward to Thursdays and the multiple listings tour. Usually she drove, but today was special: he wanted to show off his new car, and the other agent who usually came along with them had called in sick. Poor Marie. She'd missed a great tour.

Liz chuckled as Jeff pulled out onto Siskiyou Boulevard. Actually, it wouldn't have been so great if Marie had been along. Jeff was all business whenever anyone else was around. It was only when they were alone that he flirted with her. She loved it, even though she sometimes felt a little guilty.

"What's that last address?" he asked, braking for the red light at the Wightman Street intersection. He turned his head and stared directly into her eyes. His gaze didn't flicker away even when a noisy motorcycle roared up next to his car.

Liz forced herself to glance down at her list. Every time Jeff looked at her like that, another little chunk of the icy barricade melted from around her heart. The warmth crept into her cheeks, and she knew she was blushing. Even worse, she knew *he* knew she was blushing. And he knew why. She met his eyes again as she said, "Top of Morton Street. One of those new houses they've been building for rich Californians."

She grimaced, thinking how much Fletcher hated what California money had done to Ashland—and how little he respected realtors for capitalizing on it. He was a rarity, though, along with Sheri—two of the few people she knew who'd been born and reared in Ashland. Everyone else was from someplace else.

"Or rich real estate brokers." Jeff smiled at her until someone behind them honked to let him know the light was green. "One of those rich Californians, I'll bet," he said. "They're always in a hurry."

Liz sneaked little glances at him as they zipped along the boulevard. She couldn't keep herself from wondering what he looked like without clothes. Not that he didn't look good with them—he had great shoulders and narrow hips and when he wore a polo shirt, his chest and arm muscles bulged in a way that was definitely not unsightly. He was a swimmer, and those little Speedos they wore were almost the same as naked.

A smile tugged at her lips. Maybe she'd start swimming laps again. She'd given it up after Brookie was born because there just didn't seem to be enough hours in the day. Jeff swam every morning at six o'clock, she knew. If she went to bed a little earlier, she could—

She shook her head. She was almost thirty-seven years old, at her sexual prime. She was slim and pretty and people told her she looked ten years younger than her age. Still, it had been eight months since Fletcher had touched her. She was horny, goddamn it, and he refused to see a counselor. "It's because we're both so busy," he'd said. "How can a counselor help that? Besides, it'd just be one more thing to schedule. I don't have time."

Well, that was a pile of shit. He didn't choose to *make* time. He had plenty of time to take on all those *pro bono* cases for the Earth First! people who'd been arrested for sitting-in around some old growth trees to keep them from being cut down. Now he was thinking about running for the state senate. If he won, she'd never see him. She couldn't just close down her agency and go off to Salem with him.

As Jeff turned off the boulevard and headed up Morton Street, Liz stared at the For Sale signs sprouting from half a dozen lawns on the way up the hill. The real estate business was hot right now, and it was the money she made that supported them so well. Fletcher gave away so much of his time they'd barely be able to afford a modest home in Ashland if they had to rely just on his income from the law practice he shared with Meredith.

"Deep thoughts?" Jeff parked the Mercedes behind several other realtors' cars and pulled on the parking brake.

Liz shrugged, smiling at him. She could go for days without saying anything to Fletcher, and he probably wouldn't notice, let alone care what she was thinking. Jeff seemed to be able to read her mind, though, and the few occasions he couldn't, he asked. It was a wonderful novelty to spend time with a man who paid attention to her—and who didn't expect her to cook his dinner or do his laundry. Sometimes she thought Fletcher saw her as simply another household convenience, like a vacuum cleaner or a dishwasher, only more trouble because she made demands on him.

But how could she tell any of that to Jeff? Whatever there was between them was unspoken. They joked and flirted and talked seriously about business, but so far they'd both avoided confiding anything important about their lives outside of Elizabeth Berenson Real Estate and Property Management. All she knew about Jeff's personal life was that his first marriage had ended in divorce several years ago and that there'd been a bitter custody battle over his two daughters, which he'd lost; all he knew about her was that she was married to a busy lawyer who spent a lot of time trying cases in the federal courts in Eugene and Sacramento and that her small daughter Brooke practically lived in day care, which she felt guilty about.

"Nothing important," she said, finally.

He looked at her for a long time before he got out of the car. She knew he was disappointed in her answer, but personal revelations didn't come easily to her. She was reluctant to admit to anyone that her life wasn't perfect, and especially to someone who didn't know her really well. Even Meredith and Naomi and Sheri didn't know how unhappy she was with her marriage.

"Would you have lunch with me today?" Jeff asked as they climbed the long flight of steps up to the front door. A worry line furrowed his smooth brown forehead, and his green eyes seemed to grow darker.

Liz's heart stopped for a second, and her hand trembled when she touched the doorknob. He was only asking her to lunch, she reminded herself. It wasn't like an invitation to go to bed with him—besides, she'd always thought Jimmy Carter was silly for worrying over a little bit of mental lust. If it weren't for imaginary sex, she'd be completely celibate.

Jeff's hand closed over hers and tightened. "I think we need to talk," he said.

He leaned toward her, and for a minute she thought he was going to kiss her. Holding her breath, she stared up at him, completely incapable of pulling her eyes away. A wave of desire suffused her body with warmth. She had to resist it, she knew, but she sure as hell didn't want to.

He removed his hand from hers and stepped back. "Please," he said.

46

She should say no. There was no such thing as an innocent date with Jeff, not when she felt the way she did about him.

"All right." The words seemed to come of their own volition. She opened the door and stepped inside before she could do anything else stupid. Jesus Christ, she had the willpower of a worm.

CHAPTER 7

It was sure taking Professor Whittier a long time to get around to the announcement. Sheri swung her long legs to the other side of the uncomfortable student desk and wished he'd get it over with. She'd spent the whole weekend reminding herself that she was too old to play Kate, especially since Petruchio was bound to be about twenty-one, at the most. If she got a female role at all, it would probably be the Widow.

In a way, that might be the best thing. Playing Kate would mean many more evening rehearsals than playing the Widow, and that would be a big problem. She'd managed to face Mike down about the plumber, but the confrontation had used up all the courage she'd been stockpiling for a year. If only she'd told him about the Shakespeare class when she'd first started it. He'd have been pissed, but it would have been mild compared to what would happen if he found out now.

She caught her lower lip between her teeth as Professor Whittier talked about how pleased he was with the quality of the auditions. He smiled directly at Sheri, and she ducked her head and stared at the scribbles in her notebook. Maybe it wasn't so hopeless after all. Maybe he didn't care about the age difference.

Even if she got the part, though, how could she ever hide two more evenings out a week from Mike? He hated the three nights she worked as it was. She held her breath for a second. That was it. If she temporarily dropped one cocktail shift at the Mark Antony lounge and then told Mike she'd added another night to pick up some extra money for Christmas, he'd complain a little, but he wouldn't suspect anything. She'd be out four nights a week, two working and two rehearsing. Best of all, the kids would be asleep before she left home, and Mike would be passed out by the time she got back.

She drew some more squiggles in her notebook, then colored them in and put a whole row of exclamation points at the bottom of the page while Professor Whittier continued on about how exciting it was that the Shakespeare Festival was going to let him stage the play in their indoor theater during their hiatus and what an opportunity it would be to work with some of the directors and actors who'd volunteered to help out. He was right about that. Although her secret goal was to act in movies, she'd auditioned for the festival a couple of times before she married Mike, hoping to get some real dramatic training.

But the festival's actor training days were already long past, even then. More and more of the actors carried Equity cards, and those who didn't usually had college degrees in drama. All Sheri had to her credit was a lot of experience in community theater. Everyone always said she had talent, but it hadn't been enough. Then she'd met Mike, stuffed her collection of reviews and programs, along with her dreams, into a storage box, and hidden it in the attic.

Methodically, she crossed out each exclamation point. What was the use of opening the box again? Mike would just make life miserable. Besides, Professor Whittier wasn't going to choose her anyway. Now he was smiling at the gorgeous strawberry blonde in the back row, Heather Austin. She'd been pretty good, and she was the right age.

Professor Whittier cleared his throat. "Now for the cast list for *Taming of the Shrew*." He rattled off the names of the students chosen for the male parts, then paused a few seconds. "Laura Evans, the Widow. Heather Austin, Bianca. And, finally, our shrew—Sheri Riley."

Richard wanted a cigarette. He'd quit years ago, but illicit sex didn't seem complete without a smoke when it was all over. It never occurred to him to want a cigarette after he and Naomi made love. It hadn't with Olivia, or Jean either, for that matter. Married sex didn't call for anything more afterward than a handful of Kleenex.

Propping himself on an elbow, he let his eyes drift over Heather's sleek body. Jesus, she was beautiful—tanned, slender, fit, young. Not even twenty-three yet. And he was going to be fifty in a week. Of course, he wasn't bad-looking for fifty—still had all his thick black hair, even if there was quite a lot of gray in it now. He worked hard to keep his body in shape, had to with the way Naomi cooked. It was too damn bad she didn't do the same.

Heather stretched like a cat and grinned at him. "I've missed you. It's been too long."

"Yes," he said. "But there wasn't anything I could do about it." He didn't tell her his child would always come first, but it was the truth. He'd been so worried about Leah after her seizures that he'd made sure Naomi could reach him at all times—and that had meant no dalliances with Heather until Leah started taking the phenobarbital. The doctor had assured them that it would probably take care of everything, and there hadn't been any more seizures since. Still, he wasn't entirely comfortable about being away from a phone, so he'd made it clear to Heather that he couldn't stay for as long as usual.

She ran her fingers through the hair on his chest, then trailed them down his belly to his penis. "Let's make up for lost time," she said.

"I wish we could. But I've got to get back to the office. Besides, I'm getting old. I probably couldn't get it up again."

She stuck out her lower lip and pretended to pout. "You didn't have any problem with that a month ago. I think you're getting tired of me."

Of course he denied it, but it was closer to the truth than she realized or than he was ready to tell her. He'd had a disconcerting revelation while they were screwing: he wasn't really in love with her. But he didn't know how to tell her that gracefully, not yet anyway. She was tenacious and strong-willed; and, quite frankly, he was worried she'd throw some sort of public tantrum if he ended things before she was ready to give it up. The thought was not appealing, especially after what had happened at NYU, not to mention the recent law the Oregon legislature had passed about student-teacher relations.

She let go of his penis and rolled to her other side, her backside toward him. "Well, go then. No point in hanging around here. You got what you came for."

He massaged her shoulder. "Come on, Heather. You know that's not true. I'd really like to stay. But I can't."

She shrugged, and something about the sullen set of her mouth reminded him of Kristin. Jesus Christ, Heather was only eight years older than his teenage daughter and not a hell of a lot more mature. Even worse, she was two years younger than Sara, his oldest child. He'd always prided himself on being rational, but everything about his affair with Heather was starting to look completely irrational—and it was getting harder and harder to pretend to himself that he wasn't a total asshole. What had been the beginning of another mighty erection shriveled into a pathetic little worm.

He patted Heather on the butt and got out of her bed. "I'll call you," he said. "Soon."

He knew he would. The only thing he didn't know was why.

Meredith picked up the phone, stared at it, put it back down again. She had to tell someone, and her mother seemed like the logical person. But she was afraid. Would Eva believe her? She couldn't bear it if her own mother told her she was crazy. On the other hand, Eva might have suspected there was something wrong with Dad—perhaps that had something to do with why she divorced him. Meredith had been thirteen at the time; then Dad had been killed in a car wreck three years later. Meredith had been so stoical about his death that it had worried Eva. But Meredith had insisted that she was fine and refused to talk anymore about it. How could she tell her mother that his death had been almost a relief? At the time, she hadn't even known why.

Now that she did, she couldn't think of anything else—and she was in danger of turning Yvonne's case into a kind of surrogate vengeance of her own. If she didn't talk to someone about it soon—

She glanced at the clock. A quarter after three. Justie would be waking up from her nap soon, and then it'd be too late. She wouldn't be able to call later that night because Ted would be home, and she wanted to tell Eva before she said anything to him.

She stood and paced to the kitchen sink, turned on the water, and soaked the sponge. Peanut butter and bread crumbs from Justie's lunch still speckled the table. She swiped at them, sweeping the crumbs into her hand, suddenly not so sure anymore what exactly she wanted to tell Eva. Maybe she should just ask some questions about Dad. It'd been years since they'd talked about him.

Relieved, she dumped her handful into the garbage and tossed the sponge into the sink. That was a good idea—start out with some small talk, then lead up to the big bomb. Or not, if it didn't feel right. She grabbed the receiver and pushed the buttons before she could back out, then changed her mind again as soon as she heard the first ring. Eva answered before Meredith could hang up.

"You must have been sitting on top of the phone."

"Next to it, actually. I twisted my ankle at the golf course last week, and I've been babying myself." Eva laughed. "I've got everything I need to sustain life within an arm's reach—a pitcher of water, a good book, and the telephone."

"All you're missing is a husband." Meredith tried to keep her tone light, but Eva's long pause let her know she'd failed. Damn! It always irritated her the way her mother could practically read her mind. Now it was going to be Eva asking the questions, controlling the discussion. Meredith made another attempt. "Just a joke, Mother."

"Is everything all right?"

Eva's worried-mother voice told Meredith it hadn't worked. She thought of the old Parkay commercial: Never try to fool Mother Nature. Never try to fool Mother, period.

"To tell the truth, no." Meredith swallowed hard. Tears flooded her eyes. Jesus Murphy, that was all she needed now, an opportunity for Eva to move in for the kill.

"What's wrong, sweetie? Is it Ted?"

"No." Meredith took a deep breath to bring her shaky voice under control. "It's about my father."

For once, Eva remained silent, and Meredith's careful plans fizzled.

"He forced me to have sex with him, Mother. When I was five years old. Did you know that?"

"Oh, my God. It can't be true." Eva's voice trembled too.

"It *is* true. I remember it. I'd forgotten it, but now I remember. More and more every day." Meredith clenched her jaw, speaking through gritted teeth, but her words still came out as a harsh cry. "Why didn't you stop him?"

"Oh, sweetie, I didn't know. If I had, I'd have killed him." Eva didn't bother to disguise her sobs. "It's a damn good thing the son of a bitch is already dead, or I'd blow his head off now."

Meredith's legs melted under her, and she sank to the floor, her muscles so limp she could barely clutch the phone. Eva believed her, and she blamed Dad, not her. "Thank you," she whispered.

"I'm coming to Ashland, and I don't want to hear a word of argument from you, Meredith. I'll be there in three hours."

Meredith hung up. For the first time in her life, she didn't feel a bit like arguing with Eva.

CHAPTER 8

Suppressing a yawn, Sheri leaned against the bar. Wednesday nights during theater hours were pretty slow at the Mark Antony, especially in the late fall when the play season was winding down. Many of the locals didn't go out in the evenings until Halloween, the night they took back Ashland as their own in a huge celebration that closed almost the entire length of Main Street. Of course, even that had gotten real touristy lately, with those big busloads of people from Portland and San Francisco coming to watch the goings-on. It was going to be even worse this year since Halloween fell on Saturday.

She sighed, hiking her hip onto the edge of a stool and propping her elbow on the bar top. The Mark would be a zoo, but at least she'd make some extra money. Now that she'd given up working Thursdays so she could rehearse *Taming*, she could really use it, too. Mike was almost finished with that ugly fake Victorian some rich Californians were building on Granite Street, but he didn't have another project lined up yet. And there was no telling when he would get something. They might be in for a long spell without much money.

She cupped her chin in her hand and stared down at the bubbles in her glass of 7-Up. Thank God she had a night job so they didn't have to spend most of what she made on baby-sitters. She took care of the kids during the day, and Mike was there in the evening. They didn't get to see much of each other, but that was okay with her because it gave them less time to fight.

The door opened, and a blast of cold air on her back made her shiver. She turned to see who'd come in, her attention immediately drawn to the green and yellow Oakland A's cap. What in the world was Mike doing at the Mark Antony? He hated the place—too many theater people, tourists, fags. That was why she'd felt safe about changing her schedule without telling him.

She swallowed, trying to rid her mouth of its sudden sour taste. Jesus, was she lucky. If he'd walked in on Thursday, she wouldn't have been there. "Hi," she said as he sat down next to her. "Who's watching the kids?"

"Girl next door." He motioned the bartender over and ordered a Henry's. "Put it on her tab," he said, jerking his head toward Sheri.

Ed looked at her, and she tried to smile at him. "It's okay," she said. "He's my husband."

"That's right." When Mike faced her, his beer breath almost gagged her. She peered at his eyes to see how drunk he was. He could drink for hours before he slurred his words or staggered, but she'd learned to look at his eyes to see if he was going to turn mean or not. Tonight they had that glazed look that meant the worst. It was almost like Mike wasn't in there anymore. She loved him with all her heart when he was sober, but when he was drunk, he scared her so much she practically hated him.

Both doors opened, and several people stepped into the lounge. "Play's over," Sheri said. "Time to go to work." She slid off the stool and waited until most of them found seats, then nodded at Ed and moved around the room taking orders.

By the time she returned to the bar, Mike sat glaring at Jeff Haviland, the handsome real estate agent Liz had hired a few months back. Jeff was wearing pleated dark gray slacks, an expensive-looking gray tweed sports jacket, and a pink and gray striped tie—a real contrast to Mike's dirty jeans and old sweatshirt. She hoped Jeff had enough sense to agree with most of what Mike said and ignore the rest.

Mike waved his empty bottle at Ed. "Get me another."

Ed looked at Sheri, shrugged, and set another bottle in front of Mike. Her jaw tense, she rattled off the orders she'd collected, then returned to the floor to wait on some of the newcomers. Forcing herself to ignore Mike, she chatted with a table of playgoers until Ed set some drinks on the service counter.

A half hour later, the play rush was over, and the bar gradually emptied. Mike and Jeff continued their conversation, Mike's voice growing louder and more belligerent with every beer. Rather than go near him, Sheri emptied the foul-smelling ashtrays and wiped the tables, polishing them until they shone. If he didn't leave pretty soon, she'd clean the toilets, too. Anything was better than getting in his way when he was drunk.

An angry bellow stopped her short at the rest room door, and she spun around toward the bar. Mike towered over Jeff, his fists clenched and one arm drawn back.

"You motherfuckin' tailgunner, you want your face smashed in?" he shouted. His bared teeth gleamed in the dim light.

Sheri's cheeks burned, and she sucked in her breath as Ed leaned across the bar. What if Jeff told Liz about Mike? Worse yet, what if she got fired because of him? Cocktailing jobs weren't easy to come by during the off season, and they were barely making it as it was.

"Listen," Ed said, his voice sharp in the dead silence following Mike's outburst. "If you don't walk out of here right now, I'm calling the police." He beckoned Sheri. "You'd better drive him home. I can manage by myself."

Mike lurched toward the door, muttering under his breath, while Sheri grabbed her coat and purse from under the bar. She mouthed an apology to Jeff, then shrugged on the down jacket and followed Mike onto the sidewalk.

"I don't know how you can stand that fuckin' place," he said. "Bunch of fuckin' weirdos and idiots."

She'd never get away with telling him what she really thought, so she tried to keep her tone light. She had to get him into the car without pissing him off. "Yeah, but the tips are a lot better than if I worked at the Log Cabin. You have to admit that."

"Don't have to admit a fuckin' thing." He belched loudly. "Where's your goddamn car?"

Sheri was relieved that Mike wasn't planning to drive his own pickup home. She pointed up the hill. "In the Mark's lot." Her burrito dinner churned in her stomach, and she concentrated on keeping it there. "Carter said we could park there during the slow season."

When they reached the car, she unlocked the passenger door for him. Mike settled himself in the passenger seat without argument, and by the time Sheri unlocked her door and climbed in, his head lolled against the window. Holding her breath, she turned the key in the ignition, but all he did when the engine hummed to life was snore a little louder.

She backed out of the parking lot and headed down the hill. There was no way she'd be able to get him out of the car when they got home. As far as she was concerned, he could just sleep it off right where he was. She clutched the wheel with icy hands, almost wishing it was a little colder so the son of a bitch would freeze to death. It'd serve him right for everything he'd done to her.

Goddamn squawking jays made as much racket as a jackhammer. Mike eased open one eye. Where the hell was he? It was colder than a well-digger's ass, and every muscle in his body ached.

Shit. He was in the car. He pushed himself up, rubbing at the crick in his neck and struggling to remember what happened last night. He'd left the Newkirks' house an hour before quitting time, even more pissed off than usual. Goddamn assholes expected miracles and then threatened to sue him when he couldn't perform them. He'd tried to tell them about Ashland's notorious water table, but they were too fucking know-it-all to listen to a dumb contractor, and now the basement of their fancy house was leaking like a goddamn gill net.

Anyway, he'd stormed out of the place, ending up at the Log Cabin because it was on the plaza, only a block away. He'd had two or three brews there, called the baby-sitter, then headed out for the Beau Club at the other end of Main Street. By ten o'clock he was bored with the place and out of money, so he'd decided to pay Sheri a little visit at the Mark.

The rest of the night must've happened to someone else because he sure as hell didn't remember it—and he probably didn't want to, either. He stretched out his legs, massaging his knees before he got out of the car. The car, Sheri's little Chevy—not his pickup. She must have driven him home. He would have to go retrieve his pickup from wherever he'd left it.

He tripped over the curb and stumbled up the sidewalk, his legs still numb. A couple of Steller's jays screeched at him before they flew into the neighbor's maple tree, and he made his fist into a gun, pointed his finger at them, and blew them away.

By the time he reached the front door, more pieces of the night before dropped back into memory, each one a little nugget of shit. No wonder Sheri had left him in her car—she had good reason to be pissed off at him. He might have gotten her fired. Maybe he had. Jesus Christ. Just because he couldn't remember it didn't mean it hadn't happened.

He sat down on the steps, elbows on his knees, throbbing head resting in his hands. He used to get so angry at Pop for hurting Mom when he was drunk that he wanted to kill the son of a bitch. Now here he was doing the same thing to his old lady. Maybe he hadn't hit Sheri last night, but he had plenty of other times. He had to stop drinking. If he didn't, she was going to leave him one of these days—and take the kids with her. Sheri wasn't like Mom, terrified of being on her own. She wouldn't stick around if he didn't shape up, and he couldn't stand the thought of losing her. A big sob filled his chest and squeezed into his throat, but he forced it back down.

He eased himself up, keeping his head tilted to cut down on the pain, and turned the doorknob. Thank God she hadn't locked him out because he had no fucking idea where his keys were. He stepped inside, glancing at the kitchen clock on his way to the bedroom. Twenty after seven. Shit. He had to be at work in forty minutes. Goddamn Newkirks. It was their fault he'd gotten so fucked up last night.

When he reached the bedroom, he stood in the doorway and stared at Sheri, asleep in their bed, her long brown hair spread across the pillow. In the nine years they'd been together, he'd never gotten tired of looking at her, and he didn't think he ever would. She was pretty enough to be a movie star or a model, but he wouldn't be able to stand that because then she'd be some kind of public property, not just his.

She stirred, and his chest constricted. Christ, he loved her. He knelt beside the bed, stroking her hair until she opened her eyes. "I'm so sorry, babe," he said. "Will you forgive me if I promise to quit drinking?"

CHAPTER 9

Staring into the fire, Fletcher Berenson pushed his glasses back onto the bridge of his nose. For one night a year, he was glad he lived at the top of a steep hill. Every Halloween, Liz bought a big bag of candy and then ended up eating most of it herself because so few kids bothered to hike all the way up Beach Street. It was probably the most peaceful place in Ashland on Halloween.

Not that he didn't like kids. They were fine. It was Halloween he abhorred. He just didn't have time anymore for that kind of idiocy, and he hadn't particularly enjoyed it even when he had.

The Westminster clock on the mantel chimed the hour as he leaned back against the hard leather of his wingback chair and crossed his legs. Liz and Brooke should be back from trick-or-treating any time; it was already past Brooke's usual bedtime. He shook his head. The child wasn't even two yet—he didn't know why Liz bothered with it this year, but she'd insisted. It was fine with him as long as she didn't expect him to do anything.

The fire crackled, and a red ember popped onto the hearth. Fletcher rose, grabbed the shovel, and scooped it back into the fireplace. The front door slammed while he closed the screen; and a few seconds later Brooke, dressed in a green dinosaur costume, her cheeks pink and her eyes glowing, dashed into the library with Liz bubbling along after her. Fizzy Lizzie, he'd always called her in college; at thirty-six, she was still as effervescent as a bottle of shaken champagne—and about as stable. Boring was certainly not a word he'd apply to the sixteen years they'd been married.

"Look, Daddy!" Brooke held up her black and orange Halloween sack, now bulging. "Brookie got candy!"

"Far out!" Fletcher tried to sound excited for Brooke's sake. "May I see?"

Brooke thrust out her sack, and Fletcher peered inside at the mounds of candy. He looked at Liz over the top of Brooke's head. "You aren't planning to let her eat the stuff, are you?" he asked.

Liz shrugged. "It won't hurt her to have sugar once a year." She hoisted Brooke into her arms. "Come on, cutie. Time for bed." She glanced back at Fletcher as she headed toward the library's double doors. "The baby-sitter's coming in an hour. I laid our costumes out on our bed." She giggled. "You're going to make a great Surfer Ken."

"With this?" He ran his fingers through his beard and rolled his eyes. "I doubt it."

"That's what makes it funny. The perfect couple—Ken and Barbie." She grinned at him. "Of course, you could shave off the beard and wear your contacts. Your hair's certainly long and blond enough to look authentic."

Fletcher sighed, knowing she wasn't going to like what he had to say. God knows, he didn't like disappointing her, but he just wasn't into parading Main Street dressed like a lunatic surfer doll. He'd tried to tell her not to waste her time putting together a costume for him. "Why don't you call Ruth and cancel?" he said. "I'll stay home with Brooke."

Liz's normally animated face grew suddenly still, and her voice was flat. "You don't want to go?" She hugged Brooke against her chest, then shrugged. "Fine," she said. "I guess I'll just go without you. Again."

Liz inhaled the cool mentholated smoke, then opened the BMW's door and dropped the cigarette butt on the ground, crushing it out with the pointed toe of her stiletto pumps. The first thing Fletcher always did whenever he rode in her car was check her ashtray for evidence of her lack of willpower. Well, maybe she didn't have any self-control, but she did have a brain. She hadn't used the ashtray since she'd finally agreed —after months of his badgering—to quit smoking.

Her tight gold lamé dress hampering her movement, she eased herself out of the seat and locked the car door. Usually she didn't bother to lock up, but on Halloween there was no telling what might go on, especially this close to the plaza. She dropped her keys into her little gold bag and, carefully lifting the long curly strands of the blond wig, draped the long metal purse strap over her shoulder. She patted the fake hair back into place and headed toward the plaza, Cool-Times Barbie out for an evening *sans* Ken.

She shivered in the cold night air. Cool-Times was exactly right—it couldn't be more than forty degrees and she wore a skimpy mini-dress and no coat. Fletcher had commented about that as she left, but she'd just told him there wasn't any point in wearing a costume if you covered it up with a coat. Besides, she intended to keep moving, either joining the parade up and down Main Street or dancing at the masquerade ball at the Mark. She checked her purse. Yes, she'd remembered her ticket—and Fletcher's too.

Her shoulders tensed, and she forced herself to relax, to not care whether he wanted to be with her or not. It didn't make any difference to her—she could have a perfectly good time without him. God knew she got enough practice. He hadn't come with her last Halloween, or New Year's Eve either, for that matter. Now that she really thought about it, it would have been more surprising if he'd actually decided to go out with her.

The music and voices grew louder and the costumed revelers more numerous as she wobbled on her grotesquely high heels along the sidewalk bordering Lithia Park. Rubbing her arms ferociously to try to warm them up, she skirted the traffic barricade and emerged onto the plaza. Hundreds of masqueraders crammed the square and flowed into the street, and she paused for a moment at the edge of the madness, not quite ready to be swept up into it.

A pair of arms waving wildly from the top of the water fountains caught her eye. "Liz!" the thing attached to the arms yelled, then pulled off its ugly alien being mask. "It's Jeff." He jumped down and pushed through the crowd toward her.

Laughing, she waited on the sidewalk until he joined her. If she'd arranged this meeting, she'd be feeling guilty as hell right now. But she'd tried her best to get Fletcher off his dead ass, and she had no intention of letting him keep her from having a good time. "We make a great pair," she said. "Barbie and the Thing."

He grinned at her. "So that's what you are. I guessed maybe an expensive streetwalker."

"In that case, you can be the Pimp from Outer Space."

He raised his eyebrows. "Where's Fletcher? I thought you said the two of you were going to the ball."

She shrugged and snapped open her bag. "He changed his mind." She fished out the tickets and held them up. "How would you like to be my date?"

For the briefest second, his face registered surprise. Then he smiled even more broadly, his green eyes sparkling. "Last time I was at the Mark, some creep in an A's cap almost punched me out, but I'd love to anyway." He slipped his mask back on. "The best thing is that he'll never recognize me tonight—and no one will even realize I'm not Fletcher."

Liz slipped her arm through his. At this point, she'd didn't give a damn if anyone did.

.   .   .

Alec sipped his whiskey and soda, shaking his head at the craziness that swirled around him. As far as he was concerned, the Mark Antony's bar was the best place in town to see the show. Just a few minutes ago, a carton of crayons had pranced through the place, followed shortly afterward by a pack of slogan-shouting condoms. His rented Confederate officer costume was tame compared to most of what he'd seen.

The waitress paused next to his little table. "Another drink, General?"

That voice sounded familiar. He squinted at her, trying to see who was behind the black mask and can-can dancer costume. "Do I know you?"

She laughed and raised her mask.

"Cor blimey, it's Sheri Riley! What are you doing here?"

"I work here." She slid the mask back over her eyes. "I'd better get back to it before the natives get restless. Can I bring you another?"

"Sure," he said. Something gold sparkled in the doorway, and he glanced in that direction. "Isn't that Liz Berenson? Naomi told me you were friends." He nodded toward the tall, slender woman in the skin-tight metallic dress. Platinum blond hair fell in thick waves to the middle of her back, and she wore enough black eye makeup for a whole band of punk rockers, but it was still unmistakably Liz. He chuckled. In real life Liz always looked so cool and professional—almost virginal, in fact—that it was hard to imagine her any other way. It was funny the way costumes liberated people, exposing them every bit as much as hiding them.

"It sure is," Sheri said. "But that monster she's hanging onto can't be her husband. Fletcher hardly ever takes her anywhere, and that guy's at least half a foot taller than—" She bit her lip, then continued in a rush. "What was it you wanted?"

"Glenlivet and soda."

Sheri marked the order down, smiled at him, and inched her way back through the crowd to the bar. Alec stared at her until she disappeared behind a cluster of Hershey's Kisses. Goddamn it, she was pretty. And talented, too. Too bad she was married.

When he realized what he was thinking, he dismissed the idea immediately. He'd always made it a rule not to entertain even a passing thought about attractive female students.

He rattled the ice cubes against the side of his glass, then took another swig of the watered-down whiskey as Liz and her escort passed in front of his table. She glanced his way, and he doffed his cap. "Good evening, ma'am," he said, doing his best imitation of a North Carolina drawl. "You're lookin' mighty beautiful tonight."

She wiggled her hips and batted her eyelashes. "Thanks, soldier. Are you coming upstairs to the ballroom? I'll save a dance for you."

"In that case, I'll be there." Alec nodded at the creature standing next to her. "As long as he doesn't object."

The creature made ugly snarling sounds through his mask, and Liz giggled. "He's horribly jealous, but I think we can risk just one teeny-weeny dance. You wouldn't mind, would you, Ken?"

Ken grunted something unintelligible.

"He says it's fine just as long as no one tries to steal his Barbie away from him." She tugged on Ken's arm. "See you up there."

Alec waved as they made their way through the packed lounge. He wondered what had happened between Liz and her husband for her to be out with someone else. From what he knew of her, she just didn't seem to be the type who'd take cheating lightly. But she'd certainly seemed interested in Ken, pressing her breasts against his side and smiling into the eyes hidden behind the mask.

What was it Sheri had said—Fletcher didn't like going out? Sheri had stopped suddenly, as if she realized she'd betrayed a confidence. He'd bet Liz complained about her husband to her friends—and he'd bet she probably never once told Fletcher what it was she didn't like. Just like Vivianne. How many of her friends knew exactly why Vivianne had left him, knew more than he did about Vivianne's dissatisfactions?

He put his glass to his lips, tapping an ice cube into his mouth and sucking at it. For Fletcher's sake, he hoped the poor bloody bloke figured it out before it was too late.

. . .

Sitting on the edge of the bed, Ted stripped off his shorts and tossed them on the floor, then swung his legs between the freezing cold sheets. Damn! He'd forgotten to turn on the electric blanket again. He flicked it on and cranked the dial to high just as Meredith turned off the water in the master bathroom.

A few seconds later she emerged, covered from neck to toe by the ugly red flannel nightgown she knew he hated. Her "hands off" nightgown—and it was practically threadbare from being worn so much. Lately, she'd taken to undressing in the bathroom, even locking the door after he'd walked in on her a couple of weeks ago. She had a great body, but it sure didn't do him much good.

When she crawled under the covers, he scooted over next to her and pulled her into his arms. Rejection had never been his favorite pastime, but goddamn it, he was horny, and he knew from experience she'd never initiate anything. She even flinched whenever he kissed her. He'd been resigned to celibacy during her pregnancy and for several months after Justie's birth, but now his patience was worn as thin as her nightgown.

He nuzzled the back of her neck and, ignoring the way her body stiffened the minute he touched her, he slid his hand under her nightgown and up her leg. "Come on, honey," he said. "We haven't had any fun in a long time. It's Halloween. Why don't you pretend to be a stripper?" His penis finally beginning to stir, he tugged at the repulsive nightgown.

She jerked away from him. "So you can pretend to be a rapist?" Her tone was acidic.

His erection vanished immediately. "Hardly," he said. "At this point, it'd be assault with a dead weapon anyway." He couldn't help letting out a bitter little laugh as he rolled over onto his side of the bed, but he sobered abruptly. "Honestly, Meredith, I don't know what's wrong. You used to enjoy making love as much as I did. What happened?" Sighing, he smoothed his mustache.

She turned toward him and propped her head on her hand. "In all fairness, it really has nothing to do with you. It's not your fault." Her large brown eyes shone with tears. "But it's not my fault, either."

"Well, then, whose is it? Just tell me and I'll go out and punch whoever it is for you." He draped his arm over her shoulders.

"You can't. He's dead." Tears brimmed over her eyelashes and splashed down her cheeks. "Ted, I have to tell you something," she said, her voice a tortured whisper. "It was my dad. He raped me when I was little. Several times. I was never able to remember it—until just the other day."

"Jesus Christ, Meredith. You can't be serious." Staring at her, he removed his arm and sat up. "Your *real* father?" He couldn't keep the incredulity from his voice.

Her face closed up tight, she choked out, "Yes."

So that was what she and Eva stopped whispering about every time he walked into the room. Ted rested the back of his head against the brass spindles on the headboard and cracked and recracked his knuckles. He'd really stepped into it this time, a big slimy quicksand mess, and he didn't have any idea what to say or do to help Meredith.

"Mother's decided to move to Ashland," she said. "As soon as she can rent out her house in Eugene." Drawing in a shaky breath, she turned her back to him and switched off her bedside lamp. "I thought you should know why."

He nodded. For some reason, Eva'd never seemed to like him, and she hadn't taken much trouble to hide her feelings. It hadn't bothered him a lot before because she wasn't around much, but that was all going to change now. Still, it was obvious that Meredith needed her, needed *someone*, anyway. But he just didn't know if he could give her what she needed.

He clicked off his lamp, then slid back down under the covers. It sure as hell didn't look as if life was going to be much fun for the next few years.

.   .   .

Jeff pulled his car into the driveway next to the beat-up old Volkswagen bus. He switched off the ignition, then turned to Liz. Jesus, what a fool Fletcher Berenson was. Elizabeth was so beautiful and so warm, and her husband just took it all for granted. He probably had no idea how unhappy his wife was.

Jeff smiled into her eyes, deep blue and lovely even when they were smudged with mascara. She'd taken off her ridiculous wig while they were dancing and never bothered to comb her tousled blond hair, but she still looked great. More than anything, he'd like to see what she looked like in the morning, after a night of making love with him. She'd mentioned tonight that Fletcher didn't like her to touch him while he was sleeping, and the longing and loneliness in her eyes had almost brought tears to his. If he had her in his bed, he'd cradle her against him the whole night long.

So the guy was an idiot. Still, that didn't give Jeff the right to seduce his wife, no matter how much he wanted her. The choice wasn't his—Elizabeth would have to be the one who made the decision.

She leaned toward him and brushed her lips against his, then pulled back. "Thanks," she said. "It's been a long time since I've had so much fun."

He shook his head, resisting his desire to draw her against him, to *really* kiss those full, smooth lips. "Anytime," he said. "I love to dance, and you're a great partner." She was, too. He liked the way she fit so perfectly into his arms, following him with ease and grace through everything from a fifties' swing to a foxtrot to a wild mambo. Even if they never did anything more than dance, he was so much in love with her that it would be worth the torture he suffered returning her to her home and her husband.

Liz giggled, and her eyes glittered devilishly. "What the hell," she said. She laced her arms around Jeff's neck and tugged his face toward hers. "I'd love a good-night kiss. Just one. Please."

He didn't hesitate even though he knew she'd had too much to drink and it probably wasn't fair to take advantage of her giddiness. He tried his damnedest to be fair, but he wasn't a saint. He pressed his mouth against hers, softly at first, then hungrily, slipping his tongue between her parted lips and his hands between her slim legs. She arched her back and groaned, her intensity matching his.

Several minutes passed before he regained his control. Christ, *he* was the fool. What if Fletcher came out to see what was keeping Liz? Summoning all his willpower, Jeff gently pushed Liz away from him. "I'd like to make love to you right now, Elizabeth," he said. "Gearshift knob and all. But I don't think it would be a good idea."

She sighed and leaned her head against the car window. "I know you're right, but there's a big part of me that just doesn't give a damn."

He laid his hand on her thigh. "I want you. And I'm serious. I'm not interested in a casual fling. I think we both need to be rational about this."

Rationality wasn't her strong suit, especially when she'd had too much to drink, and Jeff's earnestness only made it more difficult. "I'll try," she said. She opened the car door and slipped out. "I think I'd better go." Without looking back, she shut the door quietly and walked quickly up the path to the front steps.

She propped herself against the front door as Jeff's red Mercedes backed out of her driveway and headed down the steep hill. When the car disappeared, she fumbled her key into the lock.

Inside, she dropped onto the overstuffed couch, kicked off her pumps, and rubbed her aching feet. Thank God she had tomorrow off. She checked her watch. Almost three o'clock, and Brooke never slept past seven. Maybe if she told Fletcher she was sick, he'd watch her for a while. It was Sunday, after all, and he could afford to take a few hours off.

She stood up and tripped over her shoes. She bent over to pick them up, and the room suddenly swirled around her when she straightened. Shit, she hadn't realized she was so bombed. How many margaritas had she drunk, anyway?

Good thing Jeff insisted on driving her home. He'd bought her every drink she wanted but hadn't drunk anything stronger than water himself.

Her shoes dangling from her hand, she staggered past the darkened library and up the short flight of stairs to the master bedroom, wondering what Fletcher was going to say about her being out so late. Usually, she was home long before midnight, and he was still downstairs in his library, reading or working on a brief.

The bedroom door was closed. She turned the knob carefully. Holding herself firmly upright, she stepped into the room, only dimly lit by a small night-light on the far wall. Fletcher, snoring lightly, lay on his back on his side of the king-size bed.

Asleep—or pretending to be, thank God. Talking to him would break the spell. She undressed without turning on a light, tossing her costume onto the chair next to the bed, then sliding between the sheets. She should try to go to sleep, she knew, but she wanted to stay awake anyway, to savor the delicious memories. Her whole body still tingled when she thought of Jeff's arms around her, of the way his lips tasted hers while they were kissing in his car. She'd felt electrified then, and she was still sizzling now. She wanted his hands on her body, all over her body, without clothes in the way. She wanted him on top of her, inside her. Arching her back, she caressed herself lightly, pretending her hands belonged to Jeff.

Across the vast expanse of bed between them, Fletcher snorted and rolled onto his side. Liz sighed, the magic suddenly replaced by dull reality. She was Fletcher's wife, not Jeff's. She might as well go to sleep.

CHAPTER 10

November

Sheri sipped the frothy steamed milk drink, savoring the delicious almond flavor of the Amaretto it was spiked with. The first time they'd come to Chateaulin after a rehearsal, Professor Whittier—Alec—had promised her she'd love an Almond Joy, and he was right. From now on, she'd never be able to smell almond without thinking of Alec and *Taming* and how wonderful it all was.

Smiling, she let her gaze drift around the table at the happy faces of some of the other cast members, much softer now by candlelight than they'd been under the harsh stage lights of the Bowmer Theatre earlier that evening. Even after several rehearsals, it still seemed odd to her that she belonged to a group like this, stranger even than the playgroup because, except for Alec, everyone was so young. She didn't much notice the age gap during class and rehearsal anymore, but it was harder to ignore in a purely social situation. The kids talked about stuff she'd never heard of and, for that matter, didn't much care about, so she was always real relieved when Alec made a point of sitting next to her.

He put his elbows on the table and leaned toward her. "All recovered from Saturday night? It looked as if you really had to hustle to keep up."

"It *was* pretty crazy," she said. "But the time goes a lot faster when it's busy, so I didn't mind." The tips had been great, too, but for some reason she didn't feel comfortable mentioning that to him. Money didn't seem to be the kind of thing you talked to your Shakespeare professor about, even though Alec was starting to seem more like a friend than a teacher.

"You've got one hell of a lot going on in your life—a husband, kids, college classes, a job, and now this play. I almost feel guilty that I chose you for such a big part." He shook his head. "I don't know how you manage it all. I'm sure I couldn't."

She shrugged. *Manage* was the right word. Barely. If he knew how close to coming apart it all was, he'd feel even guiltier. Not that a bit of it was his fault.

A loud roar of laughter from the other end of the table kept her from having to reply. Instead, she exchanged a tolerant, isn't-youth-wonderful, aren't-you-glad-you're-not-twenty-one smile with Alec.

When the rowdiness calmed down, he continued. "I might yell during rehearsals," he said, "but I want you to know I think you're doing a damned good job with Kate. She's a complicated woman—intelligent, strong-willed, and unhappy about her choices, or lack of them, I should say. If she were alive now, I doubt anyone would call her a shrew."

"No," Sheri said. "They'd probably call her a bitch instead." As soon as the words popped out, she wished she could take them back. She bit her bottom lip. What would he think of her?

Alec looked surprised for a second, then threw back his head and laughed as loudly as the students had a few minutes before. "You're probably right," he said, still chuckling.

72

He sounded so delighted that Sheri couldn't keep herself from joining his laughter. What a relief he hadn't been offended. Mike would have been pissed off if she'd disagreed like that with something he'd said. He thought his college degree gave him the right to the last word about everything. Her laughter trailed off as she thought about how mad he'd be if he knew she wasn't at work.

She twirled the little straw around in the foamy milk, remembering his apology the morning after he'd gotten so drunk at the Mark. His blue eyes had filled with tears as he begged her forgiveness, and then, although he was already late for work, they'd made love with even more passion than usual. She loved him so much when he was being sweet that there was no way she could keep herself from forgiving him, no matter how many times he'd promised the same thing.

Maybe this time he really *would* quit for good. She sipped at the hot milk, then glanced up at Alec. Even if Mike did give up the drinking, she still couldn't tell him about the play, as much as she hated sneaking around behind his back and as scared as she was he'd find out. What if he refused to let her go on with it?

That would ruin everything, not just for her, but for Alec, too. She just couldn't let him down. She'd promised to play Kate—and, unlike Mike, a promise meant a lot to her.

Liz covered her yawn with her hand and wished the line would move a little faster. It took a strong cup of coffee to get her going after she woke up, and there hadn't been a bean in the house this morning. Good thing the Beanery wasn't far out of her way and her first appointment wasn't until eight-thirty. With any luck, she might be able to actually drink the stuff at the café instead of taking it with her in a paper cup and risk spilling it all over her new Anne Klein suit.

Idly, she stared at the fancy imported chocolates on the counter while she waited for her turn to order. She listened for a few minutes to the women behind her discussing their husbands' shortcomings, then shifted her attention to the cars whizzing by on Walker Avenue. When the girl behind the cash register asked what she wanted, she blinked a couple of times, spaced out, as Fletcher would say. "A cup of the Sumatra—" She glanced at the clock. "For here."

The girl handed her the white mug full of steaming, rich-smelling coffee, and she looked around the crowded room for an empty table. Every damn one was taken, and it was too cold to sit outside on the terrace. Maybe she could share a table with someone—

"Come sit with me." The familiar voice came from behind her.

Jeff. Her empty stomach fluttering, she turned slowly toward him. As usual, he looked as if he'd just stepped out of a Ralph Lauren ad. Impeccable. Thick shiny hair with a beautiful widow's peak, gleaming white teeth, perfect straight nose. "Good morning. I've never seen you here before."

He smiled at her. "I started coming after I saw you walk in with one of their paper cups. I figured I'd run into you one of these mornings." He pointed to a table next to the window. "I've been saving that chair for you for weeks."

Concentrating on keeping the hot coffee inside the cup, Liz followed him to the table. Whenever he said things like that, her insides quivered the way they had the first time she'd fallen in love in high school, and she wanted to grab him and run away from him at the same time. Her whole body ached for him, but now that the excitement of Halloween was over she was scared. Her life, the life she was living now, was at stake.

In fact, her life had changed already—and all she'd done was kiss Jeff good night. What went on in her head was different; she didn't see things the same way any more. Instead of trying feebly to get through to Fletcher, she'd given up. Instead of admiring what was good about him, she picked at what she hated. The way he carped at her if she didn't separate the recyclable stuff from the garbage. The way he cringed when she let go at a party. The way he looked through her as if she weren't there.

And she couldn't force herself to stop. It was like smoking—the harder she tried to quit the more she wanted a cigarette. Self-denial just wasn't her specialty. As soon as she decided to give something up, she wound up becoming obsessed with it. All the more reason not to make herself quit whatever it was she was doing with Jeff. It was probably wiser just to let the infatuation run its course. If she tried to cut it off now, she'd end up in bed with him, sure thing. At least it was still only a possibility at this point.

She set the brimming cup on the table, then eased into the chair opposite Jeff. Fiddling with the paper napkin, she delayed meeting his eyes for as long as possible, afraid he'd be able to read the turmoil there as easily as he intuited everything else about her.

"Hard weekend?" he asked. "You look tired." He rested his elbows on the table and leaned toward her. "Your eyes are sad, not lively and shining the way they usually are."

All she could do was squeak, "They do? I mean, they are?" Fletcher would never have noticed something like that. Her eyes could be swollen shut, and he'd never say a thing. Hell, she could hop in with one leg cut off at the knee, and he'd probably mumble, "Hello, dear," and keep reading his damned brief.

She sipped the steaming coffee to give herself a few seconds to regain her poise. "I didn't sleep well last night." Because she'd been thinking about him, she added silently.

"I know what you mean. I'm not in the best shape, myself." He sighed and shook his head. "Pamela has decided to move to Eugene, and she's determined to take the girls with her."

Liz froze, her cup halfway to her mouth. Jeff was crazy about his daughters, but he seldom mentioned his ex-wife. If she hadn't been so preoccupied with her own problems, she'd have seen the unhappiness in his eyes, too. Maybe she deserved Fletcher, after all; she certainly hadn't been any more sensitive than he usually was. Even worse, her situation seemed pretty damn simple compared to Jeff's—nobody was threatening to take Brooke and move away.

"Oh, I'm sorry," she said, setting the cup back down. "What are you going to do?"

"Hire a lawyer and go back to court." He wadded his napkin into a little ball. "Does Fletcher handle custody cases?"

Liz shook her head. "Not anymore. He specializes in environmental law. But his partner does family law. Meredith Marshall. Do you know her?"

Jeff's chuckle was devoid of amusement. "Yeah," he said. "She represented Pamela during the divorce. Merciless Meredith. I'm not looking forward to tangling with her again."

"Oh," Liz said, her voice flat. "She's one of my best friends. I've known her since college."

"Don't get me wrong," Jeff said. "She's good. I'd just like to have her on *my* side, but I hear she prefers women clients."

"She's pretty intense. But she's got a huge heart. I wish you could meet her sometime outside the courtroom." Liz's shoulders sagged. She wished she could introduce Jeff to all her friends, but they'd guess in a second that something was going on.

"I wish I could too," he said, his green eyes locking onto hers.

Liz knew exactly what he meant. He wanted everyone to know she belonged with him. She lowered her eyes and took another sip of her coffee, now lukewarm. What a mess she was getting herself into.

CHAPTER 11

Meredith perched on the edge of the wicker chair, her back straight and her shoulders tense. It had been a long time since she'd been on this side of an interview, and she wasn't sure exactly what she was supposed to do. Eva had insisted for the last month that she see a counselor, so she'd finally given in. But she still didn't know if she was ready to tell the most intimate details of her life to a woman she'd never met before. It must have taken a lot of courage for Yvonne to reveal herself the way she had at her first appointment.

Actually, it was because of Yvonne that she had agreed to see Ingrid Fromme. Now that she'd remembered her own experiences, she understood why Yvonne's case affected her so strongly, and she was beginning to wonder how ethical it would be for her to represent a client whose battle was really a surrogate for her own. There was more than a little truth to the old saying, "The lawyer who represents himself has a fool for a client." She supposed it didn't matter if she made a fool of herself, but it didn't seem fair to drag Yvonne into it as well.

She hoped counseling would help, both for her sake and for Yvonne's. Meredith crossed her legs and stared at the woman seated in the old oak rocking chair in front of her. There was something comfortingly maternal about Ingrid—perhaps it was her graying hair or the slight plumpness that softened her features. She was probably Eva's age, but she completely lacked Eva's hard-edged chic. Her face appeared open and friendly, not at all judgmental. Maybe she wouldn't be so hard to talk to, after all.

Rocking gently, Ingrid nodded at Meredith. "You said on the phone that you're an adult survivor of incest. What made you decide to seek counseling now?"

Meredith took a deep breath, relieved that Ingrid didn't question her description of herself. It still seemed almost a miracle that anyone would believe something so awful. "I only remembered it a month ago. And even afterward, I wasn't sure it had really happened. It all seemed like some kind of nightmare." Almost of its own volition, her hand fluttered in the air, then dropped into her lap. "I don't know," she said. "Sometimes I still think I must be going crazy."

"Have you told anyone else?"

"My mother. My husband."

"And their reactions?"

"Mother's been wonderful," Meredith said. "She's even rented out her house in Eugene and moved to Ashland to be near me."

"What about your husband?"

Meredith shrugged. "He tries to be sympathetic, but I think basically the whole thing just makes him uncomfortable. He gets really stiff every time I mention it." She tried to laugh, unsuccessfully. "I talk about it so much lately he's beginning to look as rigid as the Tin Man in the *Wizard of Oz*. But I just can't seem to help it. I think about it sixteen hours a day and dream about it the other eight."

"That's not uncommon. After they remember—or stop denying—what happened to them, many of my clients find themselves obsessed with it. I think it serves a purpose. How old are you?" Ingrid stilled the rocking chair and leaned forward.

"Thirty-eight."

"And when did the incest occur?"

"When I was five."

"Thirty-three years ago. For thirty-three years you've managed to repress a horrible, horrifying memory. Naturally you're obsessed with it. You can't expect to assimilate something like that overnight." Ingrid gripped the chair's arms and stared intently at Meredith. "It doesn't sound as if talking to your husband is comfortable for *you*."

Tears blurred Meredith's vision, and she clenched her teeth as if that would keep them from spilling from her eyes. She was feeling sorry for herself, but goddamn it, she had a right to. Her happy childhood was a lie, and her marriage was turning into one, too. She swallowed hard. "It isn't," she said finally.

Ingrid pulled a few tissues from the box on the table next to her and handed them to Meredith. "It's not unusual to want to talk about it all the time. But you need to talk to people who will hear you. Not everyone is capable of that. Don't blame your husband. If he could, I'm sure he would. Can you find someone else to talk to?"

"I have some wonderful friends," Meredith said.

"You trust them?"

Meredith nodded.

"Then by all means tell them. You've got a long road ahead of you. You're going to need all the love and support you can get."

Meredith wiped the tears from her cheeks. She felt a little better already, just imagining Naomi's reaction. And Liz's, too. She didn't know why, but she was less sure of whether she should tell Sheri. Maybe it was because she sensed Sheri was a victim, too.

No, she told herself, not *too*. Sheri was a victim because she still allowed herself to be victimized; Meredith was a survivor. There was a big difference.

.   .   .

79

When Meredith finished, no one spoke for a couple of minutes, the silence disturbed only by the muffled noise of the children playing in Naomi's family room where they were supervised by Kristin. Meredith, her face even more pale than usual, sat at the foot of the dining room table littered with the remnants of Naomi's delicious lunch. At the head of the table, Naomi gripped the arms of her chair and gritted her teeth. Liz's eyes glittered with tears, and Sheri's mouth still hung open in shock.

Liz leaned over, grabbed Meredith's hand, and squeezed it. "It's beyond belief," she said. "My heart hurts for you." Hard as she tried, she couldn't keep the tears from spilling out of her eyes and running down her cheeks. She could smile through her own pain, but not someone else's—and sure as hell not through something this awful. She loved her dad so much, still idolized him so totally that she couldn't even imagine such a thing happening. Poor Meredith, to have lived with the ultimate betrayal for more than thirty years and to not even have remembered it. Until now.

Red patches flamed on Naomi's cheeks. "My trigger finger itches," she said. "I haven't felt rage like this in years."

Sheri just shook her head and stared at Meredith. Her father had been quick with a belt and pretty scary when he was drunk, but the whippings he'd given her were nothing compared to Meredith's ordeal. And Meredith always seemed so perfect, so in control of her life. Her house was usually spotless, her clothes expensive, ethnic but tasteful, and immaculate—even her child never seemed to get dirty. Sheri'd always marveled at the way Meredith managed a full-time profession, a home and garden that looked like a feature story in a fancy magazine, and a handsome husband and beautiful child. The fairy tale was really a nightmare.

Naomi continued sputtering. "I agree with your mother. If the son of a bitch weren't already dead, I'd *help* her kill him. But first I'd cut off his balls with my oldest pair of pinking shears. Then his penis."

Meredith put her hand over her mouth but couldn't keep back the titter growing inside her. Liz's sympathy was so touching, and so was

Sheri's horror. But Naomi's anger was wonderful. It released something that had been pent up inside her ever since she remembered. The giggle escaped as she visualized Naomi holding up her prize, and she was relieved that her laughter was only a little bit hysterical. She didn't know why, but she suddenly felt as if it were safe now for her to recognize her own anger even though she wasn't quite ready to express it, and she understood why Yvonne was suing her father. *Really* understood, in her gut.

Naomi took a deep breath, then stood and walked to the foot of the table. She wrapped her arms around Meredith's neck and hugged her. "We love you," she said. "Don't be afraid to ask for anything you need."

Liz and Sheri nodded, and tears blurred Meredith's vision.

CHAPTER 12

Finally, Liz slid into her chair at the foot of the table, now laden with platters of roast turkey, stuffing, mashed potatoes, cranberry sauce. She sighed and exchanged a glance with Meredith, proud that once again the two of them had accomplished their annual Thanksgiving feast, a tradition they'd started when Meredith and Ted got married. Afterward, there'd be the usual mountains of dishes, but at least Fletcher and Ted always helped out with those. Maybe this year she and Meredith would just escape into the living room with Eva and the kids and let the men handle the cleanup by themselves. It had been a long day of peeling and chopping and basting—she and Meredith deserved to be the ones resting their feet and gabbing.

Especially Meredith. After she finished serving Brooke, Liz plopped some potatoes on her own plate, then passed the bowl to Eva. It had been only a few days since Meredith had confided at playgroup the awful secret she'd been carrying around. Liz's first reaction had been to suggest they cancel their traditional Thanksgiving gathering this year, but Meredith insisted they go ahead with it, claiming it wasn't fair to everyone else, and besides it might do her some good to have something else to think about for a little while.

Ladling gravy over Brooke's potatoes, Liz sneaked a look at Meredith. Except for the dark circles under her eyes, she seemed to be handling everything okay. Maybe the hubbub of producing and eating a large meal was good for her, after all. Or maybe it was easier to share the secret than to keep it.

Liz wished she had that option—even though her own secret was shallow and frivolous by comparison. She watched Fletcher carve the turkey at the other end of the table; and a sudden flush heated her face. How could she even think of comparing her situation to Meredith's? After Meredith's monstrous revelation, her own resentments looked like childish self-pity. She had nothing to complain about, really. She'd had a happy childhood; she still enjoyed a good relationship with her parents; she had a pleasant, kind husband who would stand by her no matter what. So what if he was a bit distant and dull? At least he wasn't a philanderer like Richard, a red-neck drunk like Mike, or a smug, self-centered egotist like Ted. Next to any of them, Fletcher could pass for Superhusband.

Then why was she on the verge of an affair with Jeff? She scooped some of the thyme-scented dressing onto her plate and speared a slice of turkey from the platter while Fletcher stood up and cleared his throat.

He waited for a minute until everyone was silent. "I have a lot to be thankful for this year," he said. "Good friends, a loving and supportive wife, a wonderful daughter. I want to share this important decision with you first." He paused, smiling at Liz. "I've definitely decided to run for the state senate."

"Terrific!" Ted grinned.

Meredith nodded and smiled. "I'm only surprised you didn't run for something a long time ago."

They all turned to Liz, and she tried to look like the perfect wife of the perfect candidate. Happy. Serene. Enthusiastic. Totally faithful. "I'm so pleased," she murmured. "You finally made up your mind."

After Fletcher sat down, she stared at the food piled on her plate for a long time before she forked the first bite of turkey into her mouth. She had a lot to be thankful for, too, she supposed. And she *was* thankful. But she wasn't serene or enthusiastic or happy—and now that Fletcher had even more to occupy his time and mind, chances were that "totally faithful" would join the list of what she *wasn't*.

Richard leaned back in his chair, resting his hands on his stomach and smiling at the English department members sprinkled around the big dining table. Naomi always insisted on inviting all the single professors, "orphans" she called them, to their holiday dinners, and most of them accepted with alacrity. As usual, Naomi's cooking was so outstanding he'd eaten way more than he should have. Leave it to her to make a Thanksgiving dinner something really special—roast goose stuffed with sausage, chestnut purée, braised red cabbage, and brussels sprouts simmered in cream. It meant a five-mile run tomorrow instead of two, but it was worth it. He smiled at her as she set two desserts in front of him, one a rum-soaked savarin filled with whipped cream and the other a beautifully decorated *tarte aux poires à la Bourdaloue.* All right, he thought, six miles. It was still worth it.

"Look at these," he said, and several of the department orphans groaned. He slid his arm around Naomi's waist and pulled her close. "You're amazing. I don't know how you do it."

She smiled at him. "Julia and I thank you for your compliments."

"Julia?" Alec looked puzzled. "I didn't see anyone else in the kitchen."

"Julia Child." Naomi laughed. "When Richard and I were first married, the only things I knew how to fix were hamburgers and TV dinners. He gave me six cookbooks for Christmas that year."

"And now I wear out two pairs of Nikes a year keeping the weight off." Richard stood and kissed Naomi's cheek. She'd come a long way in the last three years, from a naive graduate student to an accomplished cook and hostess, and he was proud of her. If only she'd loosen up a bit about Leah. Sometimes she acted as if she were the only person in the world to ever have a child.

Naomi grabbed a stack of plates from the sideboard and put them next to the desserts, then handed Richard a knife and pie server. "You're on stage now," she said, sitting back down at her place. She turned to Alec. "Speaking of stage, how's your play going?"

Richard bent quickly over the pear tart and sliced it carefully into quarters, then eighths. He hoped to hell Alec didn't bring up Heather or mention that Richard had attended the auditions as well as several rehearsals. He was almost positive that while Naomi knew something was going on, she didn't know whom it was going on with—and he planned to end it before that could happen.

"Couldn't be better," Alec said. "Our Petruchio is a sharp kid, and Kate and Bianca are both excellent."

"I knew Sheri could do it." Naomi glowed with pleasure for her friend. "Did she tell you about the other plays she's been in? She used to do a lot of theater around here before she married Mike. Off-Bardway, she called it."

Alec shook his head. "She didn't mention it, but she seemed so at ease on stage I suspected. I'll have to ask her what she's done some time."

"Who's playing Bianca?" Mary Lawrence said sweetly, glancing at Richard and twining a lock of her long curly blond hair around her finger. She widened her blue eyes and actually batted her eyelashes at him.

The department bitch—life wouldn't be complete without one. After two years, she was still out to get him because he'd ended their affair before she was ready. Richard slid a piece of the pear pie onto a plate. "Savarin or tart?" he asked Mary, narrowing his eyes. If she caused any problems, it'd be the last time he invited her into his home—even if leaving her out might make Naomi more suspicious than she already was.

"Both, please," she said. "I always have such a hard time choosing."

85

She smiled at him, then at Alec, her bright red lipstick still perfectly in place despite the meal she'd eaten. She tapped her long nails, also brilliant red, on the white damask tablecloth. "Now, who's Bianca?"

"Heather Austin. The textual descriptions fit perfectly. She's as blond as Sheri is dark, and she's several years younger. Quite a beauty, in fact."

"So I've heard." Mary cackled, squinting at Richard.

Richard slapped a piece of the savarin on the plate and passed it down the table to Mary. He hoped she choked on it. Anything to shut her up. "So you think Sheri's pretty good," he said to Alec.

"Bloody great. She's so funny and heart-rending at the same time that she makes her sweet little sister look like the real ball-breaker right from the beginning. Kate might be difficult, but at least she's honest. On the other hand, Bianca is her da's darling—and she's devious as hell." He nodded at Richard. "I think you're going to be impressed."

"I can hardly wait!" Naomi clapped her hands. "I wrote a paper on *Taming* when I was working on my master's, and Kate's been my favorite character ever since."

It was time to talk about something else, Richard decided. Past time, in fact. Unlike Sheri and Heather, he'd never been much of an actor—or a good liar. All his mother ever had to do to know he wasn't telling the truth was look at his face, and every one of his three wives possessed the same skill. "I hate to interrupt all this," he said, "but who wants what for dessert?" He'd break things off with Heather first thing Monday morning.

SAN FRANCISCO

Doug chewed another bite of the dry hospital turkey. Some Thanksgiving. He'd hoped to be home long before this, but lately Dr. Levison had been talking about letting him out in time for Christmas. Another month. Sometimes he didn't think he could stand another day. Still, he had to pretend to be cheerful today. For Mom and Dad's sake. They'd gone to a lot of trouble to make sure he didn't feel left out, and he'd bet the turkey on their trays had been every bit as tough as his.

His brother Andy grinned at him. "Hurry up and finish, slowpoke. Wait till you see what Mom brought."

"I'll bet it's something you like, too." Doug smiled back. Andy and Nick were great brothers. They'd had to give up a lot of stuff because Mom and Dad spent so much time at the hospital, but they never complained. Not to him, anyway.

"Yeah," Nick said. "But it's your favorite."

"Pumpkin pie? Made with real pumpkin?" Doug pushed aside his dinner plate. "I'm finished. Where did you hide it?"

"It was supposed to be a surprise," Mom said to Andy, with a stern look.

"I'm surprised," Doug said. "And my mouth is watering for some real food." He pounded on his tray with the handle of his knife. "Bring on the pie. Bring on the pie."

Andy and Nick and then Dad joined his chant, and Mom giggled. "All right." She bent over her knitting basket. After pawing through the balls of yarn on top, she pulled out a white box and opened it. Inside was a big orange pumpkin pie. "Ta da."

"Hey, it looks great, Mom." Doug leaned over and kissed her cheek. "But where's the whipped cream?"

"You didn't think we'd forget that, did you?" She pointed at the thermos. "Your dad volunteered to drink hospital coffee today."

Doug settled back against the pillows while Mom cut the pie and Dad scooped big globs of cream from the thermos onto the top of each piece. "God, that looks great, Mom. Thanks." He took a huge bite, savoring the spicy pumpkin and sweet cream despite the sores in his mouth. "Best ever."

But by the time he finished his second piece of pie, the nausea he'd been keeping at bay for the last hour flared up again. He shook his head at his mother's offer of a third helping and turned to his father. He'd avoided his daily question so far, afraid of spoiling the party before it started. But it was over now, and he had to know.

Leaning forward, he tried to keep his tone casual. "Did you hear from that lawyer in Oregon yet?"

Dad glanced at Mom, and Doug knew they had—and that the news was bad. Otherwise, they'd have told him when they got there.

"He called last night," Dad said.

"Well? What did he say? Did he get to look at the adoption file?"

"He did." Dad sighed, shaking his head. "The father is listed as unknown. And your birth mother must have used a false name because he hasn't been able to trace her."

"Shit." Doug slumped against the pillows.

Mom clasped his hand. "The lawyer suggested we hire a detective. He gave us a couple of names, and your dad's going to call one Monday."

Doug forced a weak smile onto his lips. They'd worked so hard to make a special day for him. He couldn't ruin it now. "Then there's still some hope?"

"Definitely," Dad said.

Doug nodded. He'd have to be dead before Mom and Dad gave up. Too bad he didn't have their confidence that everything was going to turn out so great.

CHAPTER 13

December

ASHLAND, OREGON

Richard uncrossed his legs, recrossed them the opposite way, and settled against the lumpy back of Heather's couch. This wasn't going to be easy, but he'd known that for months. That was why he'd put it off for so damn long.

Heather leaned against him, unbuttoning his shirt and twining her fingers through the thick hair on his chest, more gray now than black. "So, you had something to tell me." She giggled and yanked a little tuft of hair so sharply he winced. "You're going to leave your wife?"

"No." Gritting his teeth, he pulled her hand from under his shirt. He held it tightly in his and took a deep breath. "I can't. Not this time." He stared down at their intertwined fingers, at her small hand with its perfectly manicured pink nails. Naomi's polish—when she bothered at all—was usually red and chipped, and her hands were so rough she complained about running her nylons by simply touching them.

"Heather." He looked into her enormous aqua blue eyes and sighed. He might as well get it over with. "It's not going to work."

She frowned. "What do you mean?"

"I mean *us*. I can't leave—"

"You mean you *won't*." She jerked her hand from his and crossed her arms over her chest. "Asshole," she muttered. "Fucking asshole."

He closed his eyes for a minute. She was right. He *was* an asshole. But for the first time, he was trying to do things the right way instead of the most diverting way. Always before it'd been easier to move on, to leave his wife and child for his lover, to escape from the boredom of the known to the excitement of the new. The only problem was that the new became the known so quickly; and now his pattern was so transparent it was almost embarrassing. He was a hunter, not a tiller of the soil, no matter how rich it was. Instead of nurturing the crop until harvest, he devoured his prey and then started looking for another. He'd shattered the happiness of his first two wives and disrupted the childhood of his two oldest daughters—and look how they'd turned out. Sara was bright, but she changed majors, jobs, and boyfriends the way most twenty-five-year-olds changed the color of their lipstick, and with about as much thought. Kristin was so angry and so hostile he'd swear she could turn a warm room chilly just by walking into it. She hated him; she hated her mother; she hated Naomi; and most of all she hated herself.

It had taken him a long time to accept that his actions had contributed to the unhappiness of so many people he cared about. While it was true he didn't feel the same passion for Naomi now that he had at first, that didn't excuse his affair with Heather. Once again lust and self-gratification had triumphed over love and commitment.

Love and commitment. He almost laughed but caught himself in time. He was fifty years old and he still wasn't sure what those two words really meant. He'd known for weeks that he wasn't in love with Heather, that in fact he didn't even like her very much. She was spoiled and demanding and a little bit mean. She claimed she loved him, but he doubted whether she knew what love meant any more than he did.

He stood and walked to the door. "I'm sorry," he said. "But I don't think we should see each other anymore."

She sucked in her breath with a sharp hiss. "You've found another bimbo to fuck, haven't you? Because that's how you've always thought of me. I loved you, but I was just a silly little college girl for you to play house with. Who is it now—that brunette in Whittier's class? I saw you talking to her the other day." She lifted her lip and sneered at him. "Nah. She's too old for you."

Richard raised his hand. "Wait a minute. I don't want it to be like this."

"You mean, let's just be friends?" She bared her teeth at him. "Fuck you, Professor Chandler. Go be friends with your wife. I'm in love with you, and you've just told me you don't want to see me again. What did you expect me to do? Kiss your cheek and say, '*Adiós, amigo*'? Or 'It's been grand; call me again when you're between bimbos'? Sorry. I'm not like that."

"Maybe we should talk later." He twisted the doorknob and eased the door open.

"Get out of here!" Tears oozed from her eyes and slid down her cheeks without disturbing her mascara. She looked even more beautiful when she cried, if it was possible—unlike Naomi, whose eyes got red and puffy and ringed with black makeup. Heather grabbed a pillow off the couch and hurled it at him.

Thank God she hadn't gone for the cactus in the clay pot. He deflected the pillow, then picked it up and tossed it into the chair by the door. "I'll call you tomorrow," he said. "When you're—"

"Forget it!" She rushed at him and shoved him out the door. "I'll do the calling. And it won't be you I talk to," she shrieked. "It'll be your wife."

Liz dumped a stack of paper plates into the trash can. Another reason to be glad Fletcher hadn't made it to her office holiday party. If he saw all the stuff she was throwing out instead of recycling, he'd spend the rest of the night carping at her. She put her hands on her hips and surveyed the mess. Of course, she could have been really frivolous and bought a brand-new set of china just for the occasion, but then she'd have to waste all that soap and water washing it.

Jeff held up a handful of plastic cups. "Do you want to save these?"

"Are you kidding?" Maybe next year. Not tonight. All she wanted to do tonight was crawl into Jeff's arms and stay there for as long as she could before she had to go home. She smiled at him. "Thanks for helping. I'd be here until morning if I had to clean this up by myself." Not a bad excuse, now that she thought of it. "You should have seen the mess," she could always say to Fletcher if he awoke when she came home at dawn. "Next year I'm going to give the party on a Saturday night and hire a crew to clean up on Sunday." He'd believe it. Not believing would require too much effort for something so trifling.

Which was exactly how he classified everything except his campaign now that he'd announced his candidacy. You'd think he was running for king the way he obsessed about it. King? She snorted. Hell, God was more like it.

Jeff tossed the cups into the wastebasket, then pulled her into his arms. "Glad to help," he said, nuzzling her hair. "I'd rather do this with you than just about anything with someone else."

She grinned up at him. *"Just* about anything?"

"Well." He drew the word out. "I *do* have some perfectly natural desires." He laughed. "But I have no intention of satisfying them unless you—"

She stood on her toes and kissed him. "Yes," she said. She relaxed against him, relief suddenly pulsing through her body now that the decision had been made, almost without a conscious effort after months of considering every angle, every nuance, every ramification.

He pulled away, holding her arms and staring into her eyes. "Are you sure?"

The only thing she was sure of was that she didn't understand anything about what had been happening to her since she'd met Jeff. In fact, she wasn't even certain that meeting him was what had started it all. She *was* sure, though, that she was crazy about him, but she had no idea if what she felt was truly love. It didn't feel the same as what she'd called love when she'd gotten married, but for months, years maybe, the only thing she felt when she looked at Fletcher was irritation, sometimes mild, sometimes not. If that was what happened to true love, she might as well enjoy the infatuation—or whatever it was—while it lasted.

She shrugged, smiling into Jeff's eyes. "I think so." She stepped back into his embrace, and he tightened his arms around her.

His mouth quivered, and his green eyes grew dark and shiny. "Jesus Christ, Elizabeth. I'm so glad." He nuzzled her hair, his whole body trembling against hers. "I don't want to take you back to my place—I'm afraid you'll change your mind before we get there."

It was a possibility, she admitted to herself, but she murmured a protest anyway.

He shook his head. "I also don't want you to regret anything. It means too damn much to me. I already feel like a jerk for letting myself go this far, but I couldn't help it. I wanted you from the minute I saw you, and I tried to deny it. I can't anymore." He kissed her, his lips soft and warm and slow at first, then harder and hungrier.

She returned his kiss, matching his impatience with her own and molding her body to his. He picked her up and cradled her against his chest, then carried her into her office and shut the door behind him.

Keeping her in his arms, he lowered himself into the big chair in front of her desk. "I want this more than anything. But only if you do, too. If you change your mind, tell me. I promise to stop." He hesitated for a few seconds, his eyes locked on hers. "I love you, Elizabeth," he said, his voice deepening.

Tears blurred Liz's vision, and she blinked them away. "Thank you," she said. She still didn't know whether or not the tight, tingly, hard-to-breathe feeling in her chest was love, but it was certainly overwhelming. She couldn't stop him now if she wanted to—and suddenly she knew clearly that she didn't.

Her eyes refusing to open, Naomi groped for the alarm clock on the nightstand for several seconds before she realized the noise that had awakened her was the doorbell, not the alarm. Groggily, she forced her eyelids up and peered at the red numbers: 3:09.

Dad. She shivered with sudden cold. His lung cancer was worse. He was back in the hospital, maybe even dying, and Mother couldn't get through by phone, so she'd sent a telegram. Naomi wrapped her arms around herself, trying to keep the throat-constricting hysteria under control. Ashland was a little town—even if there was a Western Union office, they probably didn't deliver in the middle of the night.

She hoisted herself up and shook Richard's shoulder. "Somebody's at the door."

"Jesus, it's the middle of the night. Are you sure? I didn't hear anything." He frowned at her, and the chime sounded again. He groaned and rolled out of bed, slinging on his robe as he stomped down the hallway to the stairs.

Naomi eased herself up and sat on the edge of the bed. Straining to ignore her heartbeat pounding in her ears, she cocked her head and listened, but she couldn't hear anything. Finally, she jumped up and grabbed her robe off the hook on the back of the door. Not knowing didn't make anything easier, especially since she always imagined the worst. She threw on the robe and tied the sash, then crept to the top of the stairs and peeked down into the entryway.

Kristin stood on the porch with two blue-uniformed policemen. A sneer hiked a corner of her lip. Her hair, dyed deep burgundy the week before, was disheveled, and her dark red lipstick was smeared up the side of one cheek. She crossed her arms over her breasts and glared first at the policemen, then at her father.

Naomi sagged against the railing, relief followed quickly by anger.

What the hell was Kristin doing out at this hour? The girl had gone to bed earlier than usual at ten. She'd looked sound asleep when Naomi had checked on her and Leah before going to bed herself. She must have sneaked out after they were asleep.

"Curfew is the least of it," the taller policeman said to Richard. "The boy she was with was holding. He's in jail."

"Holding?" Richard sounded puzzled.

Naomi couldn't see his face, but she'd bet he was squinting the way he always did whenever he concentrated on figuring something out. "Drugs, you idiot!" she wanted to shout at him. Damn, he was obtuse sometimes. He lived in his world of literature and faculty politics and sex with beautiful undergraduates. Wives and babies and teenagers on the verge of going wrong simply didn't interest him. That was the only explanation she could come up with. She'd warned him that Kristin was headed for trouble, but he'd called her a Cassandra and told her she worried too much about everything.

Well, that might be true, but at least she worried about things that were distinctly possible, things that *mattered*. As far as she was concerned, Leah's health and Kristin's rebellion were far more important than the distinctive voice of the narrators of Anthony Trollope's novels —and it wasn't because she didn't think literature a worthwhile pursuit. She'd majored in English because she loved it, and one of these days she was going to finish her thesis and get her degree. But Shakespeare's heroines and Trollope's narrative voice would still be there long after the crises of rearing children had passed.

"Marijuana and LSD," the policeman continued. "Your daughter was clean, though, and it was the first time she's been picked up." He stared hard at Kristin. "If there's a next time, you'll have to come down to the station and get her."

Kristin rewarded him with a scowl hostile enough to daunt a homicidal psychopath, then stepped into the entry. "I'm going to bed." She brushed past Richard without looking at him.

He grabbed her arm and forced her to stand next to him. "Thank you," he told the policemen. "I appreciate this." They nodded, and he closed the door. He glanced up the stairs at Naomi. "I know it's late, but I think it's time we had a talk."

Naomi pulled the sash on her robe a little tighter and descended the stairs. She hoped it wasn't too late for Kristin.

CHAPTER 14

Elbows resting on the bar, Mike jiggled the ice cubes in his vodka and tonic glass. He'd had a couple, but Sheri'd never be able to smell the vodka on him. Maybe one more wouldn't be such a bad idea, after all. He deserved a little celebration for sticking with that son-of-a-bitching project on Granite Street. Christ, it felt good knowing he'd never have to go back there again. Just one more drink wouldn't hurt. Still, there was the baby-sitter to take home, and he *had* promised—

Bob raised his eyebrows. "Well?" he said. "Got time for another?"

Mike took a deep breath, then shook his head. "Better not. I was planning on surprising Sheri with these tonight." He patted the dozen red roses lying on the bar next to his empty glass. "I wanted to give them to her at work." He glanced at the clock behind the bar. "Time to get going. Sometimes she gets off early on Thursdays." He got up, put on his down vest, and stuck the bouquet under his arm. "Catch you later."

"Sure." Bob saluted him and winked. "Have a good one."

That was exactly what he had in mind. Grinning, Mike pushed out the door. Things were looking a lot better with him and Sheri now that he'd cut back on his drinking, and he planned to keep it that way. Shit, he'd even started remodeling the bathroom—Sheri'd been after him to do something about it since they'd bought the damn house. He felt better, had a lot more energy when he didn't drink. Only thing he missed was tying one on with the boys now and then, but he figured Sheri'd never complain about an occasional fishing or hunting trip.

Ice sparkled on the windshields of the cars parked along Main, and he zipped his vest as he walked toward the Mark Antony. When he reached the door, he hid the roses behind his back. She was going to look worried and a little pissed off when she saw him, and then he was going to pull out the flowers, the first ones he'd ever given her. He could hardly wait to see the expression on her face.

He stepped inside, and the warm air enveloped him. Except for the bartender and a couple sitting in a corner booth, the lounge was empty. Frowning, he let the roses dangle at his side as he slid onto a stool. Maybe Sheri was in the head.

"What can I get you?" The bartender slapped a napkin down in front of him.

Mike laid the bouquet across his lap and glanced around the room again. "A Coke," he said, finally. Too bad Sheri wasn't there to hear his order.

By the time he'd finished half his Coke, she still hadn't come back. He waved the bartender over. "Pretty slow tonight," he said. "Did Sheri go home?"

The bartender raised an eyebrow. "Sheri doesn't work on Thursdays. Hasn't for the last month or so." He stared at Mike for a few seconds. "Say, you're her husband, aren't you?"

"Yeah." Mike grasped the seat with both hands and gritted his teeth. What the fuck was the bitch doing if she wasn't working on

Thursday nights? Heat boiled up his neck to his cheeks, and his eyes burned as he reached the only possible conclusion. He swept the roses off his lap and onto the floor, then pushed aside the Coke. "Bring me a double shot of Jack Daniels," he said. "And a beer back."

As she always did on rehearsal nights, Sheri held her breath when she rounded the corner onto Cambridge Street. Thank God. She exhaled with a hiss. Mike's pickup was in the driveway, and the house was dark. Everything looked normal, except that Mike had forgotten to turn on the porch light for her.

She pulled in next to Mike's green Silverado, turned off the ignition, and rubbed the back of her neck with one hand, forcing herself to relax. Only a few more weeks and the play would be over. All she had to do between now and the end of the term was make sure Mike didn't see anything about her in the newspaper—and that would be easy enough, since he hardly ever picked up the *Tidings* except to look over the TV listings and the sports page.

She got out of her car and eased the door shut as softly as she could manage, then walked carefully up the icy sidewalk. It was always easier when Mike was already asleep and she could just slip into bed beside him and not have to say anything. Acting might come naturally to her on a stage, but she wasn't so good at it in real life. Quietly, she closed the front door, took off her shoes, and tiptoed into the kitchen, where she turned the faucet on to a trickle and filled a glass with water. She swallowed a mouthful to relieve the scratchy feeling in her throat and hoped she wasn't coming down with a cold so close to opening night.

After she finished the water, she set the glass in the sink and headed down the hallway to the bedrooms. She stuck her head into her daughter's room to make sure Felicia hadn't kicked off her covers. Last year, when she'd turned seven, Felicia had announced she was too old for sleepers with feet and she wanted a nightgown instead. Sheri had given in, but she'd been sorry ever since because a lot of the time things ended up with the nightgown around Felicia's neck, the blankets on the floor, and a shivering little girl creeping into bed with her in the middle of the night.

Everything looked fine tonight, though, so Sheri pulled the door almost shut and peeked into the next room at Timmy. He lay on his tummy with his arms and legs spread out and his face turned toward the door. She thought for a second about flicking on the light so she could watch him sleep but decided against it since he always let out a surprised little yelp when something woke him up. There wasn't any point in taking a chance on waking Mike just because Timmy looked so sweet when he was asleep.

Trying to ignore the fluttering in the pit of her stomach, she left Timmy's door slightly ajar and slid her stockinged feet through the worn pile of the old brown carpet. Despite the fact that everything looked perfectly normal, she couldn't get rid of her uneasiness. She turned the knob of her bedroom door slowly. She felt like a teenager coming back late from a date with a boy her father didn't approve of. Living with Mike was like going back home again.

Except that Dad was dead and Mike had taken over his job as chief intimidator, a man to be handled as gingerly as a vial of nitroglycerine on a roller coaster ride. At least that was what it felt like—then, and now. If only she'd been smart enough to see that side of Mike before she'd married him.

But he'd been different then. Something about marriage had changed him. It was almost as if she'd become his property the day they'd said the vows, just like buying a pickup or a gun—and when he got drunk, he wrecked those things, too. Once she belonged to him, he didn't have to consider her happiness at all, any more than he'd worry about whether his golden retriever was content with her lot. When Goldie pissed him off, he kicked her. When Sheri pissed him off, he kicked her, too. Or punched her. Or pushed her around or knocked her down. What was good enough for his dog was good enough for his wife.

When he was drunk, anyway. Her arm tense, Sheri pushed the bedroom door open. The room was pitch black—the automatic nightlight plugged into the socket by the bathroom door must have burned out. She relaxed and stepped inside, pulling the door shut behind her until it closed with a quiet click.

She waited for a few seconds until her eyes adjusted to the darkness, then took a deep breath. The room smelled of stale beer and cigarette smoke, and her whole body stiffened. Mike had been drinking again. She shook her head. No. He'd promised. Maybe her nose was screwed up because she was coming down with something. Or maybe he'd been out with some friends. Her clothes often reeked like that after a busy night at the Mark, and she never drank or smoked there. Squinting, she headed toward the bed.

"Where the hell you been?"

She froze, then tried to speak. No words came out.

"Where you been? I ain't asking again." His voice was harsh, and the words slurred together.

She swallowed some foul-tasting saliva and cleared her throat. "At work," she whispered.

"The fuck you have." He switched on the bedside lamp. He sat on the edge of the bed, a bottle of Blitz dangling from one hand. Several more bottles littered the nightstand. On top of the alarm clock rested a saucer filled with cigarette butts. With a swift flick of his empty hand, he swept everything except the lamp onto the floor. His chin jutted out, and his blue eyes glinted with a kind of crazy excitement.

She'd seen that look before. It didn't matter what she said now. Her knees trembling, Sheri backed away. If he hit her in the face, she'd never get over the bruises in time for the play.

"Whore! Where the fuck were you?" He pitched the bottle at her.

She jumped aside, and it exploded against the bedroom door. "I— I'm in a play. I was at practice."

"Shit! You expect me to believe that?" He jumped up, bounded across the room, and jammed his fist into her stomach.

Bent double, Sheri reeled backward, gasping for air. Pain worse than childbirth blackened her vision, and she braced herself against the wall. Hatred surged through her body. She forced herself to straighten. "No," she managed to blurt out. "That's why I never bothered to tell you."

He grabbed her and shoved her into the open closet. "Don't you ever jaw me, woman," he shouted.

She picked herself up off the shoe rack and scrambled out of the closet, trying desperately to scoot out of his way. But she was too slow, and his kick caught her in the ribs. She rolled on the floor, sobbing. This was the last time, she crooned to herself over and over again. She'd never let him hurt her again.

The front door slammed, and a minute later Mike's pickup roared out of the driveway. Sheri crawled to the bed and heaved herself onto it, sucking in a huge breath to control her shakes, then gasping at the searing pain in her side. She had to do something—she couldn't just wait for him to come back, maybe even drunker and meaner than before. She could call the police and tell them, but then what? That would give Mike something real big to be mad about.

She shivered and hunched forward, crossing her arms tightly over her belly. No. Calling the police was out. She had to go somewhere, take the kids someplace safe. Going to her mother's wouldn't help— that would be the first place Mike would look. If it weren't for the play and disappointing Alec, she could just get in her car and drive to Portland, stay with her aunt up there.

A motel. But that was only temporary. Very temporary, since she only had enough money for two nights, even in the cheapest place in town. And this time she wanted more than a two-day vacation from hell. She wanted out.

But she needed help. Admitting it quieted the trembling that racked her body. She grabbed the phone book and thumbed through it until she found the listing for the Help Line. With cold but steady fingers, she dialed the number.

"Crisis Intervention Services." The female voice was calm but warm.

Sheri's throat constricted, and it took her a few seconds to get her voice back. "I need to find out about the women's shelter. Dunn House. My husband hit me, and I'm afraid he's going to come back."

"He's gone now?"

"Yes. But he's drunk, and I don't know—"

"I'll patch you through to the Dunn House. The counselor there can talk to you."

Sheri held her breath while the phone clicked several times, straining her ears as a car turned onto Cambridge Street. A car, not a pickup. She eased the air out of her lungs.

The phone clicked again. "Dunn House. This is Joan."

Sheri's usual control evaporated, and she listened in amazement to herself as she answered the woman's questions. Could that hysterical whisper really belong to her? It vibrated in her head, but at the same time it seemed so far away. "I have to get the children away," she said hoarsely.

The woman on the other end of the line reassured her, then instructed her to take the children and her personal legal documents and drive to the Sentry Market parking lot. "Don't worry about clothing or anything else," she said. "We have everything you need. Someone will meet you there and bring you to us."

Sheri hung up, and without the phone to clutch, her hands started to shake again. She gripped the edge of the bed, then shoved herself up. First the papers. She grabbed the accordion file from under her desk and stuck it under her arm. Everything important was in there, and she didn't want to waste time pawing through it.

Another automobile rounded the corner onto Cambridge, and she froze at the bedroom door. The car hummed past, and she resisted the urge to race into Felicia's room screaming like a madwoman. She had to keep it together for the kids. It was going to be hard enough on them anyway without having her fall apart. She woke Felicia first, wrapped her robe around her, and stuck her slippers on her bare feet, then zipped Timmy into his coat while he was still asleep.

Five minutes later, she was heading down Nevada Street with two sleepy children bundled up in blankets in the backseat and the heater blowing full blast. The tires crunched on the icy street as she pulled up to the stop sign. She shivered, but she knew it wasn't from the cold. Her side ached like crazy, and she wondered if maybe Mike had cracked one of her ribs or something. She glanced at herself in the rearview mirror, the pale glow of the street light illuminating her face. No black eyes or fat lips this time, thank God. He'd only hit her in places that didn't show.

She pulled into the back of the Sentry lot, parked, and flashed the headlights twice. A car door slammed on the other side of the lot, and Sheri peered at the figure walking toward her, sudden panic turning her stomach icy. Maybe leaving wasn't the right thing to do. Mike had never laid a hand on the kids. How could she ever justify taking his children away?

The brown-haired woman knocked on the car's window. "Sheri Riley?" she asked.

Sheri nodded, then slowly rolled down the window.

"I'm Bea. I volunteer at the Dunn House. You and the children come with me."

Bea's warm but businesslike manner comforted Sheri a little. It wasn't as if she had to leave Mike *forever*. She could go back home tomorrow, if she wanted, but it just wasn't safe tonight. With Bea's help, she roused Felicia, then picked up Timmy and cradled him against her chest. He murmured and sucked his thumb noisily.

She followed Bea to a small gray station wagon, settled the children in the backseat, and then slid into the passenger seat. Her own car would be safe in the lot until she was ready to pick it up.

Bea started up the car. "You want to talk about it?"

Sheri shook her head. Now that she'd actually done something, she wasn't so sure anymore. She and Mike could be so happy together if only he'd quit drinking. Maybe coming home to an empty house would scare him enough to make him give it up for good.

She leaned her head back and stared out the window as the car headed up Pioneer Street and past the Shakespeare Theater. She didn't know what the hell she was doing or where the hell Bea was taking her, but it was too late to change her mind now.

CHAPTER 15

As soon as he saw Sheri step through the heavy blue curtain separating Chateaulin's private room from the rest of the restaurant, Alec excused himself from the cluster of enthusiastic cast members and headed toward her. She'd been terrific in the opening night—and only—performance of *Taming*, and he wanted to tell her so again, this time without the interference of the aftershow green room chaos. Even the festival people had been impressed, and she deserved to know just how good she'd been. She didn't seem to realize the extent of her talent.

Sheri paused at the entry, her face serious as she gazed around the room. When she saw Alec, she smiled and lifted her hand.

He pulled her into his arms and hugged her tightly, then planted a big kiss on her cheek. "You were smashing, love. In fact, the best Kate I've seen in years." Surprised by how much he enjoyed the moment of physical contact, he drew her to him again before she pulled away with a wince.

Immediately, he berated himself for letting his libido overcome his good sense. After almost a year without sex, though, he supposed it was only natural to get a hard-on from a brief, friendly embrace—especially when the woman in his arms was as beautiful and desirable as Sheri and despite the fact that he generally made it a rule not to entertain even a passing thought about attractive female students.

Sheri's lips quivered with the effort to keep smiling. "Thanks," she said. "But I'd say most of the credit goes to the director. You made it all seem so natural to me that it wasn't even like acting. I didn't know Shakespeare could be like that."

"Wow." Alec shook his head. "Now that's a real compliment. Thank *you.*"

She shrugged and crossed her arms. "It's the truth. I learned a lot from you." She stared down at her feet for a second; and when she looked back up at him, he realized that without the stage makeup, her face appeared tired and drawn, with dark circles under her eyes and tense lines at the sides of her mouth.

"And I enjoyed having you in my class. I hope you're planning to enroll in another of mine next term."

Glancing down again, she murmured something he couldn't hear above the increasing din, and he fought back the urge to take her by the shoulders and make her look at him. After three months of carefully nurturing her through her doubts and insecurities, he'd somehow expected her transformation to be complete tonight.

Instead she seemed more scared and withdrawn than ever. He'd gotten nowhere, really. She still had no idea of just how bloody good she was—and not just on stage, either. She was a damned bright student as well, the perceptive and enthusiastic kind any teacher welcomed in class. He frowned and bent his head toward her. "Is everything all right?"

She nodded vigorously, twisting her lips back into a smile. "I'm sorry. I'm just a little tired. I haven't been sleeping too well—nervous, I guess. I can't believe it's over and I can stop worrying."

"I know what you mean. I may not have been up there in front of everybody, but there's something intensely and enormously personal about directing. An actor can hide behind a character or a director, but really there's no one for a director to hide behind. For anyone who knows theater, the director is in some ways even more exposed than the playwright or the actors—ultimately, it's his vision that the audience sees. That's a huge responsibility."

Alec paused, embarrassed. The last thing he wanted to do was give Sheri a private lecture. He hated admitting it, even to himself, but he'd been looking forward to seeing her tonight without all the artificial divisions of student and teacher. "Sorry," he said. "I didn't mean to get carried away." He pointed to a couple of empty chairs at the long table set up in the middle of the room. "Why don't we sit down?"

She followed him to the table, and the anxious lines between her brows smoothed a little. "It would never have occurred to me to think of Kate the way you did," she said after they were seated and he'd poured her a glass of champagne. "I thought she was pretty funny at the beginning, calling Petruchio an ass and telling him that if she's a wasp, he'd better watch out for her sting. I never noticed the unhappiness underneath." Sheri's chuckle was one of recognition rather than mirth. "She kind of reminds me of a friend of mine. She's the smartest, funniest person I know, but I always get the feeling that the things she jokes about aren't really all that humorous to her. It's like she's more mad than amused, but the way she says it, it comes out funny. Everyone always laughs anyway." She wrinkled her nose. "Come to think of it, I know quite a few women like that."

Alec's mouth hung open for a minute. Sheri had just described Vivianne perfectly; without consciously realizing it, he'd used his wife as the prototype for Kate, a woman who wasn't happy until she learned to agree with her husband that the sun was really the moon. Uncomfortable, he pushed aside the thought that perhaps his interpretation was more of a wish fulfillment fantasy than he'd realized. Instead, he nodded in agreement with Sheri. "Me, too. Sort of a gallows humor about their lot." He smiled gently at her. "You're not like that, though."

Her lovely green eyes narrowed. "I can't imagine laughing about my problems," she said softly. "Not right now, anyway." She glanced away from him, surveying the room. Suddenly her face stiffened.

Alec followed her terrified gaze. A large man wearing a green and yellow baseball cap and carrying a bouquet of red roses stood in front of the curtain and stared at Sheri.

Sheri rose, her movements as jerky as a marionette. "I have to go," she whispered, backing away from the table. She caught her foot on the chair in back of her and almost tripped, but pushed away Alec's steadying hand. "Excuse me."

Suddenly cold, Sheri waited as Mike elbowed his way through the noisy crowd. There wasn't any point in trying to escape—it would just piss him off, and then there was no telling what he'd do. The counselors at Dunn House had warned her that he might try to see her like this if she didn't get a restraining order.

But she'd decided to risk it anyway, figuring that any kind of legal action would just make Mike even more determined to find her—and maybe more violent when he did track her down. Besides, he'd only be able to talk to her in public—at the Mark or in class or at the play—and he'd be less likely to do anything under those circumstances. She hoped.

She straightened her shoulders and called up some of the bitter strength of Kate the shrew when Mike grabbed her arm. "Don't touch me," she said, pulling away. Her heart raced, but she forced herself to act calm. If she could carry it off on stage, she ought to be able to convince him, for a few minutes anyway.

"Sorry," he mumbled. He took off his cap and stuck it under his arm, then held out the roses. "I just wanted to give you these and tell you how sorry I am. I'll never do it again, babe, if you'll just come back home. I promise. I'll quit drinking for good. I mean it. Just come home."

Sheri shook her head. The counselors had warned her about this too—not that she'd needed their predictions. Mike always apologized afterward, always promised that it'd never happen again, always swore he'd give up drinking. And she'd always believed him, fool that she was.

Well, not this time, even though seeing him made her want to melt, to fling herself into his arms, to rest her head against his chest and listen to his heart beating. Jesus, she'd missed him so much this last week. Hated him, missed him, hated him again. Timmy cried every night, asking for his daddy. Felicia just stared at her, refusing to talk. Christmas was only three weeks away, and she didn't have a place to live, really. She didn't know what to do. She loved him, but he wasn't good for her.

"I can't," she said. Her face felt rigid from the effort to keep from crying.

He put the bouquet into her hand. "Take these, at least." His blue eyes sparkled with tears. "I love you, babe. And I'm proud of you. I watched you up there tonight. You were great."

She bent her head over the roses and sniffed them to keep him from seeing the tears in her own eyes. She couldn't give in, not now. Gritting her teeth, she gulped in a huge breath; and the faint twinge in her side left over from their last fight bolstered her resolve. If only he'd just leave without making a scene.

She blinked back the tears and lifted her head. "Thanks."

"I don't want to keep you from your friends," he said. "It's your night, babe." He ran his fingers through his dark brown curls, then set his cap back on his head. "Promise me you'll think about what I said."

She nodded, and he winked at her before he turned on his heel and disappeared through the curtain. Sheri slumped into the empty chair in front of her just as Naomi slid into the seat across the table.

"Are you all right?" Naomi set her glass of white wine on the table. She'd seen Mike come in, but hadn't been sure what to do. Sheri had told her about the fight, about going to Dunn House, but she'd asked Naomi not tell anyone else, not even Richard. Especially not Richard, because Sheri was afraid that Alec might find out, and she was determined to go through with the play no matter what.

So Naomi had promised even though she'd longed to tell Meredith and Liz, at least. It was hard being the safety deposit box for everyone else's secrets; she felt so responsible and so alone in her responsibility. If Mike had hurt Sheri tonight, she would have felt it was her fault.

"Yeah." Sheri put the flowers next to Naomi's wineglass. "I just hope he doesn't try to follow me back to Dunn House."

"Would he do that?" Naomi couldn't keep the incredulity from her voice. Men like Mike weren't a part of her world; Richard was far from perfect, but he'd never raised either voice or hand to her. His cruelties were more subtle: comments about her still unfinished doctoral thesis, snide remarks about her weight, officious hints about exercise and diet.

"I wouldn't put it past him." Sheri pushed the roses toward Naomi. "Why don't you keep these? I don't want to explain them to the counselor."

Naomi stripped off the green wrapping paper and stuck the roses in the vase on the table. She brushed her hands together and smiled at Sheri. "Takes care of that," she said. "Now what are we going to do about getting you safely home?" She snapped her fingers. "I've got it." She fished through her purse for her car key and handed it to Sheri. "Let's trade cars. If he's watching, he'll think that I'm you and that you're driving away with a man."

"I can't—"

"Don't argue. Just give me your key. He won't do anything to us."

Sheri sighed. "You're probably right. He seemed totally sober, and he only goes crazy when he's been drinking."

While Sheri searched for her key, Naomi glanced around the room looking for Richard. He'd been part of the group congratulating the beautiful girl who played Bianca when she'd spotted Mike and excused herself.

Now the two of them were sitting at the table in the back corner, alone and engaged in what appeared to be an intense conversation. As Richard stood up, the girl grabbed his arm and pulled him back down, then leaned across the table and kissed him. On the lips.

Naomi clenched her jaw and turned quickly back to Sheri. So

Bianca—Heather, wasn't it?—was the one. No wonder Richard had tried to get out of coming to Chateaulin after the play.

But Naomi had insisted—it was Sheri's big night, and she deserved their support, especially now. Richard had been so attentive lately that Naomi had lulled herself into believing she'd imagined all those indications of yet another infidelity, and his claim of exhaustion made her worry that he was working too hard.

Fucking too much was more like it. Heather probably wore him out. Struggling to control the fury in her heart, Naomi composed her face and took the key from Sheri's outstretched hand. Sheri had enough problems of her own; she certainly didn't need to hear about her friend's woes.

Naomi closed her ears to the conversations and laughter swirling about her and ignored the horrible feelings churning inside her, focusing instead on Sheri. "Call me if you need *anything*," she said. "We've got plenty of room. You can stay with us—"

A tiny smile fluttered at Sheri's lips. "You've done enough just listening to me," she said, standing up. "I think I should go before he decides to come back."

"It doesn't seem fair, but you're probably right." Naomi stood, too, and hugged Sheri. "You've heard it a million times tonight but I have to tell you again—you were a terrific Kate. Don't let Mike keep you off the stage again. You belong there."

Sheri sniffed and pulled away. "Thanks, Naomi. I don't know what I'd do without you—and Liz and Meredith. And if I stay for one more minute, I'm going to start bawling like a baby." Ducking her head, she slipped through the crowd and vanished behind the curtain at the door.

Her hand trembling, Naomi grabbed her wineglass and gulped down what remained of the chardonnay Richard had ordered for her. She felt like crying too, but not because she was overwhelmed with success and other people's generosity. She hated it that she wanted to cry whenever she was angry. Just when she most needed her dignity, she always ended up blubbering like a baby.

This time it would be different though. She would rage without tears, or at least look coldly furious and in total control, the way her father always had.

She started when she felt a hand on her shoulder. Richard stood next to her with a wine bottle in his hand.

"More chardonnay?"

She stared at him for a minute, then held out her glass.

Richard poured the wine carefully, twisting the bottle when he finished in order to keep it from dripping. Naomi seemed a little upset; he hoped to hell she hadn't seen Heather's kiss. She'd cornered him as soon as Naomi left, hissing that if he didn't talk to her, she'd put on a scene that would make Kate look like a wussy. She was capable of carrying out her threat, too. Damn it! Why had he ever let Naomi push him into coming tonight? Sometimes it seemed as if his whole life were controlled by women—Naomi, Kristin, Leah, not to mention his mother, his first two wives and his grown daughter Sara. They all wanted something from him. And now Heather had joined the ranks of the Corps of Demanding Women.

He supposed he had to admit that he'd created the corps himself. Except for his mother, every female in his life got there because of his pecker. It led and he followed.

Naomi upended her drink, swilled down the wine, and thudded the glass on the table. "I'm ready to go," she said.

Richard raised an eyebrow. Naomi loved parties; he was usually the one who had to urge her to go home. Undoubtedly she'd seen Heather's little display, and he wasn't sure which would be the best course: stay and risk a scene in public or go and face one for sure in private. Heather's laugh shrilled out above the hubbub for a second, and he made up his mind. "I'll get our coats," he said.

"We can get them on the way out." Naomi stomped through the little cluster of people gathered around the table nearest the door.

Richard grabbed their coats and followed her out onto the street. He tried to help her on with her jacket, but she pushed him away and put it on by herself, shoving her arms into the sleeves, then flinging the belt around her waist and tying it with a jerk.

"Sheri took our car." She dangled a key from her hand. "We're driving hers home. She parked it in front of Fortmillers." Without waiting for him, she strode up the sidewalk.

Richard hurried to catch up with her. "Why are we—"

"Don't ask."

Richard knew he was definitely in for it—the deluge of tears, the recriminations, the hysteria of the woman betrayed. It was exhausting even to think about, but he supposed he deserved it. He waited while she unlocked the door and slid into the driver's seat of a small blue Chevrolet, then opened the passenger side.

She started the car and pulled out onto Main Street before he'd even fastened his seat belt.

"Get rid of her," she said.

He blinked. It wasn't her words but the deadly calm in her voice that surprised him.

"Who?" he asked. By now denial was a reflex.

She braked for the red light and turned to him. "Don't play with me, Richard. If you don't finish it with her now, I'm finished. With you."

No tears. No hysteria. He shifted in his seat. "Wait," he said. "I know it didn't look like it, but I've already broken it off. I don't know why—"

"No more lies."

"It's the truth—"

She turned onto Gresham and accelerated up the hill. "It had better be," she said, stopping at the sign and turning to look at him. "If you ever see her—or anyone else—again, you can start looking for somewhere else to live. Right now I still have some love left for you, but my patience is gone."

She parked the car in the drive and went inside without saying another word. Slowly, Richard eased himself out of the cramped little seat and trailed after her. Christ, he felt like a dumb ass. Every time he thought he understood Naomi completely, she pulled something new on him. He knew her about as well as he knew himself.

CHAPTER 16

The baby down the hall wailed again, and Sheri felt like joining him. She leaned back against the thin pillow and wriggled, trying to find a comfortable position—an almost impossible task since the headboard was the old-fashioned kind with thin metal posts. It wasn't that she wasn't grateful. The Dunn House had given her so much—safety, shelter, food, clothing for her and the children, counseling, the opportunity to meet other women with similar problems.

But the kind of help the shelter gave was only temporary, and she felt guilty about taking up space that might be needed by someone even worse off than she was. After all, she had a job—even if she didn't make enough at it to pay rent, and if she didn't work, she might be able to get a welfare check that would support her and the kids. And she had a husband who begged her to come back to him every time he saw her.

Last night there'd even been a half-page ad in the *Tidings: Sheri—I love you. Please come home. Mike.*

She kicked the newspaper at the foot of the bed, and it rattled to the floor. Damn him. If only he'd just leave her alone. It was hard enough fighting against herself. It was like they were connected by a giant rubber band or something, and the farther they got apart, the harder it was to keep going, and pretty soon she was either going to have to get out the scissors and cut the thing or else it was going to snap her right back to him.

But she didn't have the guts to use the scissors. It was like they were right there in her hands and she kept staring at them, but she just couldn't bring herself to use them. What would she do without Mike in her life? The last two weeks had been hard enough. She didn't dare imagine forever without him, never resting her head on his shoulder in bed or feeling his excitement when he held her, the way he needed her, wanted her.

She blinked her eyes to clear away the film of tears. It was almost time to wake Timmy from his nap and go pick Felicia up at school. Tomorrow was the last day before Christmas vacation—she had to figure out what she was doing by then. Even the thought of spending Christmas in a shelter home was depressing.

Timmy stirred on the little cot at the foot of the bed. Sheri peered through the footboard at him. He didn't seem to mind the Dunn House too much. He thought it was great to be sleeping in the same room as his mommy, sometimes even the same bed. He'd made some friends, and he liked the woman Sheri exchanged baby-sitting time with so she could go to work.

But he missed his daddy, even though Sheri had explained to him that Daddy had been a bad boy and was having a time out. It was such a *long* time out, Timmy cried. Would she ever make him have a time out that *long*? And what had Daddy done to be so bad?

She couldn't bring herself to tell him. Mike never raised a hand to the kids, not really. Sure, he spanked Timmy and Felicia now and then, but mostly he just yelled at them when they pissed him off. Neither of them seemed to hold it against him, just the way she'd always loved her dad when she was little, no matter how mean he got sometimes. It wasn't until she was a teenager that she'd started resenting Dad, but then that was pretty natural, she supposed.

She brushed the tears from her cheeks, then eased herself off the bed and crossed quietly to the little sink next to the closet. Peering into the scratched and cloudy old mirror above the basin, she fluffed her dark hair around her shoulders and reapplied her lipstick. She still didn't know what to do. Stay or leave? Go back to Mike now or go to Mom's, where he'd just bug her until she eventually gave up?

She might as well make life simple for everyone. Sighing, she put her brush and lipstick into the little bag she'd already packed and leaned over Timmy sleeping so peacefully on the cot. "Wake up, sweetie," she said. "We're going home."

Liz took one last drag off the Salem before she flicked it into the fire. Thank God the idea of a house full of women and children had driven Fletcher away for a few hours. It was easier without him—he was always so preoccupied with himself and his own concerns that she worried that her friends would find him rude. He wasn't really—at least he didn't mean to be. It was just that everything she did seemed frivolous to him, while his own pursuits were important and meaningful.

She closed the glass fireplace doors. Maybe he was right. Selling fancy houses didn't compare to fighting legal battles for the good of the environment, a war he intended to carry on if elected to the state senate. Giving a luncheon for her girlfriends and Brooke's playgroup didn't come close to matching the importance of a campaign dinner.

Well, it was important to her, damn it. She straightened a pillow on the leather couch facing the wall of floor-to-ceiling windows, then poked her head into the dining room to check things out. She'd set the table with a dark green damask cloth and napkins and her Christmas Spode china, the set that would have paid all of Greenpeace's expenses for a month. The silver and crystal sparkled, and the caterers had put out the desserts on the dark mahogany sideboard. The teenage girls she'd hired to baby-sit with the kids were already upstairs playing with Brooke. Everything was going smoothly.

Too bad she couldn't say the same for her marriage. She and Fletcher still went along as if nothing were different, but every time she looked at him, she thought of Jeff. In her mind, Jeff sat at their dinner table and slept next to her in their bed. He splashed in the spa in the master suite with her, and he curled up on the family room couch with her while they watched television. He rubbed her feet, massaged her back, and whispered "I love you" at all the right times. And, incredibly, he was as wonderful during the times they really were together as when she just imagined him there.

She couldn't hold back a bitter little laugh. Her imaginary Jeff was more concrete, more vivid than Fletcher in the flesh. Even when Fletcher was really there, he wasn't; even when Jeff wasn't there, he was. All she had to do to get turned on was picture Jeff lying naked on his bed, smiling and holding out his arms to her. Surely, it had never been like that with Fletcher. If it had, she couldn't remember it now.

The doorbell chimed, and almost reluctantly she pushed the last image of Jeff from her mind. She opened the big oak double doors and stepped back as the whole crew on the front porch surged into the two-story-high entry, hugging and kissing and wishing her a Merry Christmas.

Smiling, Liz greeted them all, piled their coats and hats and purses into the guest closet, and ushered them into the living room. She flicked on the intercom to the upstairs playroom. "The kids are here," she told the baby-sitters. "Why don't you bring Brookie down?" The speaker crackled, and a minute later the two girls came down the stairs with Brooke between them.

Halfway down, Brooke shook loose the girls' hands and scrambled the rest of the way on her own. Liz held her breath until she reached the bottom. Staircases and Brookie's physical impetuosity were not her favorite combination, but she knew better than to try to restrain her daughter too much, despite Fletcher's intermittent badgering. When Brooke started to crawl, she'd simply had the hardwood stairs covered with a thick pad and carpet and kept her fingers crossed. Constantly hovering motherhood just wasn't her style.

Someone in back of her gasped, and Liz knew it was Naomi before she turned around. She laughed. "It's okay. She does that all the time."

Naomi shook her head and resettled herself on the couch next to Meredith. "I don't know how you stand it. I've got gates at both ends of my stairway. Richard is always saying I need to lighten up a little and I try, but I just can't stop worrying. Especially now, with Leah's seizures."

Sheri gave Naomi a gentle smile and nodded while the baby-sitters herded the four toddlers into a little group at the far end of the long living room. "We all worry, but I've found myself worrying less about Timmy than I did about Felicia. Kids are amazing survivors."

Meredith's hands trembled a little, but her voice was calm. "I certainly agree with that." She tipped her head toward her daughter sitting quietly at the edge of the group. "I intend to make damn sure Justine doesn't have to survive what I did, though."

Liz seated herself in the blue club chair in front of the windows and studied Meredith. Except for a new tenseness in the way she held her mouth, Meredith didn't look as if she'd just taken a walk through hell. As always, her thick auburn hair curved perfectly over her shoulders and her big dark brown eyes sparkled with life, not missing a thing.

"How are you doing, Meredith?" Naomi asked. "Do you want to talk about it?"

"We can send the kids upstairs if you'd like," Liz said.

Meredith shrugged. "No, don't bother them. I'm okay." She hesitated. "Well, not really, but better than I was. My mother's been wonderful, and I really like my counselor. If only Ted—" She broke off and shrugged again, her eyes filling with tears.

Naomi squeezed Meredith's hand, and Liz motioned to the baby-sitters to gather their charges and take them to the playroom. By the time they were gone, Meredith had composed herself again. The perfectionist of the group, Meredith worked so hard to make sure everything was just right and then gave herself all kinds of shit when she didn't live up to her own incredibly high standards—an impossible task, from Liz's point of view.

"It's all right to fall apart, you know," she told Meredith. "We don't expect you to be perfect all the time, and we love you."

Meredith's attempted smile turned into a grimace of pain. "I know," she said. "I just wish I weren't so *obsessed* with it. I know all of you have your problems, too, and I feel so selfish dwelling on myself. I want to hear about Mike and Richard and Fletcher and the funny things Brookie said and how Leah's doing with her medication and if Timmy's interested in the potty chair yet . . ." She sighed deeply. "I think I'd just like to forget about myself for a little while, if it's all right with you."

Heels clicked across the dining room's parquet floor, and one of the caterers paused in the doorway. "Would anyone like champagne?"

"What a great idea," Meredith said. "Leave it to Fizzy Lizzie to turn a playgroup into a celebration."

"This *is* a special day," Liz said as the caterer handed around the champagne flutes, then left. "It's the second anniversary of the true beginning of playgroup."

"That's right." Meredith smiled, a real smile this time. "Two years ago today we all showed up at the childbirth education class with our husbands and pillows and twenty extra pounds."

"Sixty," Naomi said. "And a couple of months later we were all mothers."

Liz laughed, glad for Meredith's sake that the arrival of the champagne had shifted the focus away from her. Naomi and Sheri didn't seem to be in a mood for confidences, either; and God knew she didn't want to talk about Jeff right now, even though he was on her mind practically every second of the day. Maybe it'd be best to keep things light for a while. Well, that was her forte, according to Fletcher, who claimed she could turn the most serious topic into trivial gossip. "I sneaked a look at my chart when I was in the hospital having Brookie. Do you know what they called me? An 'elderly *primapara.'* Can you believe it—thirty-five years old and *elderly?*"

"Well, I was only thirty-two but I sure felt elderly after twenty hours of labor," Sheri said.

"I felt positively decrepit," Meredith said. "Three days of contractions and then a C-section."

"That's what happens when you wait until you're almost old enough to be a grandmother to have your first baby." Liz winked at the others, and they all laughed.

The caterer poked her head into the living room. "Lunch is served, ladies," she said.

CHAPTER 17

Ted settled back into his favorite wing chair and put his feet up on the footrest in front of it. Hell of a Christmas. All he wanted to do was relax a little, have a little fun, but it was damn near impossible in this house.

In the kitchen, Meredith banged pots and pans while she argued with Eva. They weren't shouting, but he could hear them anyway, Meredith's low voice throbbing with irritation. "Why don't you just take Justine and get out of the kitchen?" she said. "I'll bring the dessert out in a few minutes."

Eva mumbled something, and then Meredith said, "I do appreciate your help, Mother, but right now I just want to be left alone. I'm quite capable of washing dishes and serving pie by myself."

Her voice soared, and Ted gritted his teeth. Jesus Christ, he was tired of listening to the two of them. As much as he knew Meredith needed her mother right now, he sometimes wished Eva would just go back to Eugene. It didn't make it any easier knowing that Eva had never particularly liked him, and the truth of the matter was that he'd never been overly fond of the old dragon, either.

Not that the two of them were ever anything but polite to each other. But he was tired of tiptoeing around in his own house, afraid of doing or saying something wrong. In fact, it was practically impossible to say anything *right* to Meredith these days—no matter how casual the comment, she could always find an offensive element in it.

He wanted to help her—he'd even read a couple of the books about incest survivors Eva had given him—but it was so hard. Meredith was always saying, "Don't take it personally. It's not you. It's me." But the truth of the matter was that he couldn't help taking it personally. After all, he was the one being rejected time after time, not her father. The son of a bitch was dead, and Ted was paying for his crime. Every time he thought about sex lately he felt like a goddamn rapist. And it didn't help that Meredith treated him like one most of the time.

A dish shattered in the kitchen, and the voices abruptly quieted. Ted sat up straight and gripped the arms of the chair. Maybe he should go in and get Justie himself if Eva wasn't going to bring her out. But if he did that, Eva would certainly stay in the kitchen, and he'd have to keep listening to them. No, it was better to stay put. Surely, Eva would realize that broken glass and a two-year-old weren't a good combination.

Suddenly, Meredith shrieked, "Get out! Get out of my kitchen. Get out of my house. Don't tell me you didn't know what was going on. I don't believe it. I don't believe *you*! You *should* have known it. Jesus Christ, Mother. How could you *not* know it?"

Justine started crying, and then Ted heard Eva murmur something about omniscience, about not being able to read people's minds or knowing what they were doing when she wasn't present.

"You might have been a little more aware if you hadn't been so drunk most of the time." Meredith lowered her voice, but the tone was harsh, bitter.

Ted raised his eyebrows and leaned forward. Meredith had never mentioned that her mother was an alcoholic, and the possibility had never occurred to him. Eva always seemed so elegant, so shrewd, so disciplined that it was hard to imagine her with her life out of control. It made sense, though, now that he knew. He'd always interpreted Eva's avoidance of alcohol as just another example of her rigidity. It was almost gratifying to find out that she had a flaw.

Still, he didn't like the idea of Justie hearing their argument. Even though she probably couldn't understand most of what they were saying, he'd bet the emotions were upsetting to her. Why the hell didn't Meredith think of their child before letting loose at Eva? He stood, knocking over the footstool, then kicking it out of his way. Christmas dinner churned unpleasantly in his stomach as he strode into the kitchen.

Tears running down her cheeks, Justie stood up in her high chair and stretched her arms out to him. "Down," she said.

Ted scooped her up and glared at Meredith and Eva. "You two can finish this alone," he said. "We're going to visit the Berensons. It's always peaceful there." He spun around and stomped out with Justie in his arms, slamming the kitchen door behind him.

SAN FRANCISCO

Standing between Andy and Nick, Doug grinned and draped an arm over each of his brother's shoulders. "Let's open the presents! Let's open the presents!" he shouted in unison with them. It was a ritual chant they'd started when they were little kids because Mom had insisted the dinner dishes be washed before they were allowed to attack the presents. Even though they were more patient now, Christmas Eve wouldn't be the same without it. He lifted his arms from his brothers' shoulders and started clapping in time to the chant. "Let's open the presents!"

Mom lowered the video camera and smiled at them. "Now I want a photo of all of us in front of the tree."

Doug rolled his eyes, pretending whiny reluctance. "Aw, Mom," he said. "More pictures?"

Andy and Nick chimed in, and Mom stuck her hands on her hips. "Move it, you guys. Or maybe you'd like to wait until tomorrow morning?" She delivered her yearly threat with a smile.

"Oh no, not that. Anything but that." Grinning, Doug hustled his brothers in front of the big fir tree decorated with ornaments they'd made over the years—tattered paper snowflakes, bread dough snowmen, paper-mâché angels, construction paper garlands, and ragged-looking strands of ancient popcorn and cranberries. Mom kept threatening to throw the stuff all away and buy a bunch of those frilly Victorian ornaments her magazines always showed, but Doug never believed her. She was more caught up in their family traditions than any of the rest of them—she still insisted her three sons dye Easter eggs every year, even though they were teenagers now.

Mom propped the Canon on the coffee table and set the timer, then she and Dad joined them in front of the tree. The camera flashed, and Doug started the chant again. "Let's open the presents!"

God, it was great being home, being in remission and all, even if the only thing the detective his dad hired had found out was that his birth mother had been young, unmarried, and living or staying in Portland in the late spring of 1974. Mr. Obremski was still working on it, though, so there was a good chance Doug would have another Christmas. For the first time, he thought about what it would be like for the rest of them if he weren't there. He'd be dead, so what would he care? But things would never be the same for them. Sudden tears flooded his eyes. He knelt down and grabbed a package wrapped in the Sunday comics and pretended to examine it.

He sneaked his hand up to his cheek and brushed at the tears before he turned around and held out the gift. "Here, Mom," he said. "It's for you."

CHAPTER 18

January

ASHLAND, OREGON

The soft click of the front door closing snapped Fletcher back into consciousness. He rolled over and checked the clock: 3:06 glowed red in the darkness. This was the third time in the last month Liz had come in late. Despite her general flakiness, he'd always trusted her, but something about her had changed lately. She seemed determined to shut him out of her life, and he didn't know what to do or say about it.

Except that he was starting to get pissed off. Sure, she always asked first if he wanted to go wherever it was she was going, but she knew how exhausted he was with both his job and his campaign. Not only that, but it wasn't good for Brooke that her mother was gone so much—and not just with her work, but with her socializing as well.

He clenched his jaw as Liz's light footsteps sounded on the stairs. Unfortunately, tonight just wasn't a good time to confront her about it —he simply didn't have the energy to deal with her complete lack of logic. Her total disregard for the rules of debate infuriated him so much that he'd given up trying to *really* talk to her years ago. Then she complained that he never talked to her, but every time he tried, she told him that she hated being lectured at. He had to drive to Sacramento tomorrow to defend a Headwaters activist in federal court; he couldn't afford to spend the rest of the night dealing with her irrational arguments.

The bedroom door swished open, and he squeezed his eyes shut and pretended to be asleep even though a part of him wanted to cry out, "Where have you been?" If she lied to him and he found it out, he'd never be able to believe her again. On the other hand, what if the truth was something he didn't want to hear? Even the thought was enough to make him queasy.

Liz crossed the room to the bathroom, not even bothering to be quiet, it seemed to him. He heard her flick on the light before she pulled the door shut behind her. The water ran for a minute; then the toilet flushed. Fletcher's jaw ached from the strain of keeping his mouth shut, and he forced himself to unclench his teeth and fists. It was Wednesday night, goddamn it. There was nothing happening in Ashland on a Wednesday night in the middle of January, no dance music, no plays, no parties.

So what the hell had she been doing since seven o'clock? Even if she'd spent all evening wining and dining her client at the Mark, she still should have been home by midnight. That left three hours unaccounted for, at the least.

Three hours. An image of Liz naked in bed with some faceless, unknown man seared his brain. It *was* true she'd complained lately about their lousy sex life, had even suggested they see a counselor, but surely she wouldn't go that far. It wasn't that he didn't desire her; sometimes he wanted her so much he was afraid of being devoured by his own passion.

His eyes stung with unshed tears, and despite all he'd heard the last few years about the "new male" who could be both strong and emotional, he sniffed them back guiltily. He'd learned young that tears weren't acceptable to his father—in fact that almost nothing he did was quite good enough. And he'd tried so damn hard, too. Placing first in the district tennis tournament wasn't good enough because he didn't win the state meet. He should have run for student body president instead of settling for vice president. Stanford was a more prestigious school than the U of O. Corporate lawyers made more money than bleeding heart liberals who gave away their time to radical causes. *The engine is missing, stupid, because you didn't set the timing right. You pounded that nail in crooked. Boys don't cry.* Gritting his teeth, Fletcher rolled to his side just as Liz scuffed back into the bedroom.

"Fletcher?" she whispered.

He stiffened, but said nothing. Goddamn it, he loved her, but he had so many other things on his mind right now. When she slid under the covers on her side of the bed and sighed, he controlled his impulse to reach out and pull her into his arms. It just wasn't right for her to cause problems like this.

Sheri was sure there were more butterflies fluttering around in her stomach right now than there'd been the night of the performance of *Taming*. She rested her elbows on the kitchen table and watched Mike shovel in the last bite of steak. The kids had already finished their dinners, thank God, and Felicia had taken Timmy into the living room to watch one of their noisy cartoon shows. If he blew up, she didn't want them seeing it.

"All done?" She smiled at him and took his plate to the sink. "You want some cake?"

"Sure." He leaned back in his chair and twined his fingers over his belly. "Great dinner, babe."

"Thanks." She got a saucer down from the cupboard, sliced off a big chunk of chocolate cake, and settled it on the plate. This time she had to ask him. None of the last couple of months would have happened if she hadn't sneaked around and enrolled in that class without saying anything to him about it. "Want some ice cream, too?"

"Nah."

She put the plate in front of him and sat back down.

Mike lifted an eyebrow. "Fork?"

She jumped up and grabbed a fork from the drawer. Sometimes it seemed to her that her whole life was devoted to waiting on people—Mike, the kids, the customers at the Mark. Her class at SOSC was the *only* thing she did for herself, and she was probably going to have to get down on her knees and beg Mike to let her continue. She handed him the fork, then plopped into the chair again.

He took a bite and nodded. "Good," he mumbled with his mouth full.

Now was the time—it wasn't going to get any better than this. He was sober, full, and enjoying his favorite food in the whole world. "I'm thinking about taking another class from Professor Whittier this term. He said I have a lot of talent, and it's really what I want to do. I've already saved the money from my tips to pay for the tuition, and this term I won't have to buy any books because I already got the big Shakespeare—" Her cheeks got hot, and she stopped for a breath.

Mike stared at her, then slowly put down his fork. He shook his head. "Whoa, babe. You're going way too fast for me. I've got to get this straight. You're saying you want to take another class from that fag at the college?" His eyes narrowed and took on that crazy gleam that always meant the worst.

She shivered and clasped her hands in her lap, determined to go through with it anyway. He wasn't drunk; he wouldn't hit her. "Uh-huh, I mean, he's not a fag—"

"How would you know?" His voice was soft, almost a hiss. "Found out for yourself, have you? You been porkin' the guy? Is that how you got that big fat part and a fucking A? Sleeping with the fucking teacher. I knew it the minute I spotted him at that fancy-ass party, but I was so hot to have you back I didn't give a damn."

Sheri bit her lip to keep it from trembling. This was turning out worse than she'd bargained for. She'd figured he'd complain about the time and the money, but he didn't usually go insanely jealous on her unless he'd been drinking. The worse of it was now that he'd started in on it, she'd never be able to convince him otherwise. Denying it would only piss him off faster, and if she said nothing, then he'd just keep ragging on it until he actually believed it himself. Either way she was screwed. Tears of disappointment blurred her vision, disappointment at herself for falling for Mike's line again, disappointment at him for not keeping his word, disappointment at losing her only chance to make herself better. The best she could hope for now was to somehow avoid the inevitable blowup.

"Please stop," she said, unable to keep the whining note he hated so much out of her voice. "The kids—"

"Fuck the kids." He shoved the table so violently that his dessert plate fell to the floor and shattered. "I can't take it. You think I'm going to look the other way again? You belong to me. No one touches what's mine and gets away with it." He jumped up, knocking over his chair. "Where's my fucking gun? I'm going to kill the bastard."

"No!" Sheri grabbed at his shirt.

He whipped around and slapped her hard across the face. "Cunt!" he shouted.

Sobbing, she crumpled to the floor. Pain shot up her nose and spread into her cheekbones. When she touched her face, her hand came away bloody.

"Get up, goddamn you!" He grabbed her by the shoulders and hauled her to her feet. "This is your own fucking fault." He shook her so hard her head snapped back and forth and droplets of blood spattered on the kitchen floor.

She gasped, choking on her tears and blood, and tried to pull away. She had to get to the sink, clean herself up before the kids saw her. Then she had to get them to safety. Because if he touched one of them, she'd kill him—

He hooked his elbow around her neck and twisted her arm behind her back. "Where you think you're going?" he said, squeezing his arm tight against her throat.

She gagged, fighting for air, and her vision blurred, then blackened. A humming sound, like a swarm of angry bees, filled her head. Little circles of X's lit up the blackness, swirling into a whirlpool of infinity.

Suddenly, she was lying on the cold floor, wheezing and coughing, her lungs on fire and her throat raw, her head cradled in someone's lap.

Mike's face floated above her, his cheeks wet with tears. "Sheri, babe, I didn't mean to," he kept saying over and over. He sounded like he was in a tunnel, far far away, but getting closer. "God, babe, I almost killed you. I'm so sorry." Rough sobs punctuated his words, and he buried his face in his hands.

She tried to tell him she was okay, but all that came out was a hoarse croak. "I have to leave," she finally managed to whisper.

He shook his head violently. "No. I'm a fucking crazy lunatic. I love you more than anything in the world, and I almost killed you. What if I hadn't stopped? You'd be dead, and I'd spend the rest of my rotten fucking life in the pen." He hoisted her into his arms, then set her gently into a kitchen chair and tipped the table back upright. "I might be crazy, but I'm not stupid. This time I go. You stay here with the kids. I won't bother you again. I promise."

She put her hand to her aching and bruised throat. "I don't want to die," she said.

"I know. If I could do this cold sober, there's no telling—" Another sob muffled his words, and he backed toward the door into the garage. "I'll come back tomorrow and pack up my things."

A few seconds later the garage door squeaked open and his pickup rumbled to life. The TV set still blared in the living room, but she could no longer hear the children's voices. She put her head down on the table to cry, but her eyes were as dry and scratchy as her throat. Mike was gone, and she didn't feel sad or afraid or happy. She didn't feel anything except tired.

The doorbell chimed, and Naomi wiped her floury hands on her jeans. It never failed. As soon as she started kneading dough, there was someone at the door or on the phone. "I'm coming," she called when the bell rang again. She glanced at her reflection in the mirror hanging above the coat rack in the entry hall, then wiped a flour smudge from her cheek and tucked a strand of dark, curly hair behind her ear. She looked frazzled, harried. She sighed. So what was new about that? Things between her and Richard were improving, but change took time and they both had a lot to work on.

She opened the door and had to fight back a sudden wave of nausea. Richard's latest indiscretion slouched haughtily on the front porch, her thick strawberry blond hair painstakingly mussed and her carefully lip-sticked mouth arranged into a sullen but sexy pout. "Hi," the girl said, and shrugged.

Naomi stared at her, resisting the impulse to fling the door shut and run upstairs screaming obscenities. She would be calm, handle this with some of the new maturity she'd found inside herself lately.

"I'm Heather. Heather Austin. Can I come in?"

May, Naomi corrected the girl's grammar silently. What did they teach kids in college these days? Obviously her brain's primary function was as manure for her hair. Of course, when you slept with your professor, it probably didn't matter whether you mastered the subject or not just as long as you subjected the master. *Stop it,* she told herself. *Take a deep breath. Control yourself, not the situation.* She frowned at Heather but motioned her inside. If this took long, her bread was going to be ruined. "Go on into the living room," she said. "I'm just going to stick some dough into the refrigerator. I was making bread."

"How domestic," Heather murmured, following her into the kitchen.

Ignoring her sarcasm with some effort, Naomi wrapped the dough in plastic and shoved it into the refrigerator. She washed her hands and dried them, then slipped her wedding ring back onto her finger. "Okay," she said, turning around. "Would you like some coffee—or something else?" *My husband, perhaps?*

"I just need to talk to you." Heather leaned forward, and her hair framed her face, making her look like a Pre-Raphaelite's dream girl, innocence and voluptuousness at war with each other.

Except that the predatory gleam in Heather's aqua blue eyes showed there was no question as to which was the winner. Naomi pulled out the chair across from the girl and eased herself into it. Anger at Richard for bringing this unpleasantness into her life welled up inside her, but at the same time she recognized the ultimate choice was really hers. She could always refuse, send the little bitch away. The realization calmed her, and the butterflies in her stomach flew away. "So you want to talk," she said. "All right. I'm listening."

"I'm in love with Richard. I want you to let him go."

She said the words with such drama, such intensity, such absolute conviction that Naomi could only stare at her. Mama had said this would happen; Naomi could still hear her words: "He left his first wife for a student. Now he's leaving his second wife for you, a student. And he'll leave you for a student. The man is predictable."

Well, maybe Richard *was* predictable, but that didn't mean she had to be. According to Richard, both Jean and Olivia had cried until their eyes swelled shut, pleading with him to stay. A month ago she might have done the same thing. But something had changed inside her driving home that night after the party at Chateaulin. She still loved Richard, flawed as he was, and she had no desire to take her love back no matter what kind of stupid mistakes he might make. It didn't matter to her anymore whether he returned her love tit for tat; she was willing to accept him the way he was, just as she accepted Leah. And in the same way that she was learning to set limits for Leah, she'd set them for Richard. No more affairs. She deserved respect and happiness, too.

Naomi shrugged. "I'm not his jailer. He's free to leave whenever he wants."

Heather narrowed her beautiful eyes. "You know that isn't so. You've caught him in a web of guilt so sticky he couldn't possibly untangle himself. He won't even look at me anymore." She tossed her head and sent her golden-red curls flying over her shoulder.

"I doubt if that's true." Naomi couldn't suppress a little smile. It would take more willpower than Richard had to totally ignore such a gorgeous creature, even if she was a little viper. "But if he's chosen not to see you, there's not much I can do to make him change his mind." Truthfully, absolutely nothing she *wanted* to do, either.

Still, she couldn't help feeling some empathy for Heather—she'd been in her position, and she knew what it felt like to be totally, crazily in love with Richard even though she didn't love him in exactly the same way anymore. "I'm sorry you've been hurt," she said, and she meant it. "But if you look at the situation realistically, you'd know that it would never work between you and Richard, not in the long run anyway. He likes falling in love. When the feeling fades, his attention wanders." *And so does his penis,* she wanted to add, but kept the observation to herself. She'd forgiven him so there was no point in being snide.

Heather raised her chin and sneered. "I don't need your sympathy or your advice," she said. "I know I could keep him interested. He wouldn't fuck around on *me.*"

Naomi inhaled sharply. Richard had told her Heather was completely without scruples, but she hadn't really believed him, figuring that he deserved his share of the responsibility for what had gone on between them. Now she was beginning to wonder if there wasn't some truth to his claim. Her heart thumped loudly in her ears, and not even her admonitions to herself to remain calm could keep back her response. "Think again," she said. "He's fucked around on you ever since he met you. With me. And now he's chosen to leave you. For me. If he'd wanted you, he'd have left me, just the same way he left his first two wives. In fact, I see you as a kind of penance, because I was successful—he divorced Olivia and married me." Naomi smiled, but her back teeth gritted against each other. "Only a partial penance, though, because you have failed. Of course, if I add up all the other partial penances, I've more than paid my dues for full membership in the Richard Chandler Fan Club."

"Are you through?" Looking completely unfazed, Heather glared haughtily at her and tapped her long nails on the kitchen table.

Naomi took a deep breath and struggled to regain her equanimity. Heather was so young, just a baby really, and like a baby, all that concerned her was getting what she wanted. She still thought that the whole purpose of other people was to admire her and gratify her wishes and that she was the center of the universe, the sun everyone else revolved around.

Well, in Naomi's world, she was just an extremely small, extremely insignificant meteorite about ready to burn itself out, but there was no way the girl was going to recognize that. Naomi pushed back her chair and stood. It was all right to try to understand Heather, to empathize with her, but there was no point in expending any more of her own energy on trying to help or change her. "Leave my home," she said. "I very definitely am through. With you, that is."

CHAPTER 19

Meredith lined up three mugs on the counter. "Coffee?" she asked, holding the pot aloft.

"Sure," Naomi said.

Liz nodded. "Have you heard from Sheri?"

"I talked to her yesterday." Meredith filled the cups with steaming coffee, then handed them to Liz and Naomi. "She said she planned to come." Sheri had also asked Meredith questions about divorce and child support, but Meredith didn't feel comfortable telling Liz and Naomi about that part of their conversation. Gray areas always bothered her, and the line between professionalism and friendship sometimes seemed pretty fuzzy. If she erred, though, she felt better erring on the side of professionalism. Talking about Sheri's problems when she wasn't present amounted to gossip at best, to revealing privileged information at worst.

Liz poured some cream into her cup and stirred it. "Did she say anything about Mike? The last time I talked to her she was trying to figure out a way to approach him about enrolling at SOSC again."

The doorbell rang before Meredith could say anything. "That's probably her right now." She set down her cup and headed for the door, relieved that she'd escaped having to commit herself to either side of the line. She valued her professional integrity, but she hated being evasive with her friends.

Meredith opened the door, sucking in her breath when she saw Sheri. Her eyes were ringed with dark blue, purple, and green streaks, and her upper lip was still so swollen it touched her nose. "Jesus Murphy," she said. "That asshole." God, she hated men sometimes. She clenched her fists, wanting to throw her arms around Sheri but afraid to. She busied herself instead by ushering Sheri inside.

Liz and Naomi rushed into the entry hall, their cries of horror echoing Meredith's.

Sheri's mouth trembled into an awkward smile. "I'm okay," she said, her voice hoarse. "It looks worse than it feels. Especially now that he's moved out."

Naomi drew Sheri into her arms and hugged her gently. "You can't let him come back. There's no excuse for this." Her arm around Sheri's shoulders, she guided her into the kitchen.

Liz took a deep breath, then turned to Meredith. "Oh. So that's why you wanted to get together without the kids. You knew." She looked away.

Meredith stiffened at the implied criticism, but she kept her voice noncommittal. "She spoke to me as a client as well as a friend. I tried to accommodate both." Besides, she had no idea Mike had beaten Sheri so badly—she was as shocked as Liz and Naomi. She shrugged and followed the other women into the kitchen, swallowing to ease the ache at the back of her throat. Things were hard enough for her right now; she didn't have the energy to tell Liz that her words hurt, even if she was her oldest and dearest friend.

Naomi had already settled Sheri at the old oak kitchen table. The teakettle whistled, and she bustled around putting the tea bag in a cup and pouring the boiling water over it. She set the cup and saucer in front of Sheri, then plopped down next to her. "Now," she said, "tell us what happened."

Avoiding Liz's eyes, Meredith slid into the high-backed chair across from Sheri. Thank God for Naomi—she always knew exactly what to do for everyone. The sight of pain filled Meredith with so much fear she'd learned over the years to build a strong barrier between herself and other people's anguish. She wouldn't have been able to survive, especially in her career, without it, but it was damned near impossible for her to climb over her wall of self-protection now, even for a friend.

Sheri cleared her throat, but her voice was still raspy when she spoke. "You know I told you I was going to talk to Mike about my class? Well, I tried so hard to do everything right. But it wasn't enough. And he hadn't even been drinking." She lifted the tea bag from her cup and laid it on her saucer. "I'm starting to think that for Mike there *isn't* a right way. No matter what I do, it's wrong. And it's not because of me. I've been thinking about it a lot. It's not all my fault."

"None of it's your fault. You can't blame yourself. You didn't *make* him hit you." Liz rested her hand on Sheri's shoulder for a second before she sat down next to her.

"I know." Sheri smiled, then winced. "It was so obvious this time." She sipped her tea, clattered the cup back into the saucer, and cleared her throat again. "Look." She pulled down the collar of her green turtleneck. Bruises smudged the pale skin of her slender neck. "He almost choked me to death, and there wasn't a thing I could do to stop him."

Meredith narrowed her eyes and leaned forward. Sheri hadn't mentioned anything about Mike strangling her. This was even more urgent than she'd realized. "You need a restraining order," she said. "You can't risk this happening again."

Sheri shook her head. "That would just set him off even worse. He promised to leave me alone." A shudder twitched her body. "It wouldn't do any good anyway. If he decided to come back, I could be dead by the time the police got there, restraining order or not."

"Still, come see me in my office on Monday," Meredith said. "You just can't trust the bastards."

The kitchen door swung open, and Ted strode in, his stockinged feet silent on the old pine floor. He looked at Sheri and grimaced, then nodded at Liz and Naomi. Glancing at Meredith, he opened his mouth as if to say something but clamped it shut instead. He turned on his heel and stalked out, leaving the old door creaking back and forth on its hinges in his wake.

Meredith took a deep breath. How long had he been standing outside the kitchen door? Certainly, he had to be smart enough to realize that she didn't put him in the same class as Mike and his ilk no matter how poorly things had been going between the two of them lately.

She shrugged. Oh, well. There wasn't much she could do about it now.

Leah held out her messy plastic Grover plate. "Mo'," she said. "Pweez."

Naomi couldn't help smiling as she took the plate and set it next to her own. Six months ago, Leah would have screamed and flung her dish on the floor if she'd wanted another helping. Now she actually asked politely. The ability to communicate was a wonderful thing. Too bad more adults—herself included—didn't learn how to ask for what they wanted instead of throwing their own versions of fits. At least Leah'd had an excuse: she hadn't been able to talk. Naomi, on the other hand, was only a thesis away from getting her doctorate in English.

But she was learning right along with Leah, little by little. She put a sliver of chicken and a small broccoli tree on the plate and cut them up into tiny pieces. "Here you go," she said, putting the dish back on the high chair tray.

"Reminds me of Oliver Twist," Richard said. " 'Please, sir, I want some more.' Only he wasn't rewarded for asking so nicely."

"Sad." Naomi started to cut another bite of her chicken piccata, then stopped. She loved the sharp lemony taste, but she wasn't really hungry anymore. She laid her knife and fork across her plate.

"Yeah," Kristin said. "I know how old Oliver feels." Her upper lip curled as she shoved her almost untouched dinner away. "I hate lemons and capers, Naomi. I told you that."

Naomi sighed. Somebody always hated something. She worked her ass off to please them all, but it was impossible. "Scrape them off, then. Or don't eat. It's your choice."

"It's your choice. Hah. What is that—some concept in child psychology you just read about? Every time I say something, you say, 'It's your choice.' Bullshit. You know it's not true."

"Kristin," Richard said. "Please. You're being obnoxious."

The phone rang. Naomi jumped up and headed for the kitchen, glad of the excuse to escape for a few minutes. She grabbed the receiver on the third ring. "Hello."

There was a second of silence on the other end, then her mother's voice, hesitant and soft. "Naomi?"

Naomi's heart twisted painfully. Something was wrong. Daddy was worse. Mama only called on weekends, when the rates were lower. "Daddy—"

"He's gone, Naomi." A sob bubbled over the wire. "He died this morning."

Naomi leaned against the counter. Her legs were numb, paralyzed, and her throat was so tight she couldn't talk. Daddy dead? No. It wasn't possible. She wouldn't believe it.

"Are you there?"

"Yes." She managed to get the word out when all she wanted to do was scream, "No! No!" over and over again. Her head, her whole body reverberated with her silent shrieks. No matter that she'd prepared herself for this moment, no matter that she'd known it was inevitable from that day over a year ago when Mama had told her about the lung cancer. None of that helped now.

"He didn't suffer. He—"

"Mama." Naomi clenched her teeth, then took a deep breath. She was suffocating, cold and hot at the same time, but she had to control herself. *Concentrate on the mundane. Handle the details. Worry about the pain later.* "When's the funeral?"

"Monday, I think. Does that give you enough time?" Mama sounded relieved to be organizing things, too.

"If the airport in Medford isn't fogged in, I'll be there tomorrow. If I can't get out of Medford, I'll drive to Eugene or Portland. That means I'll be in New York on Friday at the latest." So many things to take care of. "Are you all right, Mama?" She didn't know why she asked when she knew exactly what her mother would say.

"I'm fine. Your aunt is here, and she's helping me with all the arrangements. Don't you worry about anything, sweetie, except getting here."

"Okay." Naomi paused. "I love you, Mama."

"I love you, too, sweetie."

After she hung up, Naomi buried her face in her hands, but the tears she'd been holding back wouldn't come. Steeling herself, she walked slowly back to the dining room.

Richard stopped mid-sentence when she entered. "Your father?"

Naomi nodded and sank into her chair.

"I'm so sorry." He stood. "Kristin, take Leah upstairs, please."

Kristin stared at him, then at Naomi. She shrugged and hoisted Leah out of the high chair, for once not arguing or complaining. "Come on," she said. "Let's go have a bath."

Leah whined a little, but she snuggled against Kristin's shoulder. Naomi forced her lips into a wavery smile. "Thanks. I appreciate it."

"Sure." The usual hostility was gone from Kristin's voice. Leah in her arms, she headed up the stairs.

Richard pulled Naomi out of her chair and led her into the living room. He put his arms around her and held her against his chest, one hand smoothing her hair.

Naomi sobbed, the tears spilling down her cheeks, tears for her father, tears for herself. He'd never really approved of her, and now he never would. Her thesis sat in a drawer, unfinished, just like so many other things in her life she tried to do to please him. Maybe if she started working on it again—

Richard sat down, cradling her in his lap. He didn't move until she stopped crying and lifted her head.

"Thank you," she said. "That helped."

He fumbled his handkerchief from his pocket and blotted the tears from her cheeks, then gave it to her. "I want to do whatever I can. I remember how difficult it was for me when my father died."

She blew her nose on his hanky. "Leah and I are going to have to leave tomorrow. I'm not sure how long we'll stay there."

"You *are* coming back, though, aren't you?" For the first time since she'd known him, she heard a note of uncertainty in his voice. "I love you, Naomi, and I want you to come back to me."

New tears blurred her vision, and she pressed her face against his chest again. She was so mixed up. She had no idea what she would do after Daddy's funeral, but there wasn't any way she could tell Richard that now. They'd both just have to wait and see what she decided.

Ted pointed the remote control at the VCR and pressed the rewind button. The tape whirred in the machine, the only noise other than the ticking of the mantel clock and an occasional sniff from Meredith, sprawled out on the couch.

"Well, what do you think?" she said, pushing herself upright and turning to him. "Did you like it?"

He shrugged. "It was okay, I guess." He'd rented *Wild Orchid* because the evening anchor had told him it was a great movie, full of passion, beautiful women and scenery, and wonderful music. Instead of arousing Meredith as he'd hoped, though, all it had done was stimulate her to comment about how bestial men could be and how foolish women were for letting them get away with it. Christ, he was tired of hearing her complaints, of feeling guilty when he wasn't to blame. All he wanted was his old Meredith back, the wife he could depend on for everything. This stranger in Meredith's body was ruining his marriage, his life.

Meredith tucked the afghan around herself as if it were some kind of magical shield. "It was sick."

Therefore, *he* was sick because he'd chosen it. Every muscle in his body tensed. "Of course that's the way you'd see it." She didn't really give a damn what he thought; all she wanted was someone to agree with her and validate her responses. Well, if he was sick, it was because he was living with her.

"He was practically old enough to be her father, and look at the awful things he forced her to endure. Like watching that couple make love in the backseat of the car. I almost threw up."

"Seems like an appropriate response to me—why didn't you?"

She threw off the afghan and stood, glowering at him. "I don't have to listen to your sarcastic bullshit."

"And I don't have to listen to your constant bitching."

"You don't listen," Meredith said. "You either tune me out or you leave. I don't feel supported by you."

"It's hard to support someone who sees you as the enemy. Jesus Christ, Meredith, do you ever think about what *I'm* going through?" He flung down the remote control, and it skidded across the oak floor. "I don't know who you are anymore. Shit, I don't know who *I* am. How can I help someone else?"

"You'll have to figure that one out for yourself. I'm going to bed." She huffed out of the room, her slippers smacking the old wood floor.

"Meredith!"

The slippers stopped.

Ted clenched his fists and stood up. "I'm moving out," he said. "I won't be here in the morning." He held his breath, trying to choke back the overwhelming anxiety rising from the pit of his stomach into his throat. Why in hell had he said that? He didn't really want to go. Shit, he didn't know what he wanted, and that was the goddamn truth.

"Fine." Meredith's slippers continued their trek down the hall; then the bedroom door slammed.

Ted sank back down into his favorite chair. Now he was the one who felt like throwing up.

CHAPTER 20

February

Meredith emptied the box of teddy bear pasta into the pot of boiling water and stirred. Macaroni and cheese was Justie's favorite dinner; usually Meredith fixed something else for Ted and herself. There wasn't any point in doing so tonight, however. Ted was gone, and everything she ate tasted like cardboard. He'd picked up his golf clubs and tennis racket that afternoon and given her his new phone number. He was really gone.

And she was angry. Angry at herself for not seeing the signs, for being so preoccupied with her own inner torment that she'd failed to see what was happening in the world outside herself, for not paying more attention to Ted. Now that he'd moved out she could look back and see the warning signs. If only she'd been more sensitive at the time.

The boiling water foamed and bubbled over the side of the pot, sizzling as it hit the burner. "Damn!" Meredith grabbed the handle and poured some of the water into the sink, then put the pan back down. She set the timer for ten minutes. "Justie," she called. "Dinner's almost ready."

Justie pedaled her little fire engine from the living room into the kitchen. "Mama," she said. "Eat." She stretched out her arms, and Meredith picked her up.

"Let's wash your hands." Meredith turned on the faucet and stuck the grimy little fingers under the warm water. The baby wiggled until Meredith set her down and handed her a towel.

"Me do." Justine snatched the towel away and carefully patted her hands. Her lower lip sticking out in a determined pout, she thrust the towel back through the rack on the cabinet door. She looked around the kitchen. "Dada?"

The plaintive note in her voice sent another spasm of anger through Meredith, but this time it was directed at Ted. He could have talked to her about how he felt. Why had he just waited and let things build up to this point? She couldn't help the agony she was going through over what had happened to her as a child. But he acted as if it were all her fault.

During her counseling sessions, Ingrid had impressed on her how blameless she'd been as a girl. She had done nothing to cause her father to rape her; she'd been an innocent child. The blame rested squarely on her father's broad, adult shoulders. She was not responsible in any way. "It *wasn't* my fault," she wanted to scream at Ted. "Stop acting as if it were." As if screaming might somehow make him hear her more clearly.

Justie tugged at her skirt. "Up."

Meredith hoisted her daughter into her arms and buried her face in Justie's silky golden-red hair. Even if Ted wasn't happy with her, he could have thought of Justine. Justie couldn't understand her daddy disappearing for three days, then showing up to throw some things into his car and leaving again.

The timer buzzed, and Meredith set Justie back down. But Justie didn't want down. The baby whined and clung to Meredith's legs while Meredith tried to dump the pot of boiling noodles into the strainer.

The water splashed onto her hand, burning her so badly she dropped the pot in the sink. "Shit!" she yelled. She turned on the cold water and stuck her hand under it, but the pain didn't stop.

Justie's whines turned to whimpers and then sobs. "Up, Mama," she pleaded.

Tears filled Meredith's eyes. She couldn't do this alone. She counted on Ted; she needed Ted. She crumpled onto the floor next to Justie, who climbed into her lap, put her thumb in her mouth, and sucked noisily.

Meredith laid her cheek on top of Justie's head. Ted's abandonment had reversed all the gains she'd worked so hard for. And it wasn't just Meredith he'd deserted. It wasn't fair to Justine, either, to be left with a mother whose life was out of control. They both needed help, and if she was too stubborn to ask for herself, she had to ask for Justine's sake.

She staggered to her feet with the baby still in her arms, carried her to the phone, and dialed Eva's number.

Giggling, Liz fell backward on the huge circular bed. Three whole days with Jeff without having to worry about being seen had relaxed her clear down to her toes—not to mention the effects of the entire bottle of champagne she'd drunk with dinner. Jeff always ordered wine for her even though he didn't drink himself, and she hadn't been able to stand the thought of letting any of the wonderful Perrier-Jouët go flat. At this point damn little remained of her guilt over deceiving Fletcher with her story about the realtors' convention in Tahoe. Anyway, he was so busy he probably hadn't even noticed she was gone. She kicked off her black pumps and opened her arms.

Jeff lowered himself on top of her, his green eyes fixed on hers. "God, you turn me on," he said. "Three times today already. I'm almost worn out, but I still want you."

"Me, too." She pulled his head down until their lips met. She traced his open mouth with the tip of her tongue, running it along his teeth and the underside of his lips. Smiling, she raised her head. "But if you can get it up, I guess I can lie here."

"Good," he said. "A moving target would take too much energy." He slipped his hand under her red silk blouse and unsnapped the front closure on her bra, then lightly caressed each breast.

Liz arched her back and rubbed her pelvis against Jeff's, sucking in her breath when she felt his erection.

Slowly, he unbuttoned her blouse, then eased it off her shoulders. The laughter left his eyes as he leaned back to look at her. "You are so beautiful, Elizabeth. I never get tired of looking at you."

Liz shivered with delight. She never tired of hearing him tell her that, either. He was so different from Fletcher, who hadn't seen her naked in two years or told her she was pretty in ten. It was as if Fletcher didn't even see her anymore. Before she met Jeff, she'd been a ghost; Jeff's love had given her substance, made her alive and real again.

Without taking his eyes off hers, he unzipped her black skirt and slid it off her hips and down her legs until it rustled onto the floor. Her black stockings were next, followed by her garter belt and lace panties. The fire crackled in the suite's huge fireplace, and she lay naked on the soft blue bedspread, her body quivering and warm.

"Your turn," she said. But before she could even begin removing his shirt, he stood and shed his clothing in seconds.

"I'm too impatient." He settled his lean, hard body atop hers. "I hope you don't mind."

She brushed her lips against his. "I hate patience." Fletcher's patience was Buddha-like—enormous and deliberate. It drove her crazy the way he controlled himself, pretending to be so placid when every muscle in his body was rigid with tension. She felt her own muscles tighten and shoved Fletcher from her mind. It was a big bed, but not big enough for the three of them.

"I'm glad." He parted her with his fingers, then glided inside her with one smooth thrust.

Liz gasped and wove her fingers into his thick hair, drawing his face down to hers. She rocked against him slowly, making herself relax and savor the full sensation growing inside her. Jeff moaned, and waves of such intense pleasure shuddered through her that it was as if the two of them became one, existing alone, suspended somewhere in a dark warm universe. Gradually, she drifted back into her body, a little saddened by the recognition of their separateness. For a moment their unity had been so real that it had felt as if it could go on forever, into a beautiful, glowing infinity. "My God," she said. "That was amazing."

Jeff withdrew himself from her slowly, tantalizingly, his eyes locked on hers even as he shifted himself next to her. "I love you," he said. "I want to marry you, Elizabeth. I'm tired of having to sneak around, having to share you. I want to walk down the street in Ashland with you on my arm, right in broad daylight."

She held her breath. The last remnants of euphoria fled, leaving her cold and empty. "Oh, Jeff," she said. "I love you, too." But before she could be with him, she'd have to tell Fletcher their marriage was over, and even imagining the scene made her tremble. She hadn't really planned on falling in love with Jeff; and even after she realized how deeply she cared for him, she'd ignored her qualms about the future and concentrated on the pleasures of the moment. She and Fletcher had been together for sixteen years—life without him didn't seem possible no matter how much he irritated her. She wanted Jeff; she wanted love; but she didn't want to be responsible for causing Fletcher pain. She sat up, crossing her arms over her midriff.

Jeff rolled off the bed and dropped to his knees at her feet. "Will you marry me, Elizabeth Ann Stewart Berenson?"

She stared down at the bedspread, tracing the diamond-shaped stitching with her finger, unable to meet his eyes. "I want to," she said. "More than anything. But it's all so complicated—Fletcher's campaign, Brookie, everything . . ."

He lifted her chin. "I know." He grasped her hands in his. "I *can* be patient when I have to. We can postpone it for a while if it makes things easier for you."

She nodded, relief slowing down her anxious heartbeat. "If we can just wait until after the primary," she said. "I don't want to do anything to hurt his campaign. If he loses, I can tell him then and move out."

"And if he wins?"

"I can tell him and let him decide whether we should continue pretending to be together until after the election."

Jeff sighed. "I hate the thought of you living with him for eight more months."

She met his eyes. "It's not going to be easy for any of us."

CHAPTER 21

It was great to be back home and with her best friends in the world. Naomi flicked on the Volvo's blinker and slowed gradually for the Mount Ashland exit. She had chains, but with any luck the snowplow would have already cleared the road and she wouldn't need them.

Sheri leaned forward from the backseat. "This is so beautiful up here," she said.

Liz winked at her. "Does it bring back fond memories?" she asked, grinning wickedly.

Sheri blushed, trying hard to maintain her composure despite her discomfort. Liz wasn't being insensitive; it just wasn't as hard for her to talk about things like that. Sheri had grown up keeping secrets, and the night she'd lost her virginity at the party on Mount Ashland had been one of her biggest. "Unfortunately, I was so drunk I have very few memories of what you're referring to. Besides, it was August. There wasn't any snow."

Liz laughed. "Sounds like last winter. Thank God it's better this year. I'm looking forward to skiing again—I haven't been on skis in ages."

"Me neither." Meredith twisted in her seat to look at her. "Not since I got pregnant, anyway."

Naomi laughed. "And that feels like a lifetime ago, doesn't it?" It was amazing how different her life was since Leah's birth. Nothing, and no one, had ever mattered to her so much before, and she'd really had no idea what unconditional love truly was until the nurse handed her that tiny being. Suddenly, she'd understood her parents for the first time. She looked on the day of Leah's birth as her initiation into maturity, her entrance into a special, adults-only club. Before she'd only pretended to be grown-up, dressed and acted the part the same way she had as a child with her mother's old clothes, clopping around the house in a pair of high heels four inches too long for her and red lipstick smeared up to her nose.

"More than a lifetime," Meredith said. "I wonder if becoming a parent changes a man's life as much as it does a woman's."

Liz snorted. "Well, Fletcher complains that he doesn't get as much sleep now."

"And Ted always bitched about the change in our sex life. Of course, he now realizes that Justine isn't the entire reason, but I think he looked at her as basically an inconvenience right from the beginning." Meredith wiggled her shoulders against the seat belt to keep them from tensing up. Every time she thought about Ted, her whole body stiffened with anger. She'd turned out to be even more of an inconvenience than Justie, so he'd deserted her.

Naomi took her eyes off the road long enough to exchange a sympathetic glance with Meredith. It had simply never occurred to her to think of Leah as an inconvenience. Perhaps Richard had, though. After all, he had two older daughters, one already graduated from college and on her own when Leah was born.

She braked carefully in advance of the upcoming switchback just in case the road was still icy in the shade. Snow banked either side, but fortunately the sun had dried most of the moisture left by the snow-plow, and the roadbed itself was fairly clear. Tall firs with clumps of white snow clinging to the branches stood like sentinels against the startling blue of the sky.

Slowing the car to almost a crawl during the worst part of the curve, Naomi said, "Maybe men are just jealous."

"Of their wives?" Sheri couldn't keep the incredulity from her voice.

"No," Naomi said. "Of their children. I used to find myself wishing for a pair of strong arms to cuddle me and a big shoulder to lean my head on, and I started feeling a little resentful because Richard just wasn't giving me enough nurturing. Then I realized that what I really wanted was my mother—someone to take care of me the way she always did. Except that now *I* was the mother."

From the corner of her eye, Naomi could see Liz squirm in her seat and readjust the seat belt. She continued. "Before Leah was born, I mothered Richard. Afterward he didn't get as much attention. He even commented one time that each of his marriages seemed to fall apart after the birth of a child."

"Sounds like me," Liz said quietly from the backseat, a tiny tremor in her voice. She covered it immediately with a giggle.

Now Naomi felt like squirming herself. Liz hadn't been her regular self lately, but she didn't seem ready to talk about whatever was bothering her yet. It was time to change the subject before Meredith homed in on Liz's unhappiness and started cross-examining her. "New York was certainly dreary," she said. "Especially compared to this." The car windows started to steam up, and she flipped on the defroster.

"Well, I for one am glad you're back," Meredith said.

"I considered staying." Naomi accelerated on the straight stretch. "But not for long."

"Really?" Meredith sounded surprised. "Is there something you haven't told me, Naomi?"

Her ploy to draw Meredith's fire had worked. Naomi shrugged. Her marital problems weren't a secret, but, assuming that Meredith had enough worries of her own, she hadn't made a point of keeping her abreast of all the developments lately. "Richard's been having an affair with one of his students."

"Oh, Naomi, I'm so sorry."

"It's over now, or so he assures me."

"But you're still hurting." Meredith stared at her.

Naomi nodded. "Less now. That's part of the reason I came back. After my father's funeral I collapsed. Richard called every day for a week, but I refused to talk to him. I couldn't keep up my rational, controlled front any longer. I had to make up my own mind, and he's so persuasive I was afraid to let him influence me. I wanted to know what *I* thought, what *I* felt, not what he wanted me to think and feel."

The car slid a little on an icy spot, and she steered with it, tapping the brakes gently. "I decided what we have together is worth saving, as long as he doesn't do it again. Since I've been back, we've actually been talking about why it happened instead of just sweeping the whole thing under the rug the way we did the last time. The way *I* did. I thought if I just pretended that it hadn't really happened that it was the same as forgiving him and everything would go on."

"Phew," Sheri said. "I know how that works."

"In the end, I just felt so sad every time I thought about not being married to Richard that I decided the pain was worth it. As long as it's temporary, that is. Now that I've admitted to myself how much it hurts, I know I can't live with that kind of suffering forever. If I left him, though, the sadness would become a permanent part of me." Naomi smiled at Meredith. "Besides, I have too many wonderful friends in Ashland to leave. I want to stay here even if Richard and I don't make it."

"I think you will," Sheri said.

"I hope you're right." Naomi turned into the parking lot and pulled into a spot next to the Tudor-beamed lodge. "I'm not making any more excuses—for either of us—if I can help it. I'm going to resurrect my doctoral thesis and finish it. I'm going to live *my* life instead of everyone else's, for a change." She put the car in park, set the brake, and switched off the engine. "Here we are," she said with a wide smile. "What a perfect day."

SAN FRANCISCO

Doug shifted in the hard hospital chair so that his shoulder didn't touch Mom's. His whole body ached from the effort of not crying. He hated the smell of floor wax and disinfectant; he hated the subdued grays and blues and purples; he hated the quiet, foggy way people always talked in hospitals. He couldn't even look at anybody.

"Doug Sommers." The admission clerk's voice was cool, professional. He was just another body to process. Pretty soon it would be the undertaker's turn.

And all because his biological mother had been some poor girl scared shitless of taking responsibility for her actions. He thought about her all the time now, tried to picture her in his mind. He wondered if she even knew who his birth father was. One minute he found himself actually sympathizing with her, imagining the anguish she must have felt; then the next waves of anger and hatred rolled over him as he pictured her taking her baby and placing it in the arms of a stranger. Placing *him* in the arms of a stranger.

He stood stiffly, pushing his mother's hand off his arm, and walked to the long gray counter. The clerk, a smiling middle-aged woman with mousy hair, pointed to a little glassed-in cubicle next to the counter. He followed her inside and sat down in one of the blue plaid chairs. Mom sat next to him, blinking to keep back the tears that glistened in her eyes.

The clerk introduced herself as Lois Bennett, then rested her fingers on the computer keyboard. "Just let me call your file up," she said. "We can simply update it rather than starting from scratch." Her manner was cheerful, sympathetic.

Doug gritted his teeth. He could guarantee her it wouldn't need any updating. His fingers itched to throw the damn keyboard right through the monitor screen. No one had made any promises about how long his remission would last, but he'd had such high hopes when they'd told him he'd finally made it. Now he had to start all over again, and this time would be even worse. He might not make it at all. Dr. Levison said it was a lot harder to induce a second remission, and even when they succeeded, it usually didn't last as long as the first.

He might as well face it—he was a goner. Maybe he should just go home and wait to die. He slumped in the uncomfortable chair, his arms dangling over the sides. When he didn't respond to Mrs. Bennett's questions, his mother answered for him, her voice a murmur.

God, he couldn't stand it—everyone so polite and calm. There wasn't anything polite about death, about dying little by little, his body swelling grotesquely and turning black with bruises that wouldn't heal. He jumped up so suddenly he sent his chair slamming into the glass wall. "You finish," he muttered to his mother, and he walked quickly to the rest room around the corner.

He banged the stall door shut and sat down on the toilet. Resting his head against his knees, he let the tears come. If only Obremski had located his birth mother. Anger at her sent a wave of heat coursing through his body. Not only had she deserted him when he was born, but she'd made it impossible for him to ever find her again.

CHAPTER 22

March

ASHLAND, OREGON

She had to let Richard handle things, Naomi reminded herself for the umpteenth time. Kristin was his daughter; it was up to him to make the decisions. In fact, he needed to be the one making them. She forced herself to take a deep breath and lean back against her pillow. The last twenty-four hours had been hell—and just when she thought everything was going so nicely. Leah hadn't had a seizure in four months; Richard's affair really seemed to be over; her grief over her father's death was easing. And on top of it all, she'd lost five pounds, was working on her thesis, and feeling good about herself. Why was it there was always something waiting out there to destroy her happiness?

She twisted the sheet in her hands, straining to hear some of Richard's phone conversation in the study across the hall. Kristin had left for school yesterday morning, and no one had seen her since. The school reported her absent; and when she hadn't shown up for dinner, they'd called all her friends, then spent the rest of the evening in an agony of waiting. Naomi had never seen Richard so distraught.

His voice stopped, the phone clicked, and he appeared in the doorway to their bedroom, shaking his head.

"No luck?"

"Nothing. The police don't know a thing, and she hasn't contacted her mother." His face was white and drawn, and the heavy bags under his eyes made him look like an exhausted old man. "Oh, God." He sat down on the foot of the bed, his shoulders slumped.

Naomi crawled from under the covers to his side and put her arms around him. "She's fine. I know it. She's done this sort of thing before."

"That's one of the reasons Olivia sent her to us." He closed his eyes for a minute. "But I can't help thinking the worst. Ashland's a small town, but awful things can happen anywhere." He sighed. "Besides, she's probably not even here, and anything can go wrong on the road. What if she got picked up by some crazy—" He clenched his fist.

Naomi tightened her arms around him, cradling his head against her chest. She wanted to shake Kristin until her head rattled, but there wasn't any way she could share her outrage with Richard. She was worried, too, but she wouldn't let herself imagine the horrible things that could happen to a fifteen-year-old runaway. This was Richard's anguish; she had to be the strong one this time. It wouldn't help anyone if she fell apart, too—and the anger kept her together. She'd feel everything else later, when it was safe.

"Kristin's smart and resourceful," Naomi said. "She can take care of herself."

Richard pushed away her arms and stood. "I keep telling myself that. Jesus Christ, I hate this. My gut is on fire; my chest aches; I can't sit still for the twitches in my legs. If she walked in the door right now, I don't know whether I'd want to slap her or burst into tears." He paced to the bathroom door, stopped in front of it, and stared inside for a long time. "I thought I had to pee," he said finally.

Naomi slid off the bed and crossed the room to him. She'd never seen Richard this way before. He'd been the calm one during Leah's epileptic attack, the one who'd pointed out that breaking down didn't help the situation. Rational, strong, controlled—that was Richard, not this wounded, bewildered man. She grasped his hand and pulled him toward her. "Come to bed," she said. "There's nothing else you can do tonight."

He took a deep, shuddering breath. "That's what's so hard. As long as there was something I could do, I was in charge, or at least I could fool myself into believing I was." Tears flooded his eyes, and he buried his face in his hands. "Christ, I've fucked so many things up, ruined my children's lives, almost lost you. Thank God you didn't run away too. That's my nightmare—an old man, all alone, detested by all the people who've loved him and whom he's hurt. Desperate, unloved—" Choking, he clung to Naomi.

She patted his back, soothing him the way she soothed Leah after a bad fall. Richard was as weak as he was strong—the realization amazed her. She led him to their bed and helped him under the covers. "I love you," she said. "I love you more now than ever before. No matter what happens I'll be here."

Sheri poured herself another cup of coffee, then sat back down at the kitchen table littered with books, pens, and wads of notebook paper. It was after midnight, and she was only halfway through the first draft of her term paper for Alec's class on Shakespeare's heroines—and the damn thing was due in two days.

She set down her cup and picked up her pen, nibbling the end of it while she reread the last page. She'd learned a lot from her research, but it was so hard bringing all of her ideas together and writing them down, especially after being out of school for so many years. Sometimes she wished she'd taken another term of the Shakespeare on Stage class instead of this one—acting was her talent, not writing. But she just couldn't afford to give up her shifts at the Mark for evening rehearsals any longer, now that Mike was gone. They'd been barely making it as it was; when he moved out, she'd had to double the number of hours she worked. Thank God she'd already saved the money for her tuition.

Her stomach tightened as it always did when she thought of money. She was so tired of never having enough even though she scrimped here and stretched this and did without that. Mike made plenty when he was working, but sometimes he went months without a job. Even when he was flush, he spent so much of it on his stuff—fancy pickups, guns, fishing gear—that they were always on the edge, having to put off one bill in order to pay another more pressing one, writing checks for groceries at the end of the month and praying that the paycheck came before the checks made it to the bank. She hadn't bought any new clothes for herself since before she got pregnant with Timmy, and all the kids' clothing were hand-me-downs from friends or used from Goodwill.

Not that any of that was different from what she'd grown up with; in fact, compared to her mother, she had it easy. She tapped her pen on the table, remembering the high school dances she'd turned down dates for because she had nothing to wear and no way to get it. Mom had cried when Sheri'd refused a nomination to the homecoming court her junior year because they couldn't afford a formal gown. She'd even tried to talk Sheri into changing her mind, telling her they'd find some way to get her the dress she needed.

But Sheri'd refused. Mom was already overworked and worn out; "finding some way" always meant that she'd take on something else or deny herself the few pleasures she had. Besides, dances didn't really matter to Sheri—she lived for her acting, even then. Until her senior year, she was too busy with the school's drama club productions to mind a lot of what she missed. Mom didn't even have that. Her life centered on her family, and she lived for her children. No wonder she'd collapsed when the last one moved out.

But this wasn't getting her paper written. Sighing, she flipped through the huge Shakespeare book, looking for Portia's lines about mercy in *The Merchant of Venice*. She found the place and read through the speech, then wondered whether or not Kate the Shrew and Portia would be friends if they suddenly found themselves in the same women's group. They seemed so different, but then so did she from

Naomi and Liz and Meredith. And yet they all had grown so close over the last couple of years.

With an effort, she wrenched her thoughts back to her task again. She yawned noisily. Her mind didn't want to focus. Maybe she should just give up for tonight and come back to it tomorrow rested and fresh.

Rested? Fresh? She didn't know what that felt like anymore. Mike's departure had been a relief at first, giving her freedom from the constant anxiety and fear she felt when she was with him. But she had to work twice as hard and endure the loneliness, especially the loneliness of their bed, where sometimes she missed him so much she cried herself to sleep.

A car or pickup roared around the corner of Cambridge Street, and Sheri tensed automatically. *Stop it,* she told herself. *You don't have to do that now.* She unclenched her fists and wiggled her tight shoulders just as the vehicle squealed into her driveway.

A car door slammed, and her throat closed. "Oh, my God," she whispered. Her whole body trembled. It was him. What was she going to do? She'd changed the locks, but she knew better than to think that would keep Mike out if he really wanted in. Thoughts of gathering Felicia and Timmy and running out the back door or calling the police flashed through her mind, but there wasn't time to do anything before he banged on the door and shouted at her to open it.

"Now!" he bellowed. "Before I break it down."

A bubble of hysterical laughter rose in her throat. Just like the wolf and the three little pigs. He was going to huff and puff—

"Sheri! Open the door, you goddamn cunt!" He kicked the cheap hollow-core door, and it cracked and splintered. Then there was a heavy thud, and a second later the door crashed into the living room.

Paralyzed, she stood next to the kitchen table while he stumbled into the room. She opened her mouth to scream, but nothing came out, just the way it always happened in nightmares.

He strode through the living room, kicking aside an end table in his way and sending the lamp on it crashing to the floor. The whole room filled with the reek of beer and cigarette smoke.

Suddenly, something snapped inside Sheri. The rubber band she always imagined pulling her back to him finally stretched too far. This was too much. This was *her* home now, and he was an invader. How could she have thought she missed him? She hated him. She never wanted to live through this again. She didn't deserve this kind of punishment no matter what she'd done.

"Get out!" she screamed.

In two strides he was in front of her. "Shut the fuck up." His hand streaked out and slapped her face before she could duck.

She didn't move, and she didn't cry. "Don't do that again." She clenched her fists, ready to fight back for the first time in her life. "I don't want you here. If you don't leave now, I'm going to call the police." She stepped toward the phone on the kitchen wall.

He stormed across the kitchen, tore the phone from the wall, and dashed it to the floor. Then he looked at the kitchen table. "What's this?" He grabbed up her notebook and started reading aloud in a slurred pinch-nosed falsetto, "Of all of Shakespeare's heroines—"

"Give me that!" Sheri tried to snatch her paper from him.

"Sure." He ripped out the pages she'd written and threw the notebook at her, then shredded the paper into tiny pieces and tossed them into the air. "There you go."

"You bastard," Sheri hissed.

A long wail sounded from Timmy's bedroom, and a moment later he toddled into the kitchen, sobbing and rubbing his eyes. He stared up at Mike, then grabbed Sheri's leg, crying even louder.

Mike blinked, and the rage faded from his face, replaced with bewilderment and sorrow. He turned on his heel and stomped out.

Sheri marched across the room and slammed the door shut behind him. She was really through this time.

CHAPTER 23

Meredith closed the door after Yvonne, then waved her arms in the air to dispel some of the cigarette smoke. Usually she requested that her clients refrain from smoking in her office, but she found it impossible to ask Yvonne to put away her cigarettes. If smoking made it easier for her, then Meredith was willing to put up with the inconvenience. She understood what Yvonne was going through.

Lately, though, she'd been able to separate Yvonne's problems more clearly from her own. She was still touched by the girl's history, but she no longer identified with it to the extent that representing her created an ethical dilemma. Meredith had her own demons, and while similar to Yvonne's, they weren't exactly the same. She felt confident at this point that she'd win a conviction at the trial in June.

The buzzer rang. She crossed the room to her desk and pressed the speaker button on the phone. "Yes?"

"There's a Sheri Riley here to see you. She doesn't have an appointment, but she says it's urgent." Melody sounded concerned. "Should I bring her to you?"

"No, I'll be right there." Meredith hurried out of her office and down the hall to the reception area. Sheri sat alone in the room, hunched over in one of the dark green leather chairs, her face hidden by the *Smithsonian* magazine she held.

Sheri looked up. Her right eye was swollen shut, and a small cut creased her lower lip. She stood and tried to smile at Meredith.

Meredith gritted her teeth. God damn the son of a bitch. Gently, as she'd seen Naomi do the last time, she put her arm around Sheri's shoulders and guided her through the double swinging doors. "Come on," she said. "I'm glad you're here."

Sheri nodded as they stepped into Meredith's office. "I'm ready now. Really ready."

"Good." Afraid that Sheri might be intimidated by the great expanse of a desk between them, Meredith pulled two of the pale green easy chairs together in front of the desk. "Let's sit."

Sheri sank into one of the chairs. "He broke into my house last night."

Meredith shook her head. She wasn't surprised. "In my experience, the likelihood of a man like Mike changing is so small it borders on impossible. He won't change unless his own pain becomes so great he's driven to seek help in order to save *his* life." She sighed. The problem was, though, that he'd probably never realize that the incredible furnace of anger he carried around was fueled by pain, so he'd spend the rest of his life striking out at others instead of healing the hurt within himself. She sat down next to Sheri and leaned forward. "What do you want me to do?"

Sheri held up a finger. "First, a restraining order." She raised another finger. "Second, a divorce. I want custody of the kids; I want adequate child support; and I want the house." She glanced at her hand, all her fingers splayed in the air, and gave a bitter little chuckle before she balled it up into a fist and lowered it back into her lap.

"Okay." Tipping her chair backward, Meredith reached over to her desk and snared a yellow legal pad and a pen. "I'm going to need some information. How long have you been married?"

"Nine years."

"What about the house? Was it yours, or Mike's, or did you buy it together?"

"We bought it when I got pregnant with Felicia."

"The money for the down payment—where did it come from?"

"It was mostly Mike's," Sheri said. "He sold his old house, and we used the money from that plus all of my savings."

"What percentage of the down payment would you say you contributed?"

Sheri paused for a minute. "About 10 percent," she said finally. "Doesn't sound good, does it?"

Meredith jotted the notes down, then looked up at Sheri. "Oregon divorce law divides marriages into two kinds—long term and short term. The goal of the court in divorce proceedings involving a long-term marriage is to establish parity—that is, to make sure whatever property a couple has accumulated is divided equally without reference to either party's actual financial contributions. In other words, a woman who has never worked outside the home should not be reduced to poverty just because her wealthy husband wants a new wife. In fact, she would have a claim on his earnings for the rest of his life. Of course, it works the other way around, too, if the woman has been the primary financial contributor."

Sheri nodded. "I understand."

"The goal is different with a short-term marriage, though. In that case, the court seeks to return each partner to his or her financial situation prior to the marriage. If one partner had considerable assets and the other very little before the marriage, then the property settlement in a short-term marriage would reflect that."

Sheri took a deep breath. "Where's the dividing line? How long do you have to be married to be considered long term?"

"That's the catch," Meredith said. "There's no absolute number; it's up to the court's discretion. Usually, though, for practical purposes, it's around ten years."

Sheri's shoulders slumped. "We're more short term than long, then."

"That would be my guess. Getting full possession of the house might be tricky if he decides to fight it. He did leave voluntarily, though, didn't he?"

"Yeah. He also came back voluntarily, too." Tears glistened in Sheri's eyes, and she sniffed.

Meredith reached behind her and grabbed a tissue from the box on her desk for Sheri. "That's a point in our favor. Then there are the children, who I can almost guarantee you will stay with you. The court doesn't look with favor on wife-beaters. Men who abuse their wives are statistically more likely to abuse their children as well."

"Mike has never—"

Meredith held up her hand. "Just because he hasn't doesn't mean he wouldn't. The truth is that violent people are potentially dangerous to everyone around them."

Sheri frowned. "Does it make sense to you to sentence my children to poverty because Mike and I have been married for only nine years?"

"We'll definitely use that angle," Meredith said. "I personally don't believe what you're asking for is unreasonable. I just want you to know that the possibility exists that you won't get it. Are you prepared for that?"

"All I know is that I can never live with him again. If I have to rent a cheap apartment, I'll do it. I'll even move back in with my mother. I'll do whatever it takes to get him out of my life." Sheri blew her nose on the tissue and crumpled it in her hand, then stood. "But I've got to go. I feel guilty taking up this much of your time."

"Don't worry about it." Meredith rose, then hugged Sheri. "In fact, don't worry about anything. When I get the papers ready, I'll give you a call. All you have to do now is take care of yourself and the kids."

Sheri hugged her back. "Thanks, Meredith. For being my friend, for everything."

.   .   .

Pointing her toes, Liz eased her foot into the expensive silk hose she always wore for Jeff. She pulled the stocking up her leg, smoothing the sleek material over her calf and thigh, then snapping the top to her white garter belt.

"Mmmm. Nice." Already dressed and grinning at her, Jeff leaned against his bedroom door. "Need some help?"

She smiled at him. "Quit it. I'm late for work already." Her smile fading, she ducked her head and tugged on the other stocking, then wiggled into her slim ivory linen skirt and zipped it up. He was only going to be gone for two weeks, she told herself. Fourteen days, not forever. She could handle it.

She forced her lips back into a smile and looked at him again as she slipped into her blouse. *Don't go*, she wanted to plead with him. *Don't leave me here all alone.* But she kept on smiling into his eyes while she buttoned the blouse. Two weeks without Jeff's touch, without his warmth, his smile. Fourteen days. Not forever, but it felt that way right now. How was she going to be able to stand it?

"I'm going to miss you," he said. "I want you to promise to call me if you need me."

She blinked back the tears threatening to spill down her cheeks. Damn it. She was acting like a baby over a simple two-week vacation. He was only driving to San Diego, not climbing Mount Everest, for Christ's sake. What the hell was wrong with her? She shrugged herself into her jacket and took a deep breath. It wasn't fair to ruin his vacation by letting him know how upset, how just plain nervous she was.

"I want you to promise me something else, too," he said. He crossed the room to her and pulled her into his arms. "Promise me you won't tell Fletcher while I'm gone. I don't want you to be alone."

"I promise." Liz rested her cheek against the cool smoothness of his brown leather jacket. "Now it's your turn. Drive carefully, okay?"

"Always. You don't need to worry. I never take chances." He kissed her softly, warmly, slowly. "I love you."

165

"Promise me you'll come back to me?"

"Absolutely." He wrapped his arms around her and held her tightly.

The shrill clang of the old-fashioned French phone on the nightstand jerked Richard from half-sleep. His chest tightening, he fumbled for the switch on the bedside lamp, clicked it on, and glanced at the clock. Eleven-thirty. He reached for the phone as it rang for the third time. Beside him, Naomi sat up, her big brown eyes opened wide and her dark curly hair frizzed around her face.

"Hello," Richard said, his voice fuzzy with sleep. He cleared his throat and repeated, "Hello."

"Richard? This is Olivia. I'm sorry to be calling so late, but I thought you'd want to know. Kristin is here."

"Oh, Jesus. Thank God." Relief washed over him, eroding the wall of stone he'd spent the last ten days so carefully constructing around his heart. His spine suddenly felt like rubber, and he couldn't feel the telephone receiver he saw gripped in his hand.

"Kristin?" Naomi whispered, clutching his other hand.

He nodded at her, then spoke into the phone. "When did she get there?"

"Just a few minutes ago. I haven't really had a chance to talk to her yet."

"Is she all right?"

"She seems fine—needs a bath, of course, but otherwise okay."

"May I speak to her?"

"Just a second."

He strained to hear the faint, scratchy conversation, but Olivia apparently had her hand over the mouthpiece. "She just got there," he told Naomi. "Olivia's—"

"Dad?" Kristin interrupted him.

The sound of her voice left him speechless for a moment as he bit back the angry words he wanted to say now that he no longer had any cause to worry. The last thing he should do at this point was scold her; that could wait until later and be approached in a more constructive fashion. He took a deep breath. "I love you, Kristin. I'm glad you're safe."

"Yeah."

He could almost see her defensive shrug, the curl of her upper lip. "I mean it. We were really worried about you." Wrong approach. He swallowed hard. "We missed you. Leah keeps going to your bedroom and saying, 'Sissy go bye-bye.' One day the door was closed, and she kicked it over and over again." He imitated Leah's voice. " 'Sissy, in. Sissy, in.' "

Kristin laughed. "Funny thing," she said. "I missed you guys, too. Even Naomi."

He sagged against his pillow and smiled at Naomi. For days the two of them had discussed how to handle Kristin when she was found, and his respect for Naomi had grown immeasurably. She really loved Kristin, and she understood the girl so much better than he, her own father, did. "Let her make some decisions for herself," Naomi'd advised him. "She needs to feel some responsibility for herself instead of always rebelling against you."

"Have you decided what you want to do?" he asked Kristin.

Naomi squeezed his hand.

"I'd like to spend a few days with Mom, if that's okay with everyone."

"Sure," Richard said. "Talk it over with her and then let us know when you want to come home."

"Okay." Kristin was silent for a minute. "Mom wants to talk to you some more. Bye, Dad."

Olivia spoke before he could tell Kristin he loved her again. "I think it's a good idea for her to stay here a while," Olivia said. "But I don't think she should miss much more school. Have you talked to her teachers?"

"I will tomorrow." He hadn't been able to face the prospect before, but now that he knew Kristin was safe, he welcomed the idea. Kristin had too much going for her for him to give up on her, even if she did everything in her power to make him believe otherwise. Like Sara, her older sister. Only when Sara had acted up, he'd been so busy thinking of himself he hadn't made the effort. He wouldn't make that mistake again. If he backed off on Kristin, it would be because she needed some autonomy, not because he was too wrapped up in his own concerns to bother.

"Good," Olivia said. "It's late. We'll talk more tomorrow."

He said good-bye and hung up. "She sounds fine," he said, pulling Naomi to him. He kissed her, and something that felt like a mild electric shock thrilled through his body when she responded. He was alive again, his penis risen from the dead. He ran his fingers over her smooth, soft skin, pausing for a moment to cup her full breasts in his hands.

"That feels good," she said.

"You mean it?" They hadn't made love in over three months, not since the night Heather had been all over him at Chateaulin. And it hadn't been just because of Naomi, either; for the first time in his life he'd actually started thinking about other people and their feelings instead of his own gratification.

"Yes," Naomi said. She caressed his erection, then kissed him. "Yes, yes, yes."

CHAPTER 24

Liz opened her desk drawer for about the tenth time and stared at the little box wrapped in red foil paper. Jeff was on his way home; he'd called yesterday from San Francisco and they'd talked for almost an hour. Christ, she'd missed him so much.

She took out the package and held it in her hands. A single diamond stud earring. He'd mentioned once that he hated rings but he'd considered having an ear pierced, and then he told her last night that he'd finally had it done while he was in San Diego. She put the box back in the drawer and fingered the earring's mate, turning it in the new hole she'd had pierced this morning. It was almost as if they were engaged, but no one else knew. A secret engagement.

She glanced at the papers strewn over her desk—offers, addenda, appraisal reports, lease agreements, inspection orders, all awaiting her attention. She felt like sweeping them into the wastepaper basket.

There was no way she could concentrate on work today. If Jeff had gotten away when he planned—she counted on her fingers—then he'd be in Ashland in another hour or so. Her whole body ached for him; all she could think about was meeting him at his apartment. She'd spent the last few days in limbo, unable to focus on anything.

She tapped her fingernails loudly on a bare spot on the desk, eyeing the pack of Salems lying next to the tiny red box, then resolutely slamming the drawer shut. Jeff hated cigarettes as much as Fletcher did, but he never pushed her to quit or made fun of her when she slipped. Just knowing, though, that Jeff didn't like smoking made it easier for her to resist, while Fletcher's carping inspired her to rebellion. Immature, she knew, but she couldn't help it.

The intercom buzzer rang, and she pushed the button, her hands suddenly shaking. If Jeff had gotten an early start, maybe—

"There's a call on line one for you," Ursula said.

"Thanks." Liz pressed the first button. "Hello."

"Elizabeth Berenson?"

"Yes."

"This is the ER nurse at Ashland Community Hospital." A radio crackled in the background.

Panic froze Liz's heart. She stifled a gasp. Something had happened to Brookie, or Fletcher. She braced herself against her desk.

"We have a patient here who had a card with your name and phone number on it in his wallet. Jeffrey Haviland. Do you know him?"

Liz nodded, but the voice on the phone didn't continue. Finally, she realized she hadn't spoken. "Yes," she whispered. She was shaking so badly it was hard to talk. "What happened? How is he?"

"He was in a car accident on the Siskiyou summit. The ambulance brought him in about half an hour ago. He's in critical condition. Are you a relation?"

"No." Liz gripped the edge of the desk with her free hand and willed herself to stop trembling. It couldn't be that bad. Jeff would be all right. It couldn't happen to her again. "He works for me."

"In that case perhaps you have some information there about his next of kin?"

His next of kin. God, it sounded so official, so hopeless. "I'm sure we do. I'll find it and bring it to you."

"That isn't really necessary. You can just call it in."

"Jeff's a close friend. I want to see him. I'll be right there." Liz dropped the receiver back into the cradle. Her heart pounding like crazy, she grabbed her purse from her desk drawer and hurried across her office. She paused at the door and forced herself to take a deep breath, inhaling all the way down to her diaphragm the way Jeff had taught her, then exhaling slowly. She pulled open her door and stepped into the main office.

The three agents working at their desks glanced up and nodded or smiled at her. She stopped at Ursula's desk. "I've got an appointment," Liz told her. "I don't know when I'll be back."

Ursula furrowed her forehead and squinted up at her. "Are you feeling all right? You look awfully pale."

Liz pushed her lips into a smile. "Guess I'd better get back to the tanning salon, then. I feel fine."

"Okay," Ursula said. "I'll take your messages."

"Thanks." Liz waved, then walked slowly out the door. Once she was out of sight, she sprinted down the sidewalk to her car. She put the key in the lock and turned, but nothing happened. Frantically, she wriggled and twisted it, tears flooding her eyes and rolling down her cheeks. She glanced around and wiped them away furiously. Finally she realized she'd put the key in upside down, and she stuck it back in the right way.

The lock clicked. She flung open the door, jumped into the car, and revved the engine. *Don't die*, she repeated to herself over and over as she pulled the car onto Lithia Way and headed north. *You can't die. You can't die.*

By the time she pulled into the emergency room parking lot, she was numb. She found a tissue in the glove box, blew her nose, and wiped the mascara from under her eyes. No one knew that Jeff was her lover, her love; she had to keep that a secret. Suddenly she realized she'd walked out without the information the hospital had requested. More tears welled up in her eyes. There was no way she was going back for the papers now.

She strode through the whooshing automatic doors and down the hall to the reception desk. "The nurse called about Jeff Haviland," she told the clerk. "I've come to see him."

The young woman looked at her, sympathy and pity shining in her large blue eyes. "Just a minute." She turned to a dark-haired woman sitting at a desk behind her. "Dr. Gregory," she said. "The person is here for Mr. Haviland."

The doctor nodded at Liz, then disappeared, reappearing in a second at the doorway to the waiting room. Offering her hand, she introduced herself to Liz. "I'm very sorry. He died a few minutes ago."

Liz stared at her. The words registered in her head, but her heart refused to believe them. She could *feel* Jeff in this place. He was alive. He couldn't be dead. Not Jeff. Not dead. Not killed in a car accident like Kevin, her high school boyfriend. She couldn't lose two men she loved the same way. It was impossible—it had to be. She could hear Jeff's voice; his face shimmered in front of her, inexpressible love shining in his eyes.

"No," she said, shaking her head. "He can't be." A loud buzzing filled her ears, but she made herself ignore both it and the sudden urge to vomit. "I want to see him." She composed her face and straightened her back. "I have to see him."

Sheri reread the final paragraphs of her essay for the third time. It didn't seem like much of a conclusion, but her mind was all out of words. Fifteen years since she'd taken a final exam—it was hard to believe it had been that long ago. If anything, she was more nervous about it now than she'd been then.

She raised her eyes and glanced around the classroom. Two other students remained, and Alec sat behind a long table at the front of the room, his head bent over a book. He looked up, caught her eye, and smiled.

Sheri returned his smile, then lowered her head and turned back to the first page of her exam booklet. One more time all the way through. She wanted to talk to Alec, but she didn't want anybody else around.

The boy in the far corner stood, shouldered his backpack, and shuffled up to Alec's table. He dropped his paper on the messy pile in front of Alec and murmured a few words before he left.

Sheri sighed and slid her gaze sideways at the girl sitting next to her. Heather slouched in the desk, staring at Alec, her mouth pursed in a sultry pout. Her pen lay on top of her exam—she hadn't written a word in at least fifteen minutes.

Gritting her teeth, Sheri checked her watch—there were only five minutes left anyway. Why the hell didn't Heather just turn in her paper and go? Ever since the cast party, Sheri had found it hard to be civil to the girl; and then after Naomi had told them all while they were skiing on Mount Ashland about her encounter with Heather, Sheri couldn't look at her without a little shudder of disgust. Maybe Heather was working on Alec now that Richard had recovered from his temporary insanity.

Sheri couldn't keep the little smirk from twitching her lips. If Alec was what Heather was after, the girl certainly had misjudged him. He was nothing like Richard.

Alec cleared his throat. "Time is up, officially," he said.

Heather shot Sheri a withering glance, rose, and handed in her paper. Alec nodded at her. "Have a pleasant holiday," he said, his tone a dismissal.

"You too." Heather slunk out of the room without looking back.

At last. Sheri gathered her books and exam and stood. "I just wanted to thank you," she said. "I've really enjoyed both of your classes, and I didn't want you to think . . ."

He lifted an eyebrow, waiting for her to continue.

She took a deep breath, and the words rushed out. "I won't be back spring term. I'd like to, but with everything that's happened, I just can't

173

afford the tuition." She flushed. She hated talking about money, but she wanted him to know that her absence from his class had nothing to do with him. "Anyway, I really appreciate everything you've done for me."

Alec stuffed the exam booklets into a battered briefcase. "Thanks," he said. "For telling me. I appreciate you, too. Students like you are rare, and I don't think you should give up. Can you meet me for lunch tomorrow? I'd like a chance to try to change your mind."

"Well," Sheri said. "Sure, I guess." She gave him her exam, and her stomach quivered the second it left her hand. There was nothing more she could do now. "Maybe you should read this first, though, before you try to talk me into coming back."

He laughed. "I'll do that. But I doubt that there's a problem with your grade even if you botched it. Your term paper was smashing—one of the best I've ever read, in fact." His hazel eyes twinkled at her. "Noon? At Geppetto's?"

Sheri nodded, her cheeks burning even hotter. "Okay." She turned and rushed out of the classroom before he could get up. She wanted to savor his compliments all by herself, replay the words over and over until she could almost believe them.

Alec followed Sheri and the Birkenstocked waitress to the booth, then slid across the dark red Naugahyde seat. Being here with Sheri made him a little nervous—whether it was because she was his student or a beautiful, but married, woman he wasn't sure. The waitress handed them each a menu, smiled beatifically, and made her way back to the cash register at the end of the narrow hall.

He spread open the menu and glanced at the offerings. "Wontons, spaghetti with pesto sauce, and eggplant burgers," he said. "Interesting."

Sheri laughed. "You know, I've lived in this town all my life, and I've never eaten here before. The wontons are famous, though—the people who work here dress up in wonton costumes and march in the parade on the Fourth of July."

"Marching wontons?" Alec lifted an eyebrow. "I hope I'll be here to see them this year."

"You might not?" Sheri closed her menu.

He shrugged. "The Shakespeare chair is a one-year position. There is a permanent, tenure-track opening and I've applied for it, but I'm not sure about anything right now." Talking about him wasn't the purpose of this meeting. Meeting, not date, he reminded himself. "I do know one thing, though: you *have* to stay in school." He patted his briefcase on the seat beside him. "I picked up some papers from the financial aid office. You're a perfect candidate for assistance, especially if you enroll full time."

The waitress returned, and Sheri ordered a salad. "I'll try the eggplant burger," he said. After the young woman glided away, he turned back to Sheri. "Well? What do you think?"

She shook her head slowly. "I don't know. I've got a job; I've got two kids." She paused a second. "And I don't have a husband anymore. Mike and I are getting a divorce."

"I'm sorry to hear that."

"Don't be." Sheri's tone was so harsh that he stared at her, not quite sure of what to say. She reddened. "Sorry," she mumbled. "But it's really for the best."

"I don't want to pry," he said. "But my wife divorced me last summer, and I'm still trying to figure out exactly what I did wrong. Why is it for the best?"

Her face stiffened. "He drank, and he hit me," she said finally.

"Oh, Jesus," he said. Thank God Vivianne would never have to say that about him. "I understand." Now some of Naomi's comments made sense.

Sheri was silent while the waitress placed their food in front of them. "I just don't see how I can possibly continue with school right now."

"It would be difficult, but not impossible. Scholarships paid my way through university; I wouldn't be here now otherwise. You have too much talent to let it lie undeveloped."

"But I don't know the first thing about applying for scholarships," she said. "Except that it takes a lot of time filling out all those forms." She picked through her salad, speared a cherry tomato, and popped it into her mouth.

"I'll help you. I've filled out so many bloody applications I can do them in my sleep."

"You'd do that for me?" Wonder lit her lovely green eyes.

Nodding, Alec studied her face and pondered his own motives. Sure, he'd done the same for other promising students without anything prompting him but the desire to help them in the same way benefactors had assisted him. But he had to admit to himself that the prospect of spending some time with Sheri pleased him even when he knew it was against his rules. Something about her touched him, reminded him of a part of himself that he'd lost a long time ago.

And then, too, he'd hate to lose Sheri as a student. She was one of those students who inspired teachers to do their best—his classes always seemed to lack something when she wasn't there. Perhaps what he offered wasn't entirely unselfish.

Still, he had no intention of taking any kind of advantage of the situation even though her impending divorce made his attraction to her seem a little less off limits.

"I'd be glad to," he said. He clicked open his briefcase, pulled out a sheaf of papers, and slapped them on the table. "We can get started right now."

CHAPTER 25

Liz stared into her closet, blinking her eyes to clear the haze of tears. Thank God Fletcher was in Eugene; at least she could get dressed for Jeff's funeral without having to pretend sincere—but distant—sorrow. Everyone understood that Jeff's death was a tragedy for his little girls, for his family, but goddamn it, it was a tragedy for her too. And no one else knew it. She was a widow, but her widowhood was secret. Even though grieving exhausted her, she had to somehow find the energy to hide her anguish.

The clothes in her closet shimmered together in a kaleidoscope of colors and shapes, and she watched her hand reach out and tug a dress off a hanger. Black, high-necked, long-sleeved. Too obviously widow's weeds. She dropped the dress, and it crumpled into a little pile of black on the white carpet.

She forced herself to focus. She didn't want to be late, to call attention to herself. She wanted to fade into the crowd of mourners.

No, she didn't. She wanted to stand beside the coffin, wailing and keening for her lost love, not caring who knew of her grief. Another storm of tears welled up from her heart and flooded her eyes. Sobbing loudly, she threw herself on the bed and cried until she couldn't cry anymore. Then she made herself breathe deeply, the way Jeff had taught her.

"God damn you!" she whispered even though she wanted to scream. "You lied. You said you'd come back to me." She leaned over the side of the bed and pulled up the bottom of the white tablecloth covering her bedside table. Beneath it lay Jeff's picture and the little red box she'd never gotten a chance to give him. She grabbed the photo and laid it on the white bedspread.

Jeff looked up at her with his sweet, perfectly even smile, his green eyes shining with amusement. She knew that look, could almost guess what he'd been thinking. Jesus, she missed him so much. She couldn't bear the thought that she'd never see him again.

New tears burned her eyes. "Why?" she sobbed aloud. Why had he gone away in the first place? Why had he driven off the side of the goddamn mountain? Why was he dead? Why did she hurt so much? Would it ever stop, this searing pain inside, these overwhelming feelings of loss and disappointment? Half the time she felt like a sleepwalker wrapped in a fog of white grief; the rest of the time she felt flayed, exposed and raw.

She took a deep, shuddering breath that reached all the way to her gut. "Get a grip," she told herself. "You have to get dressed. Now."

She pushed herself off the bed and stumbled once again to the closet. The navy blue coatdress with the white collar would do. She jerked it from the hanger and stepped into it, then buttoned the bodice with trembling fingers. She found her navy heels and slipped them on.

When she slid the mirrored closet door shut, she caught a glimpse of herself. Jesus Christ, she looked like shit. Mascara ringed her reddened eyes, and her lips and nose were swollen from crying. She hurried into the bathroom and soaked a washcloth in cold water, then held it against her feverish face. She couldn't go, not when she looked like this.

But she couldn't *not* go. She patted mascara remover under her eyes and wiped the black circles away, then reapplied her makeup. By the time she finished with the lipstick, she could feel the soft white cloud gathering around her again. She slipped into it gratefully, as if it were a warm fur coat Jeff held out for her.

"I can handle it," she said. She pulled herself up straight and marched out of the bedroom.

The crowd roared when North Carolina's forward went in for the lay-up, and Alec joined them as the basketball swished through the hoop. He'd acquired a taste for the American sport since moving to Chapel Hill; Tarheel basketball was the only reason he'd bothered buying a bloody television set for his apartment in Ashland.

The phone rang just as the Hoosier forward's pass was intercepted by the blue and white guard. "Damn," he said, annoyed at the interruption. He turned down the sound. Keeping his eyes on the telly, he backed toward the phone. He grabbed the receiver on the second ring. "Hello."

"Dad? It's Philip."

"God, it's terrific to hear your voice." Suddenly the game was totally unimportant. He stretched the phone cord across the apartment's tiny living room and flicked the television off. "How are you?"

"I'm fine. How's Oregon?"

"I like it here," Alec said. "I think you would, too. And Gwen."

The long distance connection crackled during Philip's silence. "That's what I'm calling about," he said.

Alec's heart raced, and the blood in his veins grew warmer with hope. Even though his kids were almost grown, he'd missed them a hell of a lot.

"I want to come and live with you." Philip rattled off a litany of complaints about London, from the bad food to the unrelenting fog to the dearth of friends.

"Wait a minute," Alec said. "It's fine with me. But what does your mother say?"

"She says it's all right with her."

"Well, then, when will you get here?"

"On Thursday."

Three days. "I'm looking forward to it." He paused, then cleared his throat. "Give your mother my regards."

SAN FRANCISCO

The word *detective* always made Doug think of a semi-sleazy guy hunched behind the wheel of a car watching some unfaithful husband get himself in trouble. But Ivan Obremski didn't fit that image at all. He sat behind a clean and organized modern desk with a computer behind him. There were no half-eaten lunches and wadded-up pieces of paper scattered around him, no ashtrays overflowing with cigarettes. His brown hair and beard were neatly trimmed, and he wore horn-rimmed glasses. He looked more like an accountant than a private eye.

Mr. Obremski stood and waved Doug and his father into his office. "Have a seat," he said, pointing at a couple of low-slung leather and chrome chairs.

Doug followed Dad into the room and sat down. Little nervous tremors rattled through his stomach like he was hungry even though they'd just eaten lunch. When Mr. Obremski had called, he'd said he had some news about Doug's birth mother and asked Dad to bring a recent photograph of Doug with him. Doug hoped like hell the news was good—Dr. Levison said he was getting real close to another remission, that he was progressing faster this time than the first, which was unusual with his kind of leukemia.

Mr. Obremski propped his elbows on his clean desk and bounced the fingertips of one hand off those of the other. "We have some new information about your birth mother," he said. "I don't want you to get your hopes up, but I also don't want you to give up. I'm going to send one of my associates to Oregon to follow up on it for me. Did you bring that photo I asked for?"

Dad retrieved his wallet from his back pocket, flipped it open, and took out Doug's senior portrait. "What's the angle?" he said, handing the picture to Mr. Obremski.

"We found a nurse at Good Samaritan hospital who thinks she remembers the girl, but she's seen so many patients over the years that she only has a vague image of her. All she could tell us was that she was young and that she wasn't from Portland. She talked about going to college, the nurse remembered, but she couldn't remember where exactly," Mr. Obremski said. "If Doug looks at all like his birth mother, we're hoping that his picture will help jog her memory. It's a long shot, but right now it's our best shot."

Doug's shoulders sagged, and he exchanged a disappointed glance with Dad. Long shot was right. Andy and Nick both looked exactly like Dad, nothing like Mom. What if he looked just like his birth father, too?

CHAPTER 26

April

ASHLAND, OREGON

Carrying her largest silver tray laden with coffee and cognac serving paraphernalia, Naomi followed her guests into the living room. She'd worried about tonight's dinner party, the first since Kristin's return home, but it had turned into a roaring success. Having Alec bring his son had been a *brilliant* idea, to use one of Philip's favorite words. Kristin had taken one look at the handsome young man, her jaw had dropped, and she'd been sweet and charming all evening long. Philip entertained her, and Alec entertained Meredith, Sheri, and Liz, all of them without partners. Everything was going perfectly.

Naomi set the heavy tray on the Queen Anne console table behind the sofa and turned to Richard, already seated in the wing chair by the window. "I think we should light the fire," she said. "It's snowing, after all."

Richard rose and struck a match, then tossed it into the already laid fire. Kristin joined him by the fireplace, and he draped his arm across her shoulders. "No danger of snow in Arizona in April, is there?"

Naomi watched the flames dance and sparkle, then glanced at her stepdaughter. Kristin was a beautiful girl when she was happy, without the snarl on her lips and the disdainful gleam in her eyes.

Alec laughed. "I was all set for spring after that beautiful warm weather during break. I couldn't believe it when I opened my blinds this morning. And here I was looking forward to some of that rafting on the Rogue everyone keeps telling me about. If this keeps up, I'll be cross-country skiing right from my door."

Sheri smiled at him. "I've seen it snow here in May."

"Speaking of rafting," Liz said. "Our ladies-only trip on the lower Rogue never got off the ground last year. If we go on Memorial Day weekend, we won't need a permit." She glanced around the group. "Are all the babies finally weaned?" she said, turning around and staring pointedly at Naomi.

"No problem," Naomi said, suppressing a little flicker of annoyance. Liz had only nursed Brooke for a couple of months; she'd given it up and gone back to work full-time, claiming that they couldn't afford for her to stay home. Richard couldn't possibly make less than Fletcher, and they managed on one salary. Yet she never insinuated Liz was a bad mother because she hadn't nursed Brooke for two years; her priorities were just different, that was all. It wasn't fair of Liz to imply that Naomi overmothered Leah—even if it *was* true. "Leah weaned herself two months ago."

"Great." Liz clapped her hands. "I'll organize everything, the equipment, the food. Do you all trust me to row, or shall I hire a guide?"

Naomi was silent while Meredith and Sheri chorused their approval of Liz's rowing ability. She'd definitely be more comfortable with a guide, but she knew how proud Liz was of her raft and her river-reading skills and her prowess with the oars, and she didn't want to hurt her friend's feelings even though Liz had been somewhat prickly lately. "We don't have to camp, do we?" she asked. "I'm not much into roughing it."

"Me, neither," Sheri said. "I camped out enough as a kid to last me a lifetime. Why anyone would *choose* to sleep outside on the ground is beyond me."

"Don't worry," Liz said. "I'll make reservations at Marial and Black Bar and Paradise lodges. They'll even pack lunches for us."

"We're all set, then?" Naomi said, putting more gaiety into her voice than she felt. She picked up the silver server and poured coffee into several cups. "Coffee, cognac, or both?" she asked Liz, the closest one to her, hoping they wouldn't return to the subject of rafting.

"Cognac," Liz said, and giggled. "I hope Fletcher gets here pretty soon. Our hill is going to be a mess if it keeps snowing like this, and I sure as hell am not going to be in any condition to walk up it."

Deciding that Liz had already had plenty to drink, Naomi splashed a tiny pool of Courvoisier into a crystal snifter and handed it to her. She knew Liz would scold her if she were aware of Naomi's reason for being so stingy, but she didn't care. Sometimes people *needed* someone to take care of them, and Liz had been acting a little strange lately. "Meredith?"

"Coffee, please." Meredith smiled up at her. "Great dinner, Naomi. You should write a cookbook or start your own catering service or give cooking lessons or something. Really. I'd pay to learn how you make that raspberry dacquoise."

Liz laughed. "Not me. If I could cook like Naomi, I'd have to swim two miles every morning instead of one."

Listening to the chitchat, Naomi served everyone else, then poured herself a cup of coffee and sank onto the sofa next to Liz. "I'm off duty now," she said. "But there's more if you want to serve yourself."

Philip stood, and for a moment Naomi thought he was going after a refill of coffee. Instead, though, he bent over Alec and whispered in his ear, his eyes riveted on Kristin the entire time.

Naomi caught Richard's eye and winked, knowing he hadn't missed what was happening between Kristin and Philip either.

Alec nodded, and Philip turned to Richard. "Is it all right if Kristin and I walk to the movie theater, sir? I understand it's not too far from here."

Richard smiled broadly. "Fine with me. Have fun." He kissed Kristin's cheek before she and Philip left the room together grinning at each other.

Sheri watched them through the living room window as they raced down the steps and then headed arm-in-arm down Gresham, completely oblivious to the snow. Despite his earring and his slightly punk hairstyle, Philip was a good-looking boy, and Alec was obviously proud of him.

Everyone in the living room chuckled. Sheri suppressed a sigh and turned her attention back to the conversation.

"Young love." Naomi shook her head. "It's pretty powerful."

"I still have some vague recollections," Alec said. "Not all of them pleasant, either. Sometimes it seems more like a childhood disease than a wonderful experience."

"Yeah," Sheri said. "I wish I could have been vaccinated against it."

"It was certainly never placid," Naomi said. "I remember being ecstatic one moment and practically suicidal the next. I think that's part of the pain of living with a teenager—it brings back all of those feelings you thought you'd outgrown, reminds you of their intensity and your own lack of immunity from heartbreak."

Richard glared at Alec with mock ferocity. "If your son breaks my daughter's heart—"

Naomi laughed. "It's *her* problem, darling, not yours."

Meredith nodded. "I remember my mother taking all of my problems so personally and how much I hated it. I just stopped telling her anything. It was *my* suffering, and I wanted it all for myself." She lifted an eyebrow. "Now, of course, I'm only too glad to share some of it with her—and with anyone else who's willing."

"I don't remember feeling like that," Sheri said. "I don't think I was aware that I was suffering. Looking back, I know I must have been, but I didn't realize it then. That's just the way things were." And until recently, not much had changed with her approach to problems. If something hurt, she'd avoided thinking about it. She'd managed to deny her father's insensitivity, Mike's brutality, her sorrow over her lost dreams.

But things were different now. Dad was dead; Mike was gone; and she was working on making her dreams come true. No one stood in her way anymore. A sudden overwhelming sensation of freedom filled her, exhilarating her so much she wanted to grab Alec and dance around the room. She had to grip the edge of her chair to restrain herself.

Richard smiled at Naomi. "Some things don't change. Old love can be powerful, too."

"Old love?" Alec said. "What do you mean by that—falling in love when you're over thirty, or loving the same person for a long time?"

Richard laughed. "The former, I guess. I was forty-four when I met Naomi, and I might as well have been sixteen again. My theoretical maturity—based solely on my age, you understand—didn't make much of a difference. There's something about falling in love that brings back one's childhood."

Liz drained the rest of her cognac, not trusting herself to participate in the conversation. The wine with dinner and the brandy she'd just finished had gone straight to her head, and love wasn't a topic she could express anything coherent about right now. She felt empty and filled up at the same time, so numb and so hurting.

Naomi cocked an eyebrow at Richard. "One's childhood?" she said. "Or one's childishness?"

Liz twisted the snifter in her hands. Maybe Naomi was on the right track. In some ways falling in love with Jeff *had* been a childish response to her dissatisfaction with Fletcher. Fletcher had hurt her by ignoring her, so she'd gotten even by loving someone else. Part of her had been just like a little kid; *I know something you don't know. Nah, nah, na, nah, nah.* Her love for Jeff had somehow made her feel superior to Fletcher, protected from the insult of his distance.

She glanced at her watch as the lively conversation hummed around her. Eleven o'clock, and still no Fletcher. He'd promised to get away from his campaign meeting early so he could join her. God damn him. He never considered her feelings about anything. She swallowed back the surge of anger swelling in her chest. She couldn't afford it right now; she was too close to bursting into tears in front of everyone as it was.

She set her glass on the coffee table and stood. "I'm sorry," she said. "I have to get home, and it doesn't look like Fletcher's going to make it after all. I'll just go call a taxi."

"Nonsense," Alec said. "I've got to be going myself. Let me drop you off." Liz protested, but he rose, shook hands with Richard, and kissed each of the other women on the cheek. "Thanks so much for a truly wonderful evening."

Sheri waved good-bye at the two of them, holding in her breath as if that would dull the niggling little darts of jealousy stabbing her heart. Liz was so beautiful and so sexy. Still, Alec had volunteered to take Liz home; it wasn't as if Liz was making some kind of play for him or something. And even if Liz did, it still wasn't any of Sheri's business. She had no claim on Alec. He was her teacher, and he'd taken the trouble to help her out. That was all.

She tried to drag her thoughts away from Liz and Alec, but the sore spot remained. If Alec had volunteered to take Meredith or Naomi home, she wouldn't be feeling quite the same pangs even if she did have something going with him. Which she definitely did not.

CHAPTER 27

Sheri had hoped Saturday would be one of those beautiful spring days so all the kids could play in the backyard, but the weather sure wasn't cooperating. Outside, the wind blew, and the rain fell in cold, gray sheets, backing up the storm sewers and flooding the street. Well, at least it had stopped snowing. Sighing, she turned away from the window. The living room would just have to do.

"I could use some help," she said to Felicia, who sat cross-legged on the carpet amid a huge pile of Barbie dolls and their clothes. "If you don't want the little kids playing with your stuff, you'd better pick it up and take it into your room. Remember last time when Leah almost swallowed one of Barbie's shoes?"

Felicia rolled her eyes, then reluctantly gathered her dolls and dumped them into the white plastic milk crate she used as a toy box. Grumbling, she piled the brightly colored clothing on top. "I hate playgroup," she said. "All those stupid babies messing everything up. Why do you invite them over?" She put her hands on her hips and glared at Sheri.

"Because I enjoy it," Sheri said, forcing herself to stay calm even though her daughter's behavior irritated her. She had to be patient with Felicia, she reminded herself. When Sheri had told her about the divorce, Felicia had sobbed with such anguish that Sheri's resolve had come close to disappearing. And every time Felicia came back from visiting Mike, it took her several days to settle down. Thank God the visits were going to be fewer and farther between now that Mike had decided to move.

"Well, I don't." Felicia picked up her box and flounced out of the room.

Sheri took a deep breath, then lowered herself next to where Timmy sat surrounded by his Duplo blocks. "Let's take these into your bedroom," she said. "It would be nice if all the kids played in there for a while." She helped him stack the blocks into a giant column, and they carried it together down the hall.

The room Sheri had so carefully tidied the night before was a total wreck now, toys and books scattered everywhere. Tears stung her eyes, and she stifled her first impulse, which was to start screaming. Instead, she turned around and walked out of the room. What did it really matter that Timmy's bedroom was a mess? That her whole life was a mess? A perfectly clean house wasn't going to suddenly make her life perfect, no matter what her mother always said.

And, despite the problems of supporting herself and being totally responsible for two children, things *were* better. Mike had called a couple of days ago to tell her he was planning to move to Roseburg and work for his brother, who owned a roofing company there. At least he'd have a three-hour drive so he'd have some time to reconsider things before he was tempted to break into her house again. Hell, if he was drunk enough to want to do that again, he'd probably drive his pickup into a tree or something before he made it to Ashland.

She almost chuckled at the image, then shuddered with disgust at herself. She didn't really want Mike dead—she just wanted him entirely out of her life. But until the kids were gone, that was an impossibility. She was going to have to put up with him for at least the next sixteen years, until Timmy graduated from high school. She set her teeth. Maybe she *did* want him dead. The son of a bitch almost killed her; she had every right in the world to loathe him.

She was still arguing with herself when the doorbell rang. Fifteen minutes later, she stood in her kitchen with Naomi and Meredith while Timmy, Leah, and Justine sat at the table happily scrawling away in coloring books with Timmy's crayons. "I wonder where Liz is?" Sheri asked.

"It's not like her to be late." Meredith sounded worried. "But she hasn't been herself for the last couple of weeks. Have you noticed?"

Nodding, Naomi took the cup of coffee Sheri offered her. "She doesn't seem very happy. I guess I always expect Liz to have a big smile on her face. She just doesn't sparkle the way she usually does."

Sheri frowned and looked at Meredith. Liz and Meredith had been friends since college, and Meredith usually knew what was going on in Liz's life. But even Meredith seemed mystified. "Do you suppose Liz and Fletcher are having problems?"

"If they are, she hasn't told me," Meredith said, shrugging. "Truthfully, though, it wouldn't surprise me. I've known Fletcher for almost as long as I've known Lizzie, and I've always thought they were an unlikely match. During law school, he was involved in his causes—counseling draft protesters, providing free legal aid for the poor, all that kind of stuff. Lizzie loved to dance and go to parties. Mr. Serious and Miss Congeniality."

"Mr. Dud and Miss Livewire," Naomi added. "I guess I just assumed that Fletcher had gotten stodgy in his middle age."

"He was pretty popular in high school," Sheri said. "Student body vice president, valedictorian, tennis champion, quarterback on the football team. I was in the eighth grade when he graduated, and I'd bet that everyone in town knew who he was. He was one of those 'most-likely-to-succeed' kinds of guys."

"Not 'most-likely-to-try-to-save-the-world'?" Naomi asked.

Sheri shook her head. "If that part was there, it wasn't real obvious." She lifted her shoulders. "Of course, I was still in junior high when he left town—I didn't really know him well enough to be able to say for sure what he was like back then." She forced a little smile. "Except that he was better-looking without his beard and glasses."

Meredith bent over Justie's coloring book and praised her work, then turned back to Naomi and Sheri. "You know what's funny?" she said. "Lizzie actually encouraged Fletcher to grow that beard, and she picked out his wire-rim glasses. She told him he looked too straight." Meredith laughed. "He hasn't changed a bit since then."

The doorbell rang, and they stared at each other for a second before Sheri headed to answer it. She opened the door, and Liz stood on the porch with Brooke cradled against her hip.

Liz flashed her famous grin, but Sheri decided Naomi was right—Liz's normally bright blue eyes were dull, maybe even a little reddened. "Sorry," Liz said, stepping inside. "We had a last minute crisis at our house."

Sheri raised an eyebrow, waiting for Liz to continue, but instead Liz lowered her daughter to the floor.

"Look, Brookie," Liz said, pointing at the kitchen table. "Crayons!"

The little girl clapped her hands and headed toward the table. Naomi lifted her into a chair and spread open a coloring book in front of her, then dragged the box of crayons over to her. "Go for it," she said. She smiled at Liz. "We were starting to get worried about you."

Liz blanched, and a haze of tears glittered in her eyes.

Meredith glanced at the kids, then narrowed her eyes at Liz. "Is everything all right?" she asked.

To Meredith's surprise, Liz buried her face in her hands and sobbed. Putting her arm around Liz's shoulders, Meredith steered her toward the living room sofa, an ugly brown plaid Herculon thing. "Is there anything we can do?" she said after Liz crumpled onto the couch.

Liz shook her head. Naomi and Sheri gathered up the coloring paraphernalia and hustled the children into Timmy's bedroom. Sheri knocked on Felicia's door and stuck her head inside. "I'll give you some baby-sitting money if you play with the little kids," she said. "You can be in charge."

"Really?" To Sheri's relief, Felicia sounded delighted.

Sheri and Naomi got the kids situated, then returned to the living room. "Okay," Naomi said, settling herself on the other side of Liz. "What gives? Do you want to talk about it?"

Liz nodded, gradually regaining control.

Her voice quavering, Liz told them about how miserable she'd been with Fletcher, her love affair with Jeff, and how difficult Jeff's death had been for her. Afterward Naomi circled her arms around Liz's shoulders and held her. "I'm so sorry," she said. "For all of you. Does Fletcher know?"

Liz shook her head. "You're the only ones I've told. I haven't trusted myself—and I'm not very proud of myself either. Suddenly, love seems like a damn poor excuse for lying and cheating. Jeff's death feels like a punishment—for both of us. Sometimes I even think he got off the easiest. Isn't that sick?"

"You're being awfully hard on yourself," Meredith said.

"I deserve it. Jesus, what a mess."

"I think you should tell Fletcher," Naomi said.

"I don't know. I'm not ready yet. I'm still so pissed off at Fletcher I don't think I could be rational. And if I'm not rational, he's even less likely to listen to me than usual." She gritted her teeth, then laughed bitterly. "I can just hear him now. 'That's nice, dear,' he'll say, and he won't even look up from his book."

"I don't think so," Naomi said. "I think you'll get his attention this time." She paused for a second before adding, "Maybe that's why you started the affair in the first place."

"You might be right," Liz said. "Sometimes it surprises me how much I hate him. After all, it's not as if he's beaten me up or anything."

Sheri flinched. "He threatened your basic survival instincts, though. An infant can die from neglect as well as from physical abuse."

"I guess." Liz pulled away from Naomi and sighed. "I'm okay now. Really I am. I just wanted to tell you about all of it. But I'm okay."

"What do you mean, you're okay?" Meredith asked. "You loved Jeff, and now he's dead. Jesus Murphy, Liz, you can't just stuff it, pretend it never happened."

A smile flickered across Liz's lips. "That's what I love about you," she said to Meredith. "You never let me get away with anything. But this time I've actually thought about it. I have a choice: I can suffer and carry on about Jeff as if he were the one and only true love of my life and completely destroy my marriage as well as my chances for any happiness in the future—"

Liz paused for a breath. "Or I can be honest with myself. Sure, I loved Jeff. Sure, I miss him terribly and it hurts like hell. But I still have my life. I have my child, and I have my husband, flawed as he is." Her chuckle was brittle. "Of course, I'm not such a bargain myself."

Meredith reached over and squeezed her hand. "You've told yourself for so long that you're shallow, vain, and frivolous that you've actually started believing it," she said. "I think you've got more to offer than you realize."

Sheri's dark curls caught Alec's eye as he ambled through Stevenson Union. Her head bent over the textbook in front of her, she chewed her lower lip, then underlined a passage.

He smiled and headed up the stairs toward her table at the edge of the loft. He missed having her in class this term, but he didn't feel comfortable seeking her out. A chance meeting on campus was different, though. "How's it going?"

She snapped her head up, and the surprise in her eyes changed to delight when she saw him. "Alec!"

"Mind if I join you?"

She closed the book and pushed it aside. "I'd love it. I'm tired of U.S. history. I wish I'd had room in my schedule for one of your classes."

He pulled out a chair and sat down across from her. "I'd have liked that, too."

She sighed. "I was really disappointed when I found out that the math class I needed was only offered at the same hour as your Shakespeare's Kings class. And I just don't have the time for another stage class."

He patted her hand. "Don't worry about it. I understand. Besides, with any luck, I might still be teaching here next year."

"Oh, I hope so."

Despite the constant swirl of activity and noise around him, he found it impossible to look anywhere but at her. She seemed more beautiful to him every time he saw her, but whether the difference was because of her steadily growing self-confidence or his own steadily growing attraction to her he wasn't sure.

He was sure of one thing, though: he was damned attracted to her, had been since that first day in class last September even though he'd put a lot of energy into denying it. Still, it was one thing to admit to it and another to do anything about it right now with both of their lives in a state of upheaval. He didn't know for sure that he would get the job at SOSC, and if he didn't, he'd be returning to North Carolina at the end of the summer.

"How *is* that math class?" he asked.

"Don't ask. We had the midterm today. Nice birthday present, huh?"

"Today's your birthday?"

"Yeah. Thirty-five years old and at almost exactly the same point I was fifteen years ago—going to college. I guess I *have* learned some things, but not the kind of stuff you can get a degree with."

Alec leaned forward. "Like what?"

"Well, I finally got a restraining order against Mike. Meredith said that just because someone victimizes you, you don't have to become a victim. That made a lot of sense to me."

"Good point," Alec said. "That's something I've had to learn as well."

"Really? You seem so in control of everything it's hard to imagine you victimized by anyone."

"I grew up in the worst part of London and went straight from there to Eton, from working after school in my da's fish market to wearing suits and taking classes in French and literature. I was afraid to open my mouth until I could talk without dropping my h's. Scholarship students are always at the bottom, but I was less than zero."

"Me, too," Sheri said. "Except for the drama club. The kids in it accepted me—it didn't matter to them that my dad was a logger."

"I found a group like that at Cambridge. Funny thing, though. When I went back home, I felt like an outcast among my old friends; then I'd go back to school and feel like a misfit. It wasn't until I met Vivianne that none of that seemed to matter anymore."

"I'd never have guessed," Sheri said, shaking her head. Alec always seemed so sophisticated to her that it was hard to imagine him as an impoverished student from the wrong side of the tracks, just the same as she was. She'd thought of him as a gifted but rather distant scholar when he was really as down-to-earth and unpretentious as Mike—but a hell of a lot nicer. When she tried to talk about theater or the books she read to Mike, he just made fun of her for being an egghead, even though he had a degree in the stuff—or worse yet, he got threatened and pissed off and accused her of thinking she was better than he was.

"Most Americans tend to be naive about the social implications of British accents," Alec said. "That's why I decided to come here. I was tired of kissing ass, of being on guard all the time. I thought I could be who I really was in America." He laughed. "I was a little too naive myself. I was passed over for promotion to assistant professor at my first job, largely because of my less than academically perfect accent, I suspect. Fortunately, the people at UNC didn't seem to mind."

"How weird," she said. "I love the way you talk. In fact, that was one of the first things I noticed about you—how sexy your accent was." Her face grew warm, and she knew she was blushing. Again. Damn. Why had she said that about him sounding sexy? He was her teacher, and she wasn't a nasty little flirt like Heather Austin.

Alec blushed too, but he laughed. "Ta," he said. "I'm chuffed you like it, pet."

She couldn't help joining his laughter. "You ought to talk like that all the time."

"I'd have to work at it now," he said. "Twenty years in America have softened the edges. I may sound totally British to your ears, but a Londoner would spot me as American in two syllables." He stood. "But I'm keeping you from your studies, and I know how precious your time is."

Disappointment gripped Sheri's chest, but she struggled to keep it from showing on her face. The time she spent with Alec was what was precious to her, but she didn't want to impose on him. "I'm glad you stopped by," she said, keeping her tone neutral and polite.

After a moment of hesitation, he cleared his throat. "Are you doing anything special for your birthday tonight?"

She shook her head.

"I'd like to take you to dinner, then."

She held her breath. She couldn't afford a baby-sitter, but maybe Meredith or Naomi would watch the kids. She hesitated, hashing out the pros and cons. Mike hadn't moved to Roseburg yet. What if he saw her with Alec? The thought made her stomach flop. It was too dangerous, and it wasn't fair to Alec. "I can't," she said, ducking her head to hide the sudden tears stinging her eyes. She blinked them away. "I wish I could."

Alec shrugged. "Some other time, then."

He walked away, his hands in his pockets as he shouldered open the wide glass door. She hoped he meant it.

CHAPTER 28

May

Liz followed Fletcher into the living room, promising herself that to-night she would tell him. He'd won the primary election more than a week ago, and her desperation grew with every day that passed. She *had* to tell him, or she was going to do something really stupid, like starting a careless affair with someone else and letting herself get caught.

Fletcher sat down in the leather chair by the window, propping his feet on the hassock before he picked up his briefcase and snapped it open on his lap.

A cold rage gripped her insides when she watched him bend his head over his papers. Suddenly, she *wanted* to tell him, wanted to destroy that calm self-sufficiency of his, wanted him to feel the same kind of pain and grief that overwhelmed her. Slowly, mechanically, she eased herself into the chair across from his. It wasn't just the pain and grief of losing Jeff, either. She'd been hurting before she met him—and it was Fletcher's fault. It was time for him to pay.

She drew her breath in sharply. What was she thinking? How could she possibly blame Fletcher for something she'd chosen to do? No one had *made* her sleep with Jeff, fall in love with him. Jesus Christ, she was mixed up. Nothing but a walking container for confusing emotions. Sometimes she felt so angry she had to grit her teeth to keep from spewing out the most awful accusations; then the next second tears poured from her eyes and her sadness grew as huge as the ocean and she feared she would drown in it.

"Fletcher."

He didn't look up. "Yes?"

Irritation flooded her veins like a quick-acting poison, and an almost gleeful malice seized her as she blurted out, "I had an affair with Jeff Haviland. If he hadn't died, I would have left you."

He raised his head and stared at her, his mouth gaping open. Naomi was right; she'd definitely captured his attention this time. "Oh, my God," he said. "Oh, my God."

The expression of stunned horror and pain on his face dissipated her desire to hurt him, but it was too late. She'd finally made the first move; the rest of the scene was inevitable. All she felt now was a debilitating weariness and a desire to escape from him.

"Is that all you have to say?" He sounded like a parent scolding an unrepentant child.

She shrugged. "What else do you want me to say?"

"Jesus, Liz." He gripped the arms of his chair as if to keep himself a prisoner there. "I'm glad the bastard is dead," he said through clenched teeth.

"Why? Because it saves you the trouble of killing him?" She restrained her sudden urge to hit him. "You didn't want me; he did. I was tired of living like a zombie."

He recoiled as if she'd just punched him in the stomach, and for the first time in their life together she saw tears shine in his eyes. The ice choking her heart melted a little.

"It has a lot more to do with us, Fletcher, than it does with Jeff," she said. "I've had some time to think about it."

"If you weren't happy, why didn't you tell me?"

"I tried," she said. "But I didn't know how to say it, and you didn't know how to listen. Maybe I expected you to read my mind or something, figure out what I wanted and give it to me the way we try to do with Brookie." She crossed her arms over her stomach and leaned forward. "I don't know. I just felt alone all the time. Your life is so filled with your job there didn't seem to be any room for me."

"I think I hate you. How can I love you so much and hate you at the same time?" Fletcher said.

She almost laughed, but she caught herself in time, knowing that she was only an inch away from hysteria. She was still so in love with Jeff, still so deeply grieved over his death. But she'd never really stopped caring about Fletcher. They had their history and their child, too much to throw away for nothing. She fluttered her hand in the air. "Oh, Fletcher," she said. "I'm so unhappy. I don't know what to do."

He sat stiffly in his chair, staring at her. "I don't either," he said finally.

Naomi grimaced as her ears picked up the distant sound of rushing water. It was their second day rafting on the Rogue, but she still panicked every time they came to a rapid even though Liz was an expert oarswoman, and Meredith and Sheri assured her there was nothing to worry about. Rafting was so different from skiing, where she had at least the illusion of being in control. Not so here. The river snarled at her, roaring in fury as it broke frothy and white over invisible boulders, and she was about as important as a leaf floating on the incredibly strong current.

"Hear that?" Liz said, pulling in the oars and grabbing her life jacket. "Buckle them up, ladies. We're coming to Horseshoe Bend, two little riffles followed by a class-three rapid."

Naomi gripped the raft's wooden bench. The sun was shining and it was hot for late May, but she'd refused to remove her life jacket even during the slow, lazy stretches. She'd heard the stories about the Rogue River's treacherous whirlpools and underwater caves; she had no intention of risking her life for a tan without strap marks.

Next to her, Meredith grinned and snapped the little latches shut on the jacket. She patted Naomi's leg. "Relax," she said, winking. "Skiing's a lot more dangerous. Not many people break their legs while rafting."

"Sure." Naomi looked upward. "But doesn't 'class three' mean 'prepare to meet your maker'?"

Giggling, Sheri twisted around in her seat at the front of the raft to face Naomi. "In that case, a class four would be 'kiss your ass goodbye.'"

Liz shook her head and grasped the oars. "I've been doing this for seventeen years, ever since I was in college in Eugene," she said. "And the only time I ever screwed up was at Blossom Bar about ten years ago. I got cocky and didn't scout it, and there was a snag sticking up that hadn't been there the time before."

Naomi sucked in her breath. Blossom Bar was tomorrow's main event. "What happened?"

Laughing, Liz pulled back hard on the oars. "The raft got hung up on a big rock, and we just sat there in the middle of the river until we got rescued by some intrepid kayakers. We were fine, but we couldn't pull the raft off, and it ended up in shreds." She shook her head. "The river beat it to death."

Naomi shuddered and grasped the seat even harder as Liz lined the raft up to the middle of the V-shaped current. According to Liz, all she had to do was aim the damn thing, then take a few strokes now and then to avoid obstacles, minor little things like monstrous rocks, cliff walls, and half-submerged logs. "Rafts are pretty forgiving," Liz had explained to them all at the beginning of the trip. "You can hit something and bounce off, thank God. If you're in a wooden drift boat, you have to be a lot more careful."

"Here we go!" Liz shouted over the river's roar.

They headed into the white water. Naomi screamed, but she could hardly hear herself. She bounced on the hard seat, her head snapping back and forth. A spray of cold water blasted her, and she screeched again.

Meredith held on with one hand and waved the other in the air like a cowboy on a bucking bronco. "Yipee!" she yelled.

Gritting her teeth, Naomi held on. The water pushed them straight toward the steep bank on the left, but Liz rowed furiously in the opposite direction. A few seconds later it was all over. Her heart thundered in her ears almost as loudly as the river, and she exhaled slowly. "God," she said.

Liz let the oars dangle in the oarlocks while she shrugged out of her life jacket. "Long slow stretch coming up," she said. "We can have lunch at the sandbar around the bend."

"Great," Naomi said. "I'm ready." She was ravenous. The meals they'd had were good, but hardly gourmet. Fear apparently heightened one's appetite. It was a good thing the trip was only going to last four days or she'd for sure gain back all the weight she'd worked so hard to lose.

She sighed as Liz beached the raft on the bar. Four days away from home—it was the first time she'd ever been away from Leah for more than a few hours. She hoped everything was all right; she'd hired a nanny and written reams of instructions to cover practically every minute she was going to be gone. She heaved herself over the side of the raft, waded through the cool water, and sank onto the sand. "Solid ground," she said. "You're going to have to drag me back onto that damn thing."

Sheri filled the decapitated plastic milk jug they used as a bailer in the river and flung water at Naomi. "Water fight!"

"Better watch out for the big gun." Meredith jerked her thumb toward Liz, who was pumping like crazy on the bailing pump, a devilish sparkle in her eyes.

Liz aimed the hose at them, and a huge stream of water drenched them all. "I win!"

Howling with laughter, they helped her hoist the cooler from under her seat and haul it onto the shore. A few minutes later, lunch was spread out on a picnic blanket.

Meredith munched on her turkey sandwich, the sun warming her body. It felt so good to get away from everything for a few days. Eva and Ted were taking care of Justie; she was as prepared for Yvonne's trial in mid-June as she could possibly be; and for the first time since that awful night seven months ago, she was allowing herself a vacation from processing her nightmare memories. Healing was a lot of work—she deserved the rest.

Naomi opened the cooler, grabbed a can of Henry's, and held it aloft. "Beer, anyone?"

"I'd like one," Sheri said, but Meredith and Liz declined.

Naomi handed Sheri a beer, then popped open hers. "I've decided that I'd rather die drunk," she said, then chuckled and up-ended the can into her mouth.

Meredith smiled at her. Naomi was such a good sport. For someone who worried about everything, she was doing remarkably well. Meredith herself had a hard time leaving her child; and she knew that for Naomi leaving Leah was probably close to mortal torture. Not to mention that the river scared Naomi shitless.

After she lowered the can, Naomi said, "I have an announcement to make."

"You're pregnant!" Liz said, grinning.

"I guess you could call it 'pregnant,'" Naomi said. "Not literally, though. Alec and I have decided to create something together." She smiled, then winked. "But it's not a baby."

"I'll bet Richard's happy about that," Meredith said.

"Actually, he is," Naomi said. "He's been bugging me about it for years. I've been working like crazy, and I'm almost finished with my dissertation." She paused, grinning at each of them in turn. "And Alec wants to use it as part of the book he's writing on Shakespeare's heroines. We're going to be co-authors."

• • •

Ted pulled his little white TR-6 into the drive and shut it down. He pocketed the keys, then checked his reflection in the rearview mirror, running his fingers through his wavy brown hair and smoothing his mustache. Sighing, he eased himself from the low-slung car. Time to face the old dragon.

He headed up the walk, noticing that the weeds were taller than the bright red and yellow tulips and that the hedge on the side of the house needed trimming. Usually Meredith was a perfectionist about her garden; her unhappiness must have invaded this part of her life, too.

He still found it odd to think of Meredith as less than perfect, as flawed. He'd always idolized her—she'd given him a sense of security, and he'd believed in her. The messed-up reality behind that competent facade had shattered his happiness, too.

Or maybe it was just his complacency, not true happiness. He shrugged and knocked on the door. That felt weird, too—knocking on his own door like a stranger or something. But he'd chosen to leave, he reminded himself, even if he had felt driven out at the time. Meredith had made it clear that he was welcome to come home whenever he was ready—as long as he was willing to go to counseling with her.

Christ, he missed her so much. Living alone wasn't fun anymore. At first it had been wonderful to get away from the constant tension of Meredith's inner war. Now, though, with nothing to distract him and no one to blame, he was having to face up to some of his own problems.

Eva opened the door, saving him from pursuing *that* unpleasant topic any further. "Come in," she said, stepping to the side. "I've been wanting to talk to you, and with Meredith gone, this is the perfect time."

It sounded more like an order than a request, but he decided to ignore his instant irritation. "All right." He followed her down the entry hall and into the living room he and Meredith had decorated so carefully with antiques and flea-market finds. "Where's Justine?"

"She's still napping." Eva settled herself on the sofa he and Meredith had found at an estate sale, the one with the wood trim he'd spent hours stripping and refinishing. "How much did Meredith ever tell you about what happened to her?"

Ted lowered himself into his favorite chair. "Just that her father raped her. She was five. That's about it."

Eva shook her head. "She still loves you, you know."

He could almost hear her add, "God knows why," under her breath.

"And she needs you. I didn't understand that at first, but I do now." She leaned back, clasping her hands in her lap. "She just told you the bare outline, the facts of the case. I imagine she expected you to fill in the rest." Eva fixed him with a narrow-eyed stare. "Well, have you?"

Glancing down, he chewed on his lower lip, then ran his thumb over his mustache. "Probably not," he said finally. "I didn't feel comfortable thinking about it."

"So you didn't." Eva nodded. "I know, because that was my first inclination, too. But being here with her and Justine has forced me to open my eyes." She took a deep breath. "How would you feel if Meredith's father were still alive? Would you leave Justine with him?"

"Hell, no!" The words exploded from Ted's mouth. He sucked in a lungful of air, surprised at the force of his reaction. He'd kill any son of a bitch who did something like that to his daughter. Just the thought nauseated him.

Eva raised her eyebrows. "You're on the right track," she said. "Now imagine Meredith as a little girl, loving and trusting her daddy just the way Justine loves and trusts you." She leaned forward. "Meredith is still that wounded little girl. She needs help to heal that pain, help that I can't give her. She needs *you*, but she needs for you to be understanding and trustworthy."

He closed his eyes for a few seconds. "I haven't been, have I?"

"It's not too late," Eva said.

He stood and paced to the window, staring out at the big maple in the front yard with its new green-gold leaves just emerging. "What can I do?"

"Show her you support her any way you can. Think of her welfare more than of your own convenience."

He turned back around and looked Eva straight in the eyes. She was a wise old dragon. "You're right," he said.

CHAPTER 29

June

Meredith's heartbeat quickened as the jury returned to the courtroom. Normally, she didn't have such a personal interest in her cases, and it wasn't often they were tried in front of a jury. She turned to Yvonne and squeezed her hand. "Here goes," she whispered.

Yvonne leaned toward her, a smile lighting her pixie face. "You know, it's funny," she said. "Something changed while the jury was out. It's almost like I don't care anymore what they decide. I've done what I needed to do."

Meredith nodded, understanding exactly what Yvonne meant. The girl had taken the steps she needed to for herself, for her own healing; she'd made it clear to the world that she was a survivor, not a victim. The vengeance Meredith had been afraid of at first wasn't really the issue. What was important was what Yvonne thought of herself.

Still, Meredith couldn't keep herself from wanting the verdict to be in Yvonne's favor. The smug self-righteousness of Yvonne's well-to-do, influential father galled her; he had harmed the happiness of another human being, and his depravity deserved acknowledgment, if not punishment. A verdict of guilty would hit Mr. Giroux where it would hurt him most: his pocketbook when he would be required to pay damages and his pride when his conviction became public knowledge.

She glanced at the son of a bitch sitting at the next table, smiling and steepling his fingers as the jury members settled themselves in their seats. Her hands twitched with a sudden desire to choke him, to watch that self-satisfied smirk turn into a purple face with bulging blood-shot eyes.

Which was exactly what she'd like to do to her own father if he were still alive. She forced herself to inhale deeply, exhale slowly. Deliberately, she turned her gaze away from him, twisting around in her seat to look at the rest of the courtroom.

This time her heart almost stopped. Ted sat in the last row. He inclined his head toward her, his face serious and intense. There wasn't a trace of that slightly mocking humorous gleam in his eyes, nor was there any of the hostility she'd gotten used to over these last few months.

She returned his nod, then faced the front again when the judge asked, "Ladies and gentlemen of the jury, have you reached a verdict?"

The foreman, a heavy-set man in his late forties, stood. "We have, Your Honor. We find the defendant guilty as charged. We recommend that he pay damages of $100,000 and that he be financially responsible for all past and future costs of therapy for the plaintiff for the rest of her life."

Vindication. Justice. When the law punished a wrongdoer, the victim no longer need dream of revenge. Except for the wonderfully dumbfounded look on Mr. Giroux's face, the rest of the proceedings were a blur to Meredith. Yvonne threw her arms around Meredith's neck and hugged her. Meredith returned the embrace as the lawyer shuffled Mr.

Giroux out and Ted made his way down the aisle to their table. She disengaged herself gently from Yvonne. "I'd like you to meet my husband, Ted DeCourcey," she said.

"I recognize you from television," Yvonne said, shaking his hand.

"Congratulations." Ted offered his hand to Meredith. "To both of you." He looked into Meredith's eyes. "I really mean it."

"Thanks. Your wife is one terrific lawyer. And friend." Tears brimmed in Yvonne's eyes, and she sniffed. "I have to go before I make a fool of myself," she said. "I'll call you tonight." She turned away and hurried out of the courtroom.

"You did a great job," Ted said. "I just wanted you to know how proud of you I am. I know how hard this must have been for you."

Meredith wasn't sure what to say. She narrowed her eyes. Something was going on with Ted, and whatever it was activated her suspicion radar. *Distrust what you don't understand.*

She gritted her teeth and fought back the fear of the unfamiliar. *Give him the benefit of the doubt,* she told herself. *Innocent until proven guilty, remember?*

He grasped her hand. "I know how selfish I've been," he said. "I want to do something about it. Have dinner with me tonight?"

Taken by surprise, Meredith accepted before she had a chance to consider what she was getting into.

Ted kissed her cheek. "I'll pick you up at seven." He released her hand and walked slowly out of the courtroom.

Meredith watched the tall wooden doors close behind him, almost gasping at the pain of the little fragment of hope glowing in her heart. She would be strong; she would allow it to burn like a beacon; she would not douse it with suspicion and fear.

San Francisco

The basketball swished through the hoop above the garage door, and Doug hooted with glee. He might be weak, but he still hadn't lost his touch. He was creaming Nick and Andy. And he *was* getting stronger.

Dr. Levison had said there wasn't any reason he couldn't resume his favorite activities now that they'd managed to get him into another remission. She'd cautioned him not to go overboard, but they both knew how pointless her warning was. He wanted to *live;* he wanted to experience as much as he could just in case—

Just in case. Just in case they never found his birth mother. Or found her, but too late. Second remissions, especially with his kind of leukemia, usually didn't last as long as first ones, and his first had been pretty damn short.

He shook himself, then forced his attention back to the game. Nick dribbled, then passed the ball to Andy. Doug rushed him, stealing the ball just as Mom came out the front door.

"Doug," she called. Her face glowed with excitement. "Come here."

He bounced the ball a couple of times and then fired it back to Andy. "You guys keep practicing," he said. "I'll be right back." He trotted up the walk to his mother.

She threw her arms around him. "I just got off the phone with Mr. Obremski," she said, tears sparkling in her eyes. "They've found her!"

CHAPTER 30

ASHLAND, OREGON

Smiling at Meredith, Ted set Justie on the playground pony and rocked it gently back and forth. He was glad he hadn't gone rafting on the Klamath; spending the day with Meredith and Justie was turning out to be as much fun, and he felt a hell of a lot better about himself. Ever since his talk with Eva, he'd been giving a lot more thought to the choices he made, considering their effects on the people he loved in addition to his own desires. A wry little smile twitched his lips. What a novel concept. Forty-one years old and he'd finally figured out that giving could be as satisfying as receiving—or taking. Really figured it out, that was—not just lip service, like the spirit of Christmas stuff that had been drilled into his head since childhood.

Justine threw back her head and laughed gleefully when he bounced the pony a little faster. "Mama, horse," she said. "I ride horse."

"Let me get a picture." Meredith stepped back and aimed the camera. "Ted, crouch down a little more." She clicked the shutter at just the second Justine slid off the pony. "Oh, well." She lowered the camera and shrugged. "Maybe next time."

Ted laughed and followed Justie to the slide. "You want to go down?" he asked her.

" 'Kay," she said, lifting her arms. "Up."

He hoisted her onto the platform at the top of the slide. "Sit down."

She plopped down, her little legs sticking straight out in front of her.

"Here we go." He tugged on her legs to get her started, then hovered over her until she reached the bottom.

She clapped her hands. "Do it again!"

He smiled at her. "All right." He situated her at the top of the slide again, then glanced at Meredith, who stood by the water fountain watching the two of them, her face soft and glowing. An almost unbearable sadness swept over him. Meredith had been as innocent and trusting as Justie once, and her father had stolen the joy and safety from her childhood. Then he'd come along and almost stolen the little pieces she'd managed to regain. He'd had so little sympathy, offered so little understanding.

He motioned at Meredith. "Come on," he said. She joined them, standing opposite him. Each of them grabbed one of Justie's hands and pulled, then escorted their little girl to the bottom of the slide.

He picked Justie up and looked at Meredith over the top of the child's head, compelled by a sudden strong desire to make everything all right for all of them. "You know, I've never apologized for acting the way I did," he said. "I hope you can forgive me for being such a selfish fool. I've never stopped loving you."

Tears gleamed in her eyes. "I've never stopped loving you, either," she said.

As soon as Sheri stepped out of the shower, she heard the phone ringing. "Damn!" It never failed. She grabbed a towel and wrapped it around herself, then rushed into the kitchen, dripping water on the newly waxed floor. She snared the receiver. "Hello."

"Sheri Bradshaw?" The voice was male, unfamiliar, and official sounding.

No one had called her by her maiden name in years, even though her divorce decree had officially given it back to her. Her voice stuck in her throat. Finally, she managed to whisper, "Yes."

"My name is Ethan Myers. I'm an attorney in San Francisco, and I represent Douglas Sommers. I believe he is the child you gave up for adoption in Portland eighteen years ago."

"Oh, my God." She sank slowly into the chair next to the phone. From the day they'd taken her baby from her arms, she'd prayed that she would find him again, when it was safe for both of them. Her dad was dead and Mike was gone—all the obstacles removed. Joy constricted her throat, and tears of overwhelming happiness shimmered her vision.

Douglas. His name was Douglas. She'd always thought of him as James because that was his father's first name even though he never used it, had always gone by his middle name. Jamie was Douglas. She cleared her throat. "Yes," she said. "I did. I mean, I had a baby and I gave him up. You found him?" Her thoughts raced so fast through her head she had a hard time keeping up with them. What if Douglas wasn't Jamie after all? What if there'd been some kind of mix-up? What if—

"Actually, we've been looking for you for several months now. We got a court order to open the adoption files, but we weren't able to trace you from the information given. The Sommerses hired a detective, and he traced you through a nurse at Good Samaritan who remembered what you looked like when she saw a photograph of Douglas and that your name was Sheri. Unfortunately, it took a long time. Too long. I'm afraid the matter is urgent."

"Urgent?" she repeated. He sounded so calm. "What do you mean, urgent?"

Carefully, emotionlessly, he explained the situation to her, then gave her the name and telephone number of Doug's doctor in San Francisco. "It's urgent indeed," he said. "But not hopeless. I'm sure she can explain the medical aspect of the case more clearly than I have. I suggest you call her."

New tears stung Sheri's eyes. After all these years of waiting, to find her child when he was dying. And it was her fear that was responsible. If she hadn't been so afraid of her father, and then Mike, she never would have used that phony name, and they would have been able to find her months ago, during Doug's first remission. She managed to choke out, "Thank you," before she hung up.

She lowered herself slowly into a chair at the kitchen table and stared at the phone number scrawled below her grocery list. In the living room, Timmy yelled at Felicia as channels clicked on the television set. The neighbor's dog barked, and a lawn mower chugged, then rasped to life down the street. It was summer and the world was alive while her son was dying. She knew life wasn't fair, but she couldn't help herself. *It isn't fair. It just isn't fair.* The words buzzed in her head in time to the lawn mower's rhythm.

She blinked, then forced herself to get up and cross the kitchen back to the phone. Mechanically, she pushed the buttons, counted the rings, listened as the receptionist answered, "Dr. Levison's office." She gave her name, summarized her request, and then waited while she was put on hold. *It isn't fair. It just isn't fair.*

"Ms. Bradshaw, this is Dr. Levison. I understand that you're Douglas Sommers's birth mother."

"That's right. His lawyer told me to call you." Sheri was amazed that her voice came out so cool, so rational.

"Briefly, let me explain what we're looking for. Doug has been in remission again for a couple of months, and his best chance at this point is a bone marrow transplant, especially if it can be done while he's in remission. But we need a compatible donor. By chance, do you and his natural father have any other children?"

The idea was so outlandish that Sheri almost laughed. "No," she said.

"Siblings are the most likely donors," Dr. Levison said. "It is possible, though, that either you or his father might have a compatible HL-A factor. We need a close match to cut down on the possibility of his body rejecting the marrow. Would it be possible for you to have some tests done?"

"Of course," Sheri said.

"It's Doug's best chance—and there isn't much time to waste because even after we've found a compatible donor, we'll still need at least two weeks to prepare him for the transplant. If it turns out that you're not a good match, would it be possible to find his father? Do you have any idea who he is or where he might be?"

"Yes to both," Sheri said. She knew damn well, but her stomach roiled with eighteen years' worth of anxiety at the thought of telling him he had a son.

Yet she felt she had no choice, not when it meant her child's life. "His name is James Fletcher Berenson," she said. "He lives here in Ashland."

"Shall I ask Doug's lawyer to notify him?"

"No," Sheri said. "I'll tell him myself."

CHAPTER 31

July

Sheri shifted Timmy to a more comfortable place on her lap, then wiped the sweat from her forehead with the back of her hand. Ten o'clock and it was almost ninety degrees already. Thank God she wasn't running in the race or marching in the parade; she could always move back from the curb and get into the shade when it got too much for her. She just hoped she could put aside her worry about Doug long enough to enjoy the day at least a little.

Next to her, Alec craned his neck to look up Main Street. "It should be starting pretty soon, shouldn't it?" he said.

"I hope so," Naomi said. "Parades make me as impatient as a little kid."

Sheri smiled at her. They had a good place in front of Geppetto's, thanks to Naomi and Richard, who'd arrived early with an armload of lawn chairs and set them up at the edge of the sidewalk. After the way she'd bragged to Alec about Ashland's Fourth of July festivities, she hoped he'd be a little bit impressed with the small-town fun and flavor of it all.

Up Siskiyou Boulevard the horn sounded. "Here they come!" Felicia said, clapping her hands.

"Sit here." Sheri leaned forward and pulled Felicia out of the street and onto the curb. Sure enough, the Firehouse Five in their ancient little red fire truck crept onto the boulevard. A few seconds later the band struck up some New Orleans jazz, and the crowd standing under the awnings pushed forward.

Alec grinned at her, and she made herself return his smile. More than *almost* anything, she wanted to enjoy this day with him and her kids and her friends, especially since she didn't have to worry about Mike anymore now that he'd finally moved to Roseburg. Just when everything had started to go so well, and now there was Doug. She'd spent the last two days in a nervous uproar, unable to eat, bursting into tears when she least expected it, trembling uncontrollably every time the phone rang.

And then yesterday what she'd been so afraid of had happened. The tests showed that her HL-A factor was incompatible. She wasn't going to be able to save her son's life. There was only one thing left to do, and she should have done it immediately instead of taking the risk that she might be the donor.

She had to tell Fletcher.

She dreaded the repercussions, but not as much as she dreaded the consequences of doing nothing. She'd rehearsed her approach every waking minute since that painful call—and there'd been a lot of waking minutes because she hadn't been able to sleep. She'd tried out countless different approaches, but in the end they all ended up sounding stupid. There simply wasn't a polite, smooth way to tell someone that you'd borne and given away his child, and now that child was dying.

"Look, Mommy!" Timmy pointed at a ten-foot-tall clown on stilts.

Automatically, Sheri smiled at him. There was Liz to think about, too. What was *she* going to think when she found out her husband and one of her closest friends had slept together, actually had a child? Was she going to feel betrayed—not so much because Fletcher and Sheri had done it but because neither of them had ever told her? Fletcher and Liz already had so many problems that Sheri felt awful about dumping this one on them, too. But she had no choice, she kept telling herself.

Felicia bounced up and down in front of her. "They're throwing candy, Mom. Can I get some for me and Timmy?"

"As long as you stay close to the curb and away from the tiger." Sheri wrapped her arms around Timmy to keep him from running out into the street to pet the "big kitty," a huge tiger on a pathetically small leash. She shuddered when the cat growled. If it got loose, she'd give her life to protect her children, a simple, straightforward act of impulsive courage, no thinking involved. She wished she could do the same for Doug, her oldest child, her first baby. It would be so much easier than this.

"There's Fletcher." Naomi gestured at a sleek black BMW convertible creeping toward them. "I wonder where Liz is. She was supposed to be riding with him—that's the only reason he borrowed that fancy car."

"Yeah," Richard said. "I expected to see him on that bicycle he rides everywhere."

"When I talked to Liz yesterday, she wasn't feeling well," Sheri said. She'd called intending to tell Fletcher but had chickened out when Liz answered.

"I hope it isn't something serious," Naomi said.

"Just a touch of the flu." It suddenly occurred to Sheri that with Liz absent she might be able to talk to Fletcher after the parade. Her whole body tightened. She moved Timmy to her other knee and rubbed the back of her neck with her free hand.

Caught up with her decision, Sheri barely registered the marching wontons, the Talent Tomato Festival Precision Marching Band, the lawn chair brigade, the floats and horses, antique cars and clowns. As soon as the Firehouse Five made their traditional final appearance at the end of the parade, she stood and helped Richard and Naomi fold up the chairs and tuck them away in the back of the Chandlers' Volvo station wagon.

"What now?" Alec said.

"We follow everyone to Lithia Park," Sheri said. "That's where everything is—the chicken barbecue, the bagpipers, the booths."

"Great." Alec hoisted Timmy to his shoulders.

Sheri grabbed Felicia's hand, and all of them joined the throng in the street. When they reached the entrance to the park, she spotted Fletcher shaking hands with several well-wishers crowded around him. One by one the group thinned until Fletcher stood in conversation with only a couple of young men.

Sheri turned to Naomi. "Would you guys mind watching the kids while I run over and talk to Fletcher? I'll find out how Liz is."

"Sure," Naomi said. "Give him our regards."

"I will." Sheri hurried toward Fletcher before she could change her mind. She stood behind the young men until Fletcher excused himself and approached her. She plunged in, knowing small talk would only make it harder to say what she had to. "I need to talk to you. Privately."

He lifted an eyebrow above his wire-rim glasses. "All right." He tipped his head toward the steps leading to the brick patio outside the festival theaters. "On the bricks?"

Silently, they climbed the stairs together, Fletcher nodding and smiling as they passed people on their way down to the park. When they reached the top, Fletcher suggested they sit on the low wall bordering the small grass knoll in the middle of the patio.

As he followed her to the wall, he wondered what she could possibly have to say to him that caused her such obvious agitation. Despite the fact that they'd grown up in the same town and even screwed around that one time, he really didn't know Sheri. In fact, he'd hardly recognized her when she'd turned up in the same childbirth preparation class as he and Liz.

He sat down next to her and waited.

She stared down at her hands, her lips trembling. "Fletcher, remember that night almost nineteen years ago when we . . ."

"Of course I remember," Fletcher said stiffly.

"Well, there's something that I never told you. I got pregnant that night. And I had the baby. It was a boy. I gave him up for adoption."

It took a minute for the words to sink in, but when they did, he felt as if someone had just punched him in the gut. He didn't doubt that she was telling the truth. He calculated quickly. The kid would have to be around eighteen. "Why are you telling me now?" he asked. "Is this some kind of blackmail?" Shit. Even though he and Liz had started having a sex life again, they were on rocky enough ground without this.

"I wouldn't do that." She shook her head angrily. "I gave him up for adoption on the day he was born. No one knows you're his father."

"But why tell me now?" He had no trouble believing the child was his; it had been obvious that it had been Sheri's first time, and she'd never had a reputation for being easy. Old memories trickled back into his consciousness. He'd come home to Ashland at Christmas and called Sheri's house, but her mother had told him she'd moved to Portland. He'd even tried calling her at her aunt's house a couple of times, but she'd always been out. No wonder. She'd been pregnant with his child, and she hadn't wanted him—or anyone else—to know. She was Catholic, he remembered. Although abortion had just been legalized in Oregon, it would have been out of the question for her. "Why didn't you tell me before?" Like eighteen years before.

She shrugged. "I was afraid. You were always so important, and I was nothing. You were getting ready to go to law school, and I was a pregnant seventeen-year-old. What if you insisted on doing the right thing and marrying me? What if you refused to take any responsibility at all? I couldn't let one mistake ruin your life, and I couldn't bear the thought of being rejected. I panicked, and I let my mother make the decisions for me." Closing her eyes, she inhaled deeply before she continued. "Until a few days ago, I wasn't sorry, either. I'd long ago accepted that it was the best way for all of us."

"All right," Fletcher said. "That makes sense. But you still haven't told me why everything has changed."

"Because he's dying," she said, and her green eyes flooded with tears. She wiped them away and stared at him, her face working with such raw agony he could hardly stand to look at her. "And you're the only chance he has left."

CHAPTER 32

Sheri tapped her fingernails on the Citation's steering wheel, then checked her watch again. She hoped to hell Fletcher planned to come to his office today. She felt like some kind of criminal, slouched down in the front seat of her car, praying no one noticed her. Thank God Meredith's car was already in the lot; she'd parked as far away from it as she possibly could.

Where was he? She didn't know if she could stand any more waiting. Her insides were raw with worry and frustration. She wanted so badly to talk to Doug, but she was afraid to. What if he asked about his natural father? How could she tell him that Fletcher wasn't willing to do everything he could for his son, immediately, without thinking, without regard for his own comfort and security?

She gritted her teeth against the sudden stab of pain in her stomach. Holy Mother, she'd never understand Fletcher. No wonder Liz had almost left him. He was so calculating, so cold. He had to look at all the angles before he made any decisions, he'd said.

Angles. Sheri wanted to spit. What angles? How could there be any *angles* when a boy's life hung in the balance? Fletcher was an even bigger asshole than Mike—and that took some doing.

It had taken pleading and tears for her to convince Fletcher that having the tests done wouldn't require any drastic changes or commitments from him. "Just find out," she'd said, unable to keep the bitterness from her voice. "If your HL-A factor isn't a close enough match, you're off the hook."

He'd finally, reluctantly agreed. *Reluctantly.* The bastard. The wonder wasn't that Liz had almost left him but that she'd decided to stay.

She checked her watch again. She'd give him five more minutes; then she had to get back home. The kids were at her next-door neighbor's, and Sheri didn't want to impose on her generosity any more than absolutely necessary. If Fletcher didn't show up, she'd stop worrying about being considerate and call him at home. She'd waited by the phone for hours yesterday evening, expecting him to call with his test results. Finally, she'd gone to bed at two, but then the phone had rung all night long in her dreams. She was exhausted from being startled awake at least a dozen times, sure that she'd just missed his call.

A car turned into the parking lot, and she wiggled in the uncomfortable seat, suddenly aware that she had to pee like crazy. Or maybe she didn't; maybe it was just nerves. The urge subsided, and she twisted around to see if it was Fletcher.

It wasn't, but a bicyclist followed the silver Camry into the lot. Sheri recognized his long legs and reddish-blond beard. Thank God. She threw open her car door and stepped out just as Fletcher swung off his blue mountain bike with the child seat on the back.

He hoisted the bicycle into the rack and locked it, then took off his white helmet. It dangled from his hand as he walked across the lot toward her.

"Well?" she said.

"I'm sorry I didn't get a chance to call last night. Liz and I went out, and it was late when we got home."

Fuck the excuses, she wanted to shout at him. Instead she clenched her jaw. "Did you get them?"

He nodded.

She was a fraction of an inch from losing control, but she hung on. "And?"

He sighed. "It's close enough to work."

"Oh, thank God," she whispered.

"Just a minute."

She stared at him, her heart racing. He couldn't possibly refuse to help now.

"I've got Liz and Brooke to consider as well as my campaign. I'll need a few more days to think about it."

A wave of heat flushed her face. How could he make something gray out of a situation that was so obviously black and white? "Doug may not have a few days." She fought to keep her voice under control. If she got too emotional, he'd turn her off, just the way she'd seen him do with Liz. "Dr. Levison told me that he's in his second remission, and they never last as long as the first. She told me that with his kind of leukemia a third one hardly ever happens." Tears burned her eyes, then rolled down her cheeks. "Please," she croaked, grabbing his arm.

He pulled away. "I'll think about it," he said.

Liz sat down on the edge of the pale gray spa in the master bathroom and slowly removed the little blue and white box from the paper sack. It hadn't occurred to her that she might be pregnant until yesterday, even though her period was already at least three weeks late. She'd always been so irregular—twenty-eight days one cycle, forty-five the next—that she never bothered to keep track.

But lately she just hadn't been feeling her normal, high-energy self. She fell asleep at once, as soon as her head hit the pillow, instead of planning everything she had to accomplish the next day. When she'd sneaked a cigarette last week, she'd almost thrown up after one puff. There'd been the constant queasiness, and then yesterday the little dizzy spell—the final clue that had made her pay attention and put it all together.

She skimmed over the basic instructions on the back of the box, then opened it and took out the booklet with all the details. Simple. Pee on the little stick, then put it into the solution for a minute. Then wait.

She sighed, then followed the directions. It had been so different last time. She and Fletcher had tried for months to get pregnant; they'd almost given up after a dozen false alarms, a dozen big disappointments. Then it happened, and they were overjoyed.

She removed the white stick from the test tube and put it on the stand. She wasn't so sure she wanted another baby, especially now when there was still so much tension between her and Fletcher even though they were faithfully seeing a counselor twice a week despite their busy schedules. They were working so hard just to get to know each other again, and no matter what everybody said, in her experience the reality of caring for a baby day after day wedged a couple apart instead of bringing them together. She was afraid of losing what they'd gained since their decision to give it another try.

She stared at the small window in the middle of the stick. And what if Fletcher didn't want another child? If he won the election, he'd be gone for weeks at a time.

A faint blue tinged the white window, and she blinked her eyes and looked again. Suddenly, she couldn't remember whether blue meant positive or negative. Her heart thumping, she grabbed the box and reread the directions, then glanced back at the stick. The blue line was unmistakable this time.

Positive. She was pregnant. She wanted to laugh and cry at the same time.

Fletcher pulled his VW bus into the only empty space at the Blue Mountain Café parking lot, then turned to Liz. "Are you sure you want to talk here? Maybe we should go home." The situation between them was always more tense after one of their counseling sessions, so they usually spent a half hour or so debriefing afterward. For some reason, though, today Liz had suggested they go somewhere for coffee.

It was ironic. When he needed privacy and intimacy, she pushed him away with both hands. He had to tell her about Doug; it couldn't wait any longer.

"I like their papaya scones," Liz said, smiling broadly. "In fact, I've been craving one all morning."

He knew that smile. Something was going on with her, and she had no intention of telling him about it. Every time their counselor had asked her to comment this morning, she'd flashed that grin and avoided making a direct answer. Fletcher had spent enough time questioning witnesses to recognize evasion when he saw it, and he'd learned a hell of a lot more about Liz in the last couple of months since she'd forced him to open his eyes. She was protecting herself, hiding something.

He also knew better than to push her. Sighing, he turned the engine off. "Okay," he said, opening his door and climbing out.

A few minutes later they were seated at a window table with coffee, tea, and scones in front of them. Liz hadn't wanted to sit outside on the patio; "Too hot," she'd complained, even though it couldn't be over eighty degrees.

Fletcher sipped his lemon zinger tea, then glanced at the clock. He had an appointment in half an hour, and then the rest of his day was full. Liz had told him she wouldn't be home for dinner, and he had to go back to the office after Brooke was in bed to finish up some briefs. His plane left for San Francisco at seven o'clock tomorrow morning. He'd already waited for two weeks because he was so afraid of pissing her off just when things were going a little better between them. He had to tell her now.

He scooted his chair closer to the table. "I'd rather not do this here," he said. "But I don't have any choice." Haltingly, he told her the story, from the party almost nineteen years ago to the confrontation after the Fourth of July parade, noting the way Liz's smile faded now that he was the one in the hot seat. Sympathy shone in her eyes when he told her that his son had leukemia, and when he said that he was leaving the next morning to donate bone marrow because he'd never be able to live with himself if he didn't do what he could, she reached across the table and grasped his hand.

"There's another thing," he said finally. He might as well get it over with. "Doug's mother is Sheri. Sheri Bradshaw. She's going too."

Liz was silent for a few seconds, her face registering surprise but not horror. "I see," she said at last.

"We were never in love," he said. "In fact, I hadn't thought about Sheri in years, not until we met again at that childbirth class. There's nothing between us—you have to believe that."

Liz's large blue eyes glimmered with warmth and support. "I do," she said. "I've always trusted you that way. I know that infidelity isn't one of your flaws."

"Not with another person, anyway," he said. "But there are other kinds of infidelity. I think I've betrayed our marriage with my work. It's taken me a while to admit it, but I've always put my causes first, before both you and Brooke." The last piece of resistance to the plan forming in his mind gave way.

"There's one last thing," he said. "I've decided to withdraw from the senate race."

The happiness glowing on her face was the greatest reward he could ask for.

CHAPTER 33

SAN FRANCISCO

His stomach fluttering only slightly, Doug stared through the window of his hospital room. His birth parents were due to arrive any minute now, and Dr. Levison had made a special exception for them to be able to visit him while he was in isolation.

He aimed the remote control at the television and zapped through the channels until he came to one of those stupid game shows. Man, he was bored. Funny how you could be all excited and keyed up and bored at the same time. It was the waiting. He just wanted it to be over. Two weeks in a sterile room with hardly any visitors was more than enough. Even if it was for his own protection, it felt like prison. Instead of the electric chair or lethal poison, he got huge doses of radiation and drugs to destroy his bone marrow and suppress his immune system so he wouldn't reject the new marrow cells.

He glanced through the window again. They still weren't there.

He'd asked Mom and Dad not to drop by and wave at him through the window the way they usually did every afternoon. It just seemed too weird.

Face it, he told himself. It *was* weird meeting your parents when you were eighteen, no matter where it happened. The whole thing hadn't really hit him until Sheri called last night to let him know they'd be there today. She sounded so nice he'd forgotten his bitterness while they were talking.

But it had come back as soon as he hung up. She'd carried him around inside of her and then given him away like he was a puppy or something. Sure, it had been for the best, he supposed—he loved Mom and Dad and Andy and Nick, and he knew how much they loved him.

He knew all that stuff. Still, the anger was there, made even worse by the disease inside of him and the difficulty of finding his natural parents. The whole situation sucked big time.

Attitude check time. He dragged his fingers through his hair, what was left of it. He was in remission, scheduled for a bone marrow transplant tomorrow. He had a terrific family, and Sheri and Fletcher cared enough to help him out. If the transplant worked, he had years ahead of him, good years, without pain and medication—and maybe a cure, eventually. His life wasn't shit—it was just beginning, really. Outside his window the sky was pure blue; the sun was warm; the world was beautiful. He just had to keep remembering that.

A continuous stream of people meandered along the corridor in front of his inside window. He inspected each couple in street clothes, trying to guess if they were the ones. Fletcher had long, straight blond hair, a beard, and wire-rim glasses, Sheri had told him. She had curly dark brown hair to her shoulders and green eyes.

He focused on a couple approaching his room. They matched the basic description—medium tall fair male with medium short dark female. They weren't holding hands, and they weren't talking to each other. She was beautiful, much prettier than Mom and much younger-looking. He walked like a robot, stiff and jerky—the Terminator looked a hell of a lot more natural. Doug's blond hair came from the man, but the green eyes, the straight nose, the full lips were that woman's. No wonder Obremski's man had found her by showing the nurse his senior photo.

He clicked the television off when they stared in the window at him. His heartbeat drummed in his ears like a tom-tom gone nuts. No matter what he told himself, this was freaky, much freakier than the transplant tomorrow, which for him just involved another shot.

He could see the woman's lips forming his name. He bobbed his head up and down.

They disappeared down the hall, gone to the nurses' station for their sterile masks and gowns, he supposed. He was glad he'd gotten to see what they looked like first before they came in dressed like everyone else in the place.

A few minutes later the door opened, and they stepped in, the woman first. She stood at the foot of his bed, her eyes smiling at him above the blue mask. "I'm Sheri Bradshaw. This is Fletcher Berenson."

"You had me." Christ, he couldn't believe he'd said something so stupid.

Her eyes crinkled even more. "That's probably a good way to put it. And I've hoped for and been terrified of this minute ever since."

Fletcher nodded at him, his gaze intense but warm when his eyes met Doug's. He looked less like a robot up close, but maybe it was because the gown hid his stiffness. He stared at Doug as if trying to see something of himself in him, some kind of proof that he really was Doug's father.

Doug chided himself. That was a dumb thing to think. Even if they didn't look that much alike, all those tests proved it. The dude was just feeling out of it, that was all. Just like him. Having a son sprung on you all of a sudden had to be pretty damn weird.

"I'm glad to meet you," Fletcher said.

The silence following his words wasn't a comfortable one. Finally Doug cleared his throat. "Well, tomorrow's the big day, I guess. Thanks a lot for doing this for me." He gave up. Every word that came out of his mouth sounded idiotic.

"Sheri told me you play football," Fletcher said.

"Used to," Doug said.

"Your mother said you were chosen for the all-city team last year." Sheri's eyes still smiled at him.

"Really?" Fletcher sounded truly interested, not just polite. "What position?"

"Quarterback."

"That's what I played in high school. It must be genetic." Fletcher laughed.

Doug relaxed against his pillow. The guy wasn't so bad after all. And the woman—his birth mother—was beautiful and nice. He sucked in a huge breath. They were trying. It was up to him now. "Hey," he said. "What do you think about me coming up to Oregon for a visit when this is all over?"

Sheri's eyes shimmered with tears. "I can hardly wait," she said.

ASHLAND, OREGON

Brookie screamed and screamed as Liz loosened the car seat straps and gently lifted her out, trying hard not to jar the arm she was sure was broken. Cradling the child against her, she kicked the car door shut and hurried toward the ER entrance, her chest tight and nausea threatening to overwhelm her. Poor Brookie. She was hurting so bad, and there was nothing her mommy could do to make it stop. Liz felt as if she'd betrayed her little girl in some horrible, fundamental way, as if Brooke's suffering was all her fault.

Stop it, she told herself, rushing through the automatic doors. An accident at day care was nothing to blame herself for. She nuzzled Brooke's soft blond hair. "It'll be all right," she said. "Your owie will go away." Brooke looked up at her, and the tears that had been threatening all during the drive to the hospital splashed down Liz's cheeks.

She wiped her face on her shoulder as she approached the reception desk. "I called a few minutes ago," she said above Brooke's shrieks. "I think her arm's broken."

"You can bring her right in." The tall woman doctor who'd been there when Jeff died stepped into the receptionist's office. She waved toward the door on Liz's right. "Come around this way."

Liz carried Brooke into the emergency room, then hiked her hip onto the examining table and settled Brooke in her lap.

Dr. Gregory took some keys from her pocket and dangled them in front of the child. Brooke looked at them, but continued sobbing and made no effort to grab them. The doctor dropped the keys on the table, then ran her hand carefully along Brooke's arm. "I doubt that it's broken," she said. "Dislocated elbows are pretty common with toddlers. How did it happen?"

"I'm not exactly sure," Liz said, hating herself for not knowing. Suddenly her priorities seemed totally screwed up. She'd been closing a deal on a big house up on Morton while someone else was watching her daughter. The deal meant nothing to her; Brooke meant everything. Why in hell, then, did she spend ten hours a day, six days a week working while another woman raised her child? Were the things her earnings bought more important than Brooke's welfare? Or her own happiness and sense of fulfillment? One thing she'd learned from Jeff's death was that she might not have forever. If she died tomorrow, she'd die regretting the time she hadn't gotten to spend with her family, not feeling bad about the money she hadn't lived to make or the stuff she didn't get a chance to buy.

She gave herself a little shake. "Her baby-sitter told me she was playing with some other kids and then she just started screaming bloody murder. When she didn't quiet down, Doreen called me."

Dr. Gregory nodded, touching Brooke's arm again. Slowly, she turned the child's palm up, then bent her arm at the elbow and pressed her hand toward her shoulder.

Miraculously, Brooke stopped crying.

Dr. Gregory smiled at Liz. "I thought so," she said. She held the keys out again, and Brooke grabbed them immediately. "It *was* a dislocated elbow. But we can still have X-rays taken, if you want."

"I don't think that's necessary. She seems fine." Liz stared down at

Brookie playing happily with the keys. She'd missed out on so much of her little girl's childhood, but it wasn't too late to start over with Brooke and to do it better with the next one.

San Francisco

Dressed in the sterile blue gown and mask, Sheri rapped on Doug's window. He grinned at her and motioned her to come in, then clicked off the television when she stepped through the door.

"How are you feeling?" She perched on the edge of the chair beside his bed. What she'd dreamed of, hoped for, hadn't happened with Doug, but neither had what she'd feared. She loved him with her whole heart, but she didn't know him. Jesus, she'd give anything to have that chance. Dr. Levison had told them yesterday that the prognosis was excellent, that he was showing no sign of rejecting the marrow, but that they'd know more in a week or two. Still, it was hard to say good-bye today not knowing anything for sure, not even knowing whether he would ever want to see her again.

Doug lifted his shoulders, then let them fall. "Okay. Fletcher's probably in worse shape than I am. He's not used to it."

Fletcher's voice came from the hall. "You're damn right about that," he said, limping into the room. He stood at the foot of the bed. "Don't get up," he said to Sheri. "I'm more comfortable standing." Rubbing his butt, he winked at Doug.

"I know what you mean." Doug grinned at him.

Sheri thought about the three hours she'd spent in the waiting room the day before yesterday while the doctors removed marrow from Fletcher's pelvic bone. It had seemed to last forever, but when it was all over, it felt like such a short time to save someone's life. The procedures were simple, Dr. Levison had explained beforehand. A large needle would be inserted into the front and back of Fletcher's hip and the marrow extracted from the bone. They would pass the marrow through screens to break up any particles, then inject the marrow into Doug via an IV needle. The biggest danger, other than what she called "graft-versus-host-disease," was that Doug might contract something while he lacked his normal immunity. That was why he had to remain in his sterile hospital room until the doctors were satisfied that the transplant had worked.

And if it didn't, they'd just try again. Fletcher had committed himself to doing whatever it took to save his son's life. When Sheri'd asked him what made him change his mind, he'd replied that he hadn't changed it, that it had just taken him that long to make a decision. But once he decided on the right course of action, nothing would sway him from following it.

She smiled at Fletcher now while he discussed the relative merits of various colleges with Doug. She'd gotten to know him a lot better during the last couple of days, and it was easier for her to forgive him. He was such an idealist, so guided by his conscience, that he had a hard time seeing things from someone else's perspective. On the other hand, once he knew what was right, he would give his life for his cause. No wonder he considered his decisions so carefully; no wonder he was fighting so hard to keep Liz. He might be difficult to live with because he was always so sure he was right, but at least he took his commitments seriously. If only he'd figure out it was okay to loosen up, to have fun, to enjoy at least some parts of his life without thinking he had to improve everything.

Well, if he really wanted Liz, he'd learn those things. She was certainly the most likely person in the world to teach him. Maybe that was why some people ended up with their opposites. Sheri had often wondered what had ever brought the two of them together—Liz so free-spirited, fun-loving, lively; Fletcher so controlled, tense, restrictive. Perhaps Liz had a few things to learn from Fletcher, too.

Thinking about Liz made her a little uncomfortable even though Fletcher had reassured her that Liz had taken the news well. Of course, Liz wouldn't blame Fletcher for anything; what had happened had been in the past and there wasn't a jealous bone in Liz's body. But things were always different between women. Sheri couldn't keep herself from worrying about how Liz was going to respond to her the next time they were together. Had Liz already told Meredith and Naomi, or would she leave that up to Sheri?

Doug's laughter brought her back from her speculations. She looked at him, affection and tenderness filling her heart the same way as when she looked at Felicia or Timmy. Thank God he'd been raised by such wonderful parents; giving him up had been the hardest thing she'd ever done. She still wasn't sure whether it had been the *right* thing to do—she just didn't have Fletcher's clear sense of morality—but at least it hadn't ruined Doug's life. There was something to be said for that.

"So what do you think about SOSC?" Doug was asking Fletcher. He grinned at Sheri. "Do you guys think it'd be weird for me to go to school in Ashland?"

Sheri couldn't keep her mouth from dropping open. She glanced at Fletcher, and he nodded at her. "Do you really mean it?" she said. "That would be wonderful!" Saying good-bye didn't feel like such a tragedy anymore. She wished she could throw her arms around both of them and dance around the room.

CHAPTER 34

August

ASHLAND, OREGON

Meredith rinsed the worst of the lasagna grime off the plate and handed it to Ted to put in the dishwasher. Her fingers brushed his in the exchange, and she smiled at him, then grabbed the heavy casserole dish from the counter, set it carefully in the sink, and filled it with water.

He nuzzled her neck. "That one looks pretty grungy. Why don't you let it soak for a while?"

Meredith giggled, still feeling the effects of toasting their anniversary with Taittinger before dinner and drinking the Chianti with it. Thank goodness Eva had volunteered to keep Justine at her new place overnight. Things were going so well with Ted and her lately she'd almost decided to try going to bed with him again. Almost. It was still definitely a wait-and-see situation. At least, though, she was open to the possibility for the first time in months.

And actually almost looking forward to it. Almost. But if he kept up that delicious exploration of her nape and ears—

She flicked the water off her hands and turned around inside the circle of his arms. After twelve years together, she still enjoyed looking at him, loved the way his dark brown eyes sparkled with energy and humor. She lowered her gaze from his eyes to his lips, smooth and full but clearly defined, not too soft, and usually curved in a pleasant smile even when he was just thinking.

Ted moved his face closer to hers, and in a second his lips touched hers gently, tentatively. Holding her breath, she returned his soft pressure, surprised at the warmth spreading through her body. She was actually feeling something—and now was the time to stop it if she wanted to.

She stiffened a little, and Ted responded by easing up, his mouth barely against hers. Meredith's heart quickened at his tenderness; clearly he had no intention of going any further than she wanted him to. Whether it was because of the wine or because she was getting stronger, she felt safe with him, secure.

She tilted her head back and smiled up into his eyes. "Why don't we take the rest of the champagne and go upstairs?"

His eyes grew darker, and the gleam of humor faded. "Are you sure?"

She wasn't, not entirely, but she nodded anyway and handed him the bottle and glasses. The part of her that wanted to live again, to feel pleasure, was crowding out the scared, wary little girl. This was Ted, her husband, the man she loved. She slipped her arm around his waist, and they climbed the stairs together to the bedroom.

While Ted set the champagne and glasses on the bedside table and poured, Meredith stood behind him, pressing herself against him, her cheek resting on his shoulder. She ran her finger down his chest to his belt, then unbuckled it and unzipped his pants.

"Jesus Christ, Meredith." Ted put the bottle down and pulled her onto the bed. "If you keep this up, I'm going to have a hard time stopping." He kicked off his pants and lowered himself on top of her.

He rubbed himself against her, his hands fumbling with her clothing. "See what I mean about the *hard* time?"

Meredith started to laugh, but suddenly all she could see was Ted's mustache as he brought his lips closer and closer to hers. Every muscle in her body tensed, and she pushed him away. Her throat closed. "I'm sorry," she whispered. "Something happened. I—"

She gasped, the memory filling her vision. Her father's mustache, the way she'd focused on it, counting the bristly hairs to keep from screaming as he'd pounded into her, splitting her open without mercy. "Oh, my God," she said. Ted had grown the mustache while she was pregnant, and that was when the problems between them started. "Shave it off."

He looked bewildered but not angry. "My mustache?"

She nodded, then haltingly explained. When she finished, he pulled her from the bed and led her into the bathroom, where he grabbed her razor from the soap dish on the side of the claw-foot tub.

"Here goes." He worked up a lather with the bar of soap and spread it over his mustache. Tugging his upper lip down, he scraped the dark hairs away, then rinsed them down the drain. He laid the razor down and patted his skin dry, staring at Meredith in the mirror. "Better?"

She heaved a huge sigh. Her fury and terror had diminished with each swipe of the blade. It was almost like erasing a mistake—rub, rub, gone. Just the faintest impression left until she covered it with something new.

"Shall we try again?" He turned around and cupped her face in his hands. "Or would you rather wait?"

"Let's go back to bed. Even if I can't, we can at least sleep together, can't we?"

He wrapped his arms around her and held her tightly against his naked body. "Of course."

Quickly, to cover her awkwardness, Meredith pulled away, stripped off her tunic, leggings, and underwear, and slid under the covers. When Ted slipped in beside her, she tugged him on top of her. "Kiss me again."

She kept her eyes open as he lowered his face to hers once more, slowly relaxing, then finally closing her eyes as her body, freed now from her mind's nightmare, responded to Ted's gentle, persistent touch. She arched her back and rubbed herself against his erection, his soft groans setting off little electrical charges in her heart and groin. When his fingers explored her wet inner folds, she shuddered with pleasure, letting it roll over her in slow waves.

Carefully, he entered her, his body positioned over hers on extended arms so she could look into his eyes, soft brown eyes gleaming with tenderness. "I love you," he said.

"I love you, too." She forced herself to keep her eyes focused on his as he moved inside her, slowly at first, then with increasing intensity. Finally she reached out and pulled him down against her, giving in to her growing urgency. When she came, tears flooded her eyes.

A few seconds later he gasped, clutching her even more tightly. "Good God," he said.

She reveled in his little convulsions, contracting her inner walls, then relaxing them the way he'd always liked.

"You're back," he whispered in her ear. "Thank God you're back."

"Thank God you are too," she said.

The soft breeze felt good against Liz's sticky, hot skin, and she silently blessed it. The August heat wave had started while Fletcher was in San Francisco, and she was sick of sweating. Still, when Fletcher had suggested on the way home from the airport that they celebrate his homecoming with a gin and tonic on the balcony at Alex's Plaza Restaurant, she'd agreed without hesitation. They'd dropped Sheri off at her mother's house where her kids were and driven straight downtown.

She settled herself in one of the little café chairs, smiling at Fletcher as he gingerly eased his backside onto the hard wooden seat across from her. "We could sit inside on the couch," she said. "It might be easier on your butt."

He laughed. "I'm fine. Besides, I like the view from up here."

She gazed out over the wooden railing at the plaza, then at the smooth green grass of the park entrance presided over by the Tudor-beamed Shakespeare theater. Shaded from the hot sun by liquid ambers and brightly colored awnings, pedestrians crowded the sidewalks of Main Street. "It *is* nice," she said. "Sometimes I forget to stop and take the time to appreciate it."

"I've been thinking the same thing. About me, that is, not you," he added quickly. "Actually, about us. I mean—" He paused, looking up at the ceiling. "Shit. I'll start over." He fixed his eyes on her. "What I mean is that I haven't been taking the time to appreciate you. Hell, I've made it so I don't *have* the time. I thought a lot about it while I was in San Francisco, and I just asked myself what *was* really important to me. What did it mean if I busted my ass to save the world and ended up fucking over my family at the same time? I decided to think small for a change: save myself, save my marriage, save my family. Maybe if every-body did the same, the world would get saved anyway."

Liz listened to him with astonishment. The speech had been deliv-ered with Fletcher's usual intensity, but the message was so different—not *entirely* about all of the things other people needed to do to make the earth a better place, even if he did insist on throwing that in at the end. That was just a part of Fletcher she had to accept, and she was more than willing to.

But what was even more amazing than his change of attitude was that it was almost exactly the same as hers. "I thought about things a lot while you were gone, too," she said. "And I've decided to put my money where my mouth is. I'm going to find a partner to help out at my agency. And I'm going to cut back on my hours. If you don't object, that is."

"Shit, no." He grinned at her, then grew serious, settling his glasses on his nose. "You know the money doesn't mean anything to me. Are you sure it's really what *you* want to do, though?"

She nodded. "I want more time to spend with you. And with our children."

"Children?" A blond eyebrow arched above his glasses. "Are you trying to tell me something?"

The waitress arrived to bring the orders they'd placed at the bar, and Liz just smiled as the young woman set the tonic and lime in front of her. She winked at Fletcher after the girl left and swirled her glass, clinking the ice cubes. "No gin for me," she said. "I'm pregnant." She popped the entire slice of lime into her mouth and chewed it with relish.

Chuckling, Fletcher shook his head. "That's great," he said. "You're amazing."

"You really mean it?"

"I do," he said. He reached across the small round table and grasped her hand. "Let's start over. Will you marry me, Lizzie?"

She smiled into his eyes. "I will." And this time she intended to do it right, with no evasions and no lies.

CHAPTER 35

September

A shriek distracted her from the conversation, and Naomi twisted in her chair to peer over the deck railing. The children played on the lawn below them, supervised by Kristin and Philip. Nothing was amiss, though—just a scream of pleasure from Timmy at a fast trip down the big slide. She turned back to the other women as Meredith finished her check-in, something they'd decided to try today for the first time. The idea was to give everyone a chance to talk without interruption for seven minutes—a rare luxury, they'd all agreed.

Also, next to impossible, even with two baby-sitters taking care of the kids. It was proving extremely difficult for the other women to keep their mouths shut for that long, and it was agony for Naomi. When Liz had announced that she was pregnant and had decided to revamp her agency so she could spend more time at home, none of them had been able to contain themselves; and the whole table had erupted with congratulations and advice and questions. Seven minutes had turned into twenty before they'd moved on to Meredith.

She'd been doing a little better—probably her lawyer training in summing up a case. Meredith spoke so crisply and so matter-of-factly that there wasn't as much temptation to butt in.

Now, Meredith paused, her face working as if she were having difficulty deciding what to say next. Finally a big grin lit up her face. "What the hell," she said. "It's not for sure, but I'm so happy I have to tell you anyway. Ted's probably going to move back in. I think I'm falling madly in love again with my husband."

"That's great!" Naomi clamped her hand over her mouth, then smiled sheepishly at the other women. "I'm sorry," she said. "But I just can't help it. Maybe it's a secondary sex trait or something—maybe women have a gene that *makes* them interrupt."

"It's okay," Liz said. "I felt that you were really listening to me. It's not like having someone tugging at your skirt and whining at you while you're trying to carry on a conversation."

"Or like having a man switch the subject to something entirely different right in the middle of what you were saying." Sheri wrinkled her nose.

"I agree." Meredith's head bobbed up and down enthusiastically. "Anyway, I'm finished." She tilted her head toward Naomi. "Your turn."

Naomi laughed, suddenly feeling a little awkward. "God, it's like being on stage. You're all staring at me, and I have to say something. Usually that's not a problem, as you all know." She toyed with her glass, then took a big gulp of the iced coffee. "Here goes," she said. "Alec dropped by yesterday with some really great news—"

"He's been offered the job at SOSC!" Liz clapped her hands, then cringed when everyone stared at her. "Oops. Go on."

Naomi smiled at her. "That's true, but it's not the news I'm talking about." She glanced at Sheri before she continued. "Anyway, he told me that the University of North Carolina Press has accepted our book for publication."

"Wonderful," Meredith said. "Jesus Murphy, that was quick. You just finished the thing last month, didn't you?"

"Uh-huh." Naomi settled back in the wicker chair, and it creaked. Not even Meredith could resist putting in her two cents' worth. "But they'd already tentatively accepted it based on his proposal, so this was just the final decision. I guess they liked my chapters—at least that's what Alec said. He went on and on about how original my ideas were and how great my writing was—" She flushed. "It was embarrassing, but I loved it. Then he tried to talk me into applying for a position teaching English at SOSC or Rogue Community College. I'd actually been thinking about it, but the more he talked, the more I found myself resisting. It was bizarre. It was almost as if he were my father or something."

She leaned forward and plopped her elbows on the glass tabletop. "All the time he was talking, this funny feeling came over me and I started thinking about what *I* really wanted to do, not what my father wanted or Richard wanted or Alec wanted. I knew, of course, that Alec didn't have the same kind of personal investment they did—or do—but I kind of used him to help me figure it out. So here's what I'm planning to do." She paused, grinning at them while she sipped her coffee. "I'm going to start my own catering business."

They all beamed at her. "Great idea!" Meredith said.

"I thought you'd say that," Naomi said. "It was your suggestion that got me thinking."

"I get to be your first client," Liz said. "Oops, I forgot—we're trying to be frugal now that I'm going to be making a lot less money." She winked at Naomi. "Special rates for friends?"

Naomi giggled. "I'll do it for cost if you let me practice on you and invite me as a guest, too."

"Done," Liz said.

"And I am, too," Naomi said, gesturing at Sheri. "You're on."

"I don't know where to start." Sheri poured more coffee into her glass, then stirred in some sugar. The ice cubes rattled against the crystal. A little white car pulled up at the curb below, and she stared at it while, still toying with the spoon, she gathered her thoughts. Before she could speak, the driver stepped out and waved at her.

Her heart stopped beating, and she could feel the blood drain from her face. It was Doug—a week earlier than she'd expected. He grinned and ran up the brick steps, two at a time. She rose slowly as he unlatched the gate and strode onto the deck. He'd gained weight, and his hair, though still short, was thick and glossy.

"Here's my most important news in the flesh," Sheri said, her voice quavering. "I'd like everyone to meet my son Douglas Sommers." She met Liz's eyes across the table, glad that the two of them together had told Meredith and Naomi what was going on. Liz had been so wonderful about everything, assuring Sheri that she didn't consider the secret a betrayal of their friendship since it really had nothing to do with her. If anything, they were even closer now than before. "Doug's been accepted at SOSC," she said. "He's going to live in Ashland this year."

"Fletcher told me where I could find you." Doug enveloped her in a bear hug, then greeted the other women.

"I'm Fletcher's wife, and I'm very happy to meet you," Liz said, shaking his hand when it was her turn. She pointed to Brooke, playing happily in the sandbox. "That one's your half-sister." She patted her belly. "And there's another sibling in here."

Sheri gestured toward Felicia and Timmy. "And yet two more down there. They've been beside themselves with impatience waiting for their big brother to get here."

"Well, I'd better go meet them, then." Doug kissed Sheri's cheek, then pushed her gently back down into her chair. "You stay here. I'd like to do this by myself."

Sheri watched in silence as he descended the steps to the lawn and introduced himself first to Kristin and Philip, then to the children. Felicia and Timmy stared shyly at him at first, but within a few minutes he was pushing them on the swings while they chattered at him as if they'd always known each other.

Sheri turned back to her friends. "You won't believe this, but I've got even more good news. I auditioned with Actors' Theater last week and got chosen for the lead. I'll be playing Estelle in *No Exit,* and we open at the end of September. I've decided not to go back to college because I want to have time to do more theater. At least that's what I'm hoping to do." She paused for a breath, then plunged on when Doug and the kids headed for the steps up to the deck.

"And on the personal front, I think I'm falling madly in love with Alec Whittier and he feels the same way about me."

She had just a few seconds to enjoy the astonished gapes on her friends' faces before the kids swarmed around the table. Doug hoisted Timmy onto her lap. She smiled up at him.

She couldn't wait to find out what the future held—for all of them.

ABOUT THE AUTHOR

Penny Hayden is a fifth-generation Oregonian from Gold Beach. After receiving her B.A. and M.A. degrees in English from the University of Oregon, she taught junior high and high school English for fourteen years before becoming a full-time writer. She has published three novels under another name. She has lived in Ashland, Oregon, since 1979 with her husband and three children.